Wingmom

Terra Weiss

*Patty,
Thanks for being a friend to my mom. If you like her, you'll like this book!
Kind Regards,*

AUTUMN SKY
BOOKS

To Mom.

My hero. My co-conspirator. My wingmom.

Contents

1. Encounter of the Weird Kind   1
2. Surprise Guest   11
3. Costume Party   16
4. The Board Game   21
5. Dog Eat Dog   27
6. Hell on Wheels   32
7. Caught Pantie-Handed   40
8. Buzz Kill   47
9. Cheeto Combat   57
10. The Bling Machine   62
11. Coffee Kitten   67
12. The Sweet Pad   76
13. Birthday Bash   82
14. Tangled Up in Blue   89
15. Swingers   98
16. Eating Nemo   109
17. Dolly Llama   116
18. The Sting   125

19.	Rooftop Reunion	135
20.	The Office	145
21.	Conflict of Interest	153
22.	Man's Best Friend	161
23.	Runaway Runway	169
24.	Sentimental Slippers	178
25.	Crowded Space	187
26.	The Ride	195
27.	The Big Fish	208
28.	Wedding Crashers	215
29.	In the Toilet	226
30.	The Net	234
31.	The Dirtiest Dog	237
32.	Free Falling	244
33.	The Dark Skye	251
34.	Snaked	262
35.	The Puzzle	271
36.	Princess Bride	280
37.	Rolling Stone	286
	Also by Terra Weiss	291
	About the Author	293
	Acknowledgements	294
	Copyright	297

1

Encounter of the Weird Kind

The bangs against the flip side of my motel room's paper-thin wall become more rapid and fervent.

As the ruckus escalates with a cat-like mewling, the rickety headboard I'm leaning against starts vibrating against my back. I scowl, scooting away. "Seriously? It's midnight." Some of us have career-defining presentations in the morning.

I slide my computer off my lap and hop out of bed. With the picture frame above the headboard sliding sideways, it's probably not the safest place to be right now, anyway. Determined to tune out the proverbial neener-neener to my non-existent love life, I pace the floor. Refocusing, I memorize the potential sales figures of my new product line for Fur Bebé, the Atlanta-based boutique petwear company where I work. This is my one shot for a big promotion, and I can't screw it up.

Tomorrow, I'm presenting to the board at PAW-CON, the pet industry's big annual conference kicking off at the five-star Loft Hotel. While Fur Bebé executives are staying there, the rest of us are here at the Starlite Inn around the corner. It was my idea; Fur Bebé's on a tight budget, and I wanted all employees to be able to attend.

Bravo on that recommendation.

The polyester floral bedspread rustles. The racket has finally disturbed Notorious D-O-G, my distinguished graying rescue chihuahua with a massive overbite. Narrowing his eyes, he lets out a soft, low growl. He's trying to keep his cool—he's great like that.

But it pains me to see him awake. He's got a big day tomorrow, and he needs his beauty sleep.

That's it—I jam on my hot-pink fuzzy socks in preparation to march next door and let them have it.

Then...

Blissful silence.

"Thank you." I exhale. "That was exhausting, right Mr. D?" I scratch his head. Notorious D-O-G was selected among thousands of entries to be this year's spokes-pup for Fur Bebé. I jumped at the chance to be his adopted parent.

I straighten the framed print of a fruit bowl above the bed before sitting back down on the saggy mattress and returning the computer to my lap. Notorious D-O-G does a few circles before settling in beside me.

My phone buzzes, and my heart races faster than my fingers reaching for it. No one calls this late unless something terrible is happening. "Unknown" glows on the screen.

I fumble as I snatch my phone off the nightstand. "Hello?"

"Devastating news, Sophie."

"Mom?" My breath hitches. "What's going on?"

"Wanda didn't invite me to Lulu's wedding. Can you believe that? After everything I've done for that woman!"

I hold back a groan. I love my mother, but I really have to get this presentation done.

But it's *Mom*, so I set my laptop aside and keep the irritation out of my tone when I ask, "Why are you calling from an unknown number?"

"Because I blocked my name. This is an emergency, and I wanted to make sure you took my call."

"That's ridiculous. I take all your calls. Ten of them a day." I lean against the headboard.

"You didn't answer yesterday."

I scowl. "I didn't pick up your sixth call yesterday because I was in the shower. Anyway, I answered now. After midnight."

"Yeah, but you were up," she says, indignant. "I checked your activity log. You've burned seven active calories in the past ten minutes."

I should've known better than to become workout accountability partners with Mom. She doesn't give a crap about exercise—she just uses the app to track me. Well, track me *more*. I yawn. "So, why didn't Wanda invite you to Lulu's wedding?"

"Wanda says it would be upsetting to Lulu, and I know that's not true because I talked to Lulu. She wanted me there."

"Wait." My face puzzles. "How did you talk to Lulu?"

"It wasn't easy—she was out of town this week, camping in the Blue Vine Mountains."

"I meant how did you talk to Lulu because she's a dog."

Mom scoffs. "Telepathically. Duh."

Right, of course. Not wanting to get into the weeds of *that* particular discussion, I say, "And you placed Lulu for adoption. I can understand Wanda's concern about upsetting her." After fostering Lulu, a pug, Mom had a terrible time letting her go.

"That's total crap," Mom plunges on. "Lulu understands, and Wanda promised me I could go to Lulu and Yoda's wedding. That was part of the adoption. And it gets worse. Wanda posted a wedding announcement in the paper, and she didn't even list me as 'Foster Mother of the Bride.'"

I stifle a gasp. "Wanda announced the dogs' wedding in the newspaper?"

"In *The Grape Vine*. That's how I found out about it. Lulu wore a gorgeous set of pearls and a shimmering taffeta veil. Yoda had on a white tuxedo vest. My heart is shattered."

Mom had told me that Wanda is traditional and doesn't want Yoda and Lulu—both fixed—to dry hump unless they're married. As far as the telepathy thing goes, communicating with animals is a new level. Apparently, I was wrong thinking Mom's "gift" was limited to humans and aliens.

Keeping my tone soft, I say, "I'm sorry you weren't invited to Lulu's wedding. That must be very painful."

"It is."

My eyes drift shut as I renew patience for another round of Mom's neon shade of eccentricity. I always try to deal, but I'm exhausted. "Shoot, Mom, I really gotta finish my presentation."

"What's happening with your big promotion?" she says in her usual voice. Her ability to snap back from devastation is almost a superpower.

"It's a done deal." I'm ready to put my paycheck-to-paycheck past behind me and do something I once thought impossible—become an executive at twenty-eight. "Well, it's almost a done deal." It will be after tomorrow's presentation.

It has to be. I've exceeded all quarterly sales goals and developed our best-selling parent-pet matching sleepwear, Petjamas. I've done everything the board has asked of me and more.

"Hmm—" Mom blows out a long breath. "I have a bad feeling. I'm gonna burn your picture under a gold candle in a success prayer."

Into candle magic, Mom believes the energy of the flame strengthens her powers of manifestation. Or something like that.

"They have to give me the promotion—they promised. It's only fair."

"Fair is a place for rides, Sophie. Someday you're gonna have to learn that." Mom tsk-tsks. "So, what's up with *Bridesmaid to Bride* Missy Mulligan?"

I try to keep my voice light. "Missy's still working at Fur Bebé, but she wants to move from sales to my product design team." Missy Mulligan is an influencer and a celebrity... of sorts. She'd chosen her "one and only" on season two of the *Bridesmaid to Bride* reality show, proposing to Eben in the final episode. Four months later they were over, but she lives on in infamy.

Instead of Mom's voice, I hear typing—Mom's signature hunt and peck style.

I furrow my brows, shifting on the hard mattress. "What are you doing?"

"I love her new bejeweled nails," Mom coos.

"Wait." It takes me a second to compute how Mom is seeing Missy's fingernails. "Are you one of her FaceSnap followers?"

The line goes silent.

"Mom?"

"Has she moved on okay after Eben?" More typing echoes through the phone. "That was one tough breakup."

My lip curls. "I have no idea. Why don't you check Missy's Chirper feed?"

"Already did. Four times." The typing stops.

Unbelievable. "Missy seems fine." Notorious D-O-G is shivering, so I swing out of bed and rifle through my suitcase until I find the turquoise velvet sweatsuit with a lightweight hoodie—the prototype I designed for the line I'm introducing tomorrow named Pet Sweats. After I slip the suit on Mr. D and tuck him under the covers, I say, "Okay, I really have to get back to work on my presentation." The new CEO will be at the board meeting tomorrow—some uppity Harvard alum from Wall Street. I'm almost certain they held off my promotion so they could get his approval first. He has zero pet industry experience, but he's the nephew of a board member. Nepotism at its finest.

Suddenly, the wall banging erupts again with salacious intensity. The cat-like sound has graduated into a high-pitched wail, and I yell, "Oh, for crying out in the night!" realizing my words apply figuratively and literally. Notorious D-O-G has had enough too, as he starts barking.

"What's going on?" Mom asks.

"I gotta go—my neighbors at this hotel are having *way* too much fun."

I'm waiting for Mom to make some sort of wisecrack when she says, "I'm gonna be late!" Keys jangle into the phone. "I'm going undercover." She disconnects.

Undercover? What is she talking about? And where is she going at midnight? Mom lives in Blue Vine, a tiny vineyard town two hours north of Atlanta. Nothing there is even open at midnight.

I try to call her back, but she doesn't answer. I text her but get no response. We were *just* talking, for Pete's sake!

And Mom always responds.

###

With growing frustration at the clamor, I bang on the wall, but the noise doesn't stop. Maybe if I knock on my neighbor's door and pretend to be hotel security, they'll keep it down?

I hop out of bed. In the grimy wall mirror, I catch a shadowed glimpse of my Minnie Mouse cotton tank top and matching fuzzy pajama pants. I consider throwing on a bra, but who cares? It's not like anyone besides the Energizer Humping Bunnies is going to see me.

I flip the deadbolt to prop my door open before heading to the neighbors, my socks snagging on the roughly worn carpet. I'm no princess, but this place is gross. I'm debating whether I should toss the socks when a heavy groan blasts from my neighbor's room.

I knock, then in the firmest voice I can muster, I say, "This is hotel security. Can you keep it down, please?"

The door swings open, revealing a guy wearing only his flannel Batman pajama bottoms. He puts his palms up and yells, "It's not me, I swear!" Then he points to the air conditioner in his room, which is squealing and shaking so much it looks like it's preparing for liftoff.

"Just turn it off," I yell over the noise.

His brows dive. "No kidding. I tried, but it won't—that thing's possessed."

I rush past him and into his room before flipping up the flap that covers the A/C unit. I press the off button several times, putting my full body weight into it.

It doesn't shut off.

"Told you," he says with a tinge of attitude.

After backing up, I give the unit a hefty karate kick. It sputters and coughs to a halt, squealing as it takes its final gasp—maybe forever.

I glance at Batman Jammies to see his face flushed as he looks at me bug-eyed. "Impressive. Um. Thank you." The attitude is gone.

"Welcome. I have some experience with air conditioners on the fritz." And no money to pay someone to fix them.

I open my mouth to say something else, but I shut it because I can't remember what it was. My thoughts jumble as I stare at Batman Jammies.

Broad shoulders; long, muscular legs. Strong jaw in need of a shave, although his stubble is sexy. My eyes roam to his golden chest, nicely cut, not too bulky.

"I turned it off when it started making noise." His rich, baritone voice pulls me out of my haze. "But then I turned it back on when it got too hot in here—"

"Then it wouldn't turn off again." I finish his sentence.

"Right." His eyes flicker to my chest, so I fold my arms. He blinks, finally meeting my gaze with his dark, piercing eyes. "Hotel security, huh?"

I shrug, my cheeks hot, and I'm not sure if it's because I'm self-conscious, or it's a million degrees in this room. Empathizing with this guy, I blurt, "You should take a cold shower."

He blinks. "Come again?"

I swallow hard, realizing how that sounded. "Because it's sweltering in here."

"Right. Of course." He nods, combing his fingers through his silky black hair.

I wave a hand. "I mean, you don't stink or anything."

He hesitates, studying me. "Good to know."

"Cool." I wring my hands. "And I'm sorry I was curt before. I thought the noise was... you know. Wild hanky-panky."

"Hanky-panky? Does anyone say that anymore?"

I scowl. "I do."

A hint of a smile hides in one corner of his mouth. "Well, no hanky panky here. Unfortunately."

I laugh, and his sexy half-smile grows. "Right."

And it's not just his smile that's sexy. *He's* sexy.

The confidence he exudes, even in his pjs. The way his lip twitches before he speaks, as though he's carefully considering each word. The timbre of his voice that's soothing to the ears.

Looking past him, I notice an electric toothbrush in the shape of The Flash sitting on his bathroom sink. What's up with this guy and superheroes?

Despite myself, I grin when I imagine The Flash vibrating as he cleans teeth at lightning speed.

Realizing I probably look like a weirdo smiling at his toiletries, I straighten my face and point to the air conditioner. "Anyway, I should've known it was something else. No woman makes that sound."

"I dunno..." An eyebrow shoots up as he shrugs.

"Don't get me wrong. The fake Os can take on that—" I wave my hand around "—pet cemetery kind of mewl."

Wow, Sophie. Bold.

Riley, my best friend, would be proud.

His face twists and his lips tick as he appears to scramble for a reply. Finally, he says, "Hey, I can tell. Trust me."

"Sure you can." I nod, playing it cool. "But I'll have to take your word for it."

Batman Jammies and I lock gazes, a tension hanging in the air. I don't know what's come over me—my insides never get this twisted from a stranger's gaze.

But when Notorious D-O-G barks, the tension drops away, like that silly roadrunner-chasing-coyote in old cartoons.

With an awkward wave, I mumble, "Well, I should go. I've got a big presentation to the new CEO tomorrow. Some Harvard brat."

Batman Jammies face crumples as he tilts his head.

It's either his vibe or the fact that we've been forced past pleasantries, but whatever it is, I feel like I can be honest with this guy. "My new boss is a bougie trust fund baby who wipes his butt with hundred-dollar bills. Zero qualifications, but he's related to the president of our board." I cup my palm. "Here, Your Majesty, the CEO position on a gold-encrusted platter."

"Wait." He swallows hard, his Adam's apple traveling along his throat. "Your name isn't Sophie Fox, is it?"

My stomach plummets and my arms turn to gooseflesh. "Uh, yes," I squeak.

He hesitates, blinking, before a cocky smirk spreads across his face. When he extends his hand for a shake, he says, "I'm your new CEO. Your Majesty, Lucas Nevarez."

"Oh," I croak, sweat filming my body. Batman Jammies is my new CEO? As I shake his hand, I struggle for a firm grip with my clammy palm.

If he's an executive, why isn't he at the Loft Hotel?

My face is so hot my cheeks burn as I scramble for words. When the silence seems to hit a note so high my ears ring, I lift my chin and say, "I'm so sorry. I'm running on coffee and fumes... and it's after midnight. You know how Cinderella turns into a pumpkin? Well, *I* turn into a late-night comedian." My voice cracks. "Yup. Just one big joke-teller." *Shut up, Sophie.* "Well, nice meeting you, Mr. Nevarez. See you bright and early tomorrow."

"Looking forward to it." His tone is smooth, confident.

I back away and rush into my room, fumbling with the deadbolt before accidentally slamming the door shut with a thunderous boom.

2

Surprise Guest

At the unholy crack of dawn, I arrive at the Loft Hotel to put the finishing touches on my presentation before the PAW-CON breakfast meet and greet. My hair is in a careful bun, my makeup natural, and I'm wearing my best professional Kate Spade black dress with a thin suede belt.

Walking through the deserted lobby, I mumble, "I have to make VP," then realize how strange that sounds. Growing up volunteering at shelters, I never thought I'd work in corporate America. I took this job at Fur Bebé because I needed cash, but soon realized how much I loved designing petwear. If I get this promotion, it'll help me launch more lines.

I'm also determined to make a dent in animal homelessness. For years, Fur Bebé has been talking about changing the structure of our company so that a portion of proceeds go to pet rescue organizations, but that deal always gets narrowly shot down. If I get promoted, I'll be a voting member of the board.

I'm fighting to open the door of our reserved conference room when a folder slips from my fingers and hits the floor, scattering papers everywhere.

"Let me help you." A familiar baritone voice echoes behind me.

I whip my head around to see that it's him—Batman Jammies. Or, rather, Lucas Nevarez.

Memories of last night flood my mind, and I wonder if flames are actually licking my cheeks.

He's seen me in a tank top, braless. I called him, "Your Majesty."

And sweet mother. He knows my thoughts on fake Os!

He strides over and begins picking up the papers off the floor, one by one.

Batman Jammies. Here an hour early. On his knees.

A million thoughts—including a few censor-worthy ones—swirl through my head as I stand, unable to speak. If I thought shirtless Lucas Nevarez was hot, that was nothing compared to all-business Lucas Nevarez. His suit fits as though it's been tailored for his body, and his chestnut shirt and tie make his eyes heavenly, like truffle confections. "Mr. Nevarez. You're here bright and early." I finally manage to form words.

He towers over me when he stands. "Please. Call me Lucas. And I'm a little short on experience in this industry—as you pointed out." He clears his throat. "I came to do my homework."

"Oh." Is he here now because of the things I said? When his smell of fresh soap and warm skin hits me, my brain buzzes.

He glances at one of my papers. "Pet Sweats, huh?"

"Yes," I chirp, excited to have a tension-breaker. "It's an idea I thought of last winter when I saw so many people jogging in the cold with their pets. Our four-legged friends need to stay warm too."

The corner of his mouth lifts. "That they do." He studies the paper. "And these potential sales figures look phenomenal."

"I've been crunching the numbers for months, and they've only gotten better. I mean, who doesn't love activewear?"

"Good point."

"Thanks." I bite my lip. "I'm sorry about last night. Again—"

"Don't worry about it. It was a bizarre set of circumstances."

"Why weren't you with the other executives at the Loft Lounge?"

He shrugs. "There was no need to spend company money on that. I'm not picky. Well, except about A/C in Atlanta. In August."

"Yeah, that's pretty diva-ish."

He smiles as he ushers me inside the conference room, and after we're seated, I'm thrilled that Lucas asks me more questions about Pet Sweats.

I take out my sample. "Look, the hood is lightweight and hangs loosely on the neck," I say, leaving off the part that I'd prefer pet clothing not have hoods at all. Most of the time, the animals don't need them, and the added bulk around the neck is uncomfortable. But I know jackets sell better with hoods, so I had to come up with a compromise.

As I continue going over more ideas, my phone buzzes in my pocket, and I check to see that it's Mom. I still don't know what's happening with her, but she did text me back last night saying that she'd call today and tell me everything. My phone starts continually buzzing as she goes into a call-text-leave-a-voicemail frenzy. Then she sends me the message, "911."

Drat!

Although... Mom uses "911" for crap like a death in a TV show she's watching. If it's a real emergency, she just texts me what's going on. This is her code to trick me into calling, which I'll do the second I'm done talking with Lucas. I *have* to show him that I'm more than the blundering mess he met last night.

Right now, conversation with him is easy, and before I know it, we've been chit-chatting so long, it's time to join all the PAW-CON attendees at the breakfast social in the hotel lobby. This is my chance to lay the foundation for my pitch to the rest of the board.

We join the attendees, and I'm grabbing coffee when I hear a voice with a strong Boston accent. Turning, I see Hugh Nevarez, our founder and president of the board. With a round belly and a beard that matches his graying hair, Hugh could pass for Santa Claus if it weren't for his designer Italian suit.

After I approach Hugh, Brock Bing, our new Chief Information Officer, cuts in front of me. Then he proceeds to talk to Hugh… and talk, and talk, and talk. I stand and wait patiently—and awkwardly—until Brock finally has to inhale. Darting forward, I blurt, "Mr. Nevarez. I have a new marketing idea for Petjamas." The line of parent-pet matching sleepwear I designed is flying off the shelves so fast, it's even made it into infomercials.

"I'm listening." Hugh folds his arms.

I square my shoulders when I say, "Let's sleep together."

Both pairs of eyes stare at me, wide as jumbo pizzas. The perma-buzzing Brock goes blissfully silent. My eyes flip from him to Hugh. Still nothing. I wave a hand as if that'll awaken them from their trance. "Imagine: the parent wearing the Petjamas onesie, the matching pet sleeper modeled on Notorious D-O-G. Above, it says, 'Let's sleep together.'" I let the words linger in the air for a beat. "It applies to the matching Petjamas and the animal since most of our customers sleep with their pets."

Finally, Brock moves, blinding me with his set of pearly whites, the reason the sales team calls him "Jaws." There's a running debate on whether it references the shark or the Bond villain. "The tagline could also be used to highlight that parents and pets sleep better with Petjamas because they're made from hemp cotton. Not bad, Sophie Fox!" Brock booms.

"That sounds great, actually." Hugh rubs his chin. "Creative, catchy, and definitely has shock value."

"Thank you." My smile broadens. When Brock starts up again, I politely excuse myself from the conversation. It's best to leave on a high note.

Through the crowd, I can't see Missy Mulligan, but I hear her shrill voice say, "Who are you again?" followed by murmuring. Missy's voice hits a pitchy soprano. "Do you just need money? If I give you some cash, will you go away?"

"I'm Sophie's mom. Let me in!"

Oh, no. No, no, no. I forgot to call Mom back!

I shimmy through the bodies to the entrance. It *is* Mom. And what in the holy cheese whiz is she wearing?

3

Costume Party

Mom stands in the lobby, crammed into a skimpy, skintight dominatrix outfit. Her chest spills out of the top of her cherry-red corset with spikes. Her bare midriff is covered in chains. Cobweb nylons held up by leather garter straps stretch their way into knee-high shiny black boots. Those have spikes on them, too. She's wearing the Lady Gaga wig with the incandescent blond hair shaped into a bow. Her red lipstick is so bright, it probably glows in the dark.

"Mom? What're you doing here? Looking like—*that*?" I scold in a fierce whisper.

"Wait, this is really your mom?" Missy's jaw hits the floor, joining mine.

"You wouldn't answer my calls, Sophie! I was so worried—I had a terrible feeling. Last night I had a vision you were bloody and mangled, guts spilling out everywhere." Mom turns and waves. "Hi everyone, I'm Sophie's mom, Skye. Sorry about the outfit, I was working undercover. Remember the 'Pantie Bandit,' Soph? Well, I just caught him." She looks around, making eye contact with various unlucky souls. "The mayor of Blue Vine is a pantie-collecting cheater, and it's gonna be on the cover of *The Grape Vine* when the story breaks. Which should be soon."

Everyone holds back laughter as they offer patronizing congratulations. I jump in with, "Wow, that sounds like big news, Mom. Excellent work." But when I glance at myself in the lobby mirror, my face is a shade of red that rivals Mom's lipstick.

Mom approaches Brock. "You're handsome." She looks around, raising her voice when she says, "Doesn't he look so much like Ken? You know, from Barbie and Ken. A dead ringer."

He flashes a smile of a million lumens and returns the handshake. Brock glances at the guests before he booms, "Why thank you, Ms. Fox."

"Call me Skye. Fox was my maiden name, which was about five last names ago!" Mom stomps through the room, chains jingling on her belly. "Oh, there's the hotel bar. I could use a drink after the all-nighter I just pulled. I'd love a stiffy."

I force my mouth into an upward curve as sweat beads on my brows. "It's nine a.m., Mom. And you didn't tell me you were in town."

"Sorry." She turns to me. "I tried to call you a zillion times."

Riley, my best friend and coworker, comes in for the rescue. "So, you work undercover, Skye?"

"Sophie, you didn't tell Riley?" Mom regards me with heavy eyes before she straightens her shoulders and returns her gaze to Riley. "I just got my cheater-buster's certification."

Riley shifts back and forth on her crisp Jimmy Choo boots, flashing me a guilty look before saying to Mom, "Sophie told me stuff, but I just didn't know you worked undercover."

"That's a new thing," I mumble, picking at my freshly manicured nails, a habit I'd quit until now.

Mom looks at me. "That reminds me, Soph, can you help me download and print my certificate? I have a frame ready. I can't believe I've just cracked a high-profile case. My phone's gonna be ringing off the hook!" Mom plops down at a cocktail table with Mason Carlisle from Pet IQ's accounting department before smiling at all the attendees. "I found the mayor's collection of different women's underwear, so I set up a trap and caught him."

"That's great news." I force a smile, desperately wishing she had a mute button. "So, how about I take you to my hotel room where you can change?"

"No need. I still have a few details to tie up. No pun intended!" Mom bursts into laughter. Alone. She elbows Mason, who gives her a nervous smile. Then his eyes dart around as though scouting an escape route.

I pan the crowd, finding Lucas. He's watching Mom with a smile that seems genuine. Then, as though he can feel my eyes on him, he meets my gaze. His smile grows, which makes things better… for a second.

It ends when Brock hands Mom a glass of amber liquid on ice, grinning when he says, "That's awesome. What else do you do?"

No, Brock. *Please* stop. I slam my eyes closed. I can't watch this.

Mom lifts her chin. "I'm a psychic white witch specializing in candle magic, although I also do past life regressions, spirit channeling, and tarot card readings. Oh, and standard entity lifts, but not full-blown exorcisms."

Muffled snickers echo around the room, notably Hugh Nevarez and our Chief Financial Officer, Mark McCoy. I'm struggling to inhale, and the sweating has become a full-body predicament.

Mom takes a hefty swing of her drink. "Anyway, Mayor Hayden kept making 'business' trips to Atlanta." She speaks loudly, confident all attendees want to hear her story. "Too many business trips. I followed him to the Lace 'n Leather parade and told him he could *earn* my panties. It was a setup, and he took the bait. He found me irresistible in this outfit. Of course." She lets out a satisfied sigh.

"That's a great thing you did." I keep my tone calm, but I grab her by the arm. I'm done trying to handle her without making a scene. "We're going back to my room. I have to check on Notorious D-O-G."

Mom slams her drink and sets the glass down before I give her a hefty tug.

"Back soon!" she calls out as I coax her toward the exit.

As I rush Mom out the door, I catch Hugh's scowl, and a wave of nausea hits. My chances of making VP surely dwindled with each word out of her mouth.

Once we're outside, Mom's face turns pouty. "I can't believe you yanked me away. I almost spilled my Johnnie Walker!"

"How could you just show up here dressed like that? Those people in there are my colleagues and bosses. They all think you're bonkers."

"I *told* you I was going undercover! What else was I supposed to do when you wouldn't answer? And you didn't mention that this was all hoity-toity." She waves her hand in the air with her pinky up. "You said you had a conference thingy, which I figured hadn't started yet. It's only nine a.m. I was just coming to check on my daughter."

Out of energy, I groan.

"Did you get all moved?" As usual, Mom shifts gears like a Porsche.

"Yes, at least that's all done." Everything I own is packed in my suitcase at The Starlite Inn. A year and a half ago, I found an amazing rental deal on a beautiful Tudor style home in Buckhead, the Beverly Hills of Atlanta. I moved in with Riley, and we lived there happily until the owner sold the home. We had to be out a few days ago, and now, Riley is staying with her parents. I haven't found a place yet. I'm going to Airbnb after this conference is over; I don't want to rush into anything.

Mom puts her palm on my forehead. "I'm getting a strong psychic vision that you're close to finding your soulmate. A man that understands and appreciates you for you."

I let out an exasperated sigh. "Are you missing an empathy chip? You think now's a good time to discuss my finding of a soulmate?" The blank look on Mom's face tells me that my words aren't computing, so I move on. "You told me your psychic gift doesn't work with family."

"True. I could call Veronica for an outside consult, although she's not really gifted with relationships. She told me I'd never get married again, and that was three husbands ago. Oh, I got it! A truth water prayer. That always works. You'll get the truth in thirty-six to forty-eight hours."

Picking up my pace, I say, "No outside psychic consults or water prayers."

Mom stops walking. "You know what? I can't help you if you won't help yourself."

"I didn't *ask* you for help," I say, louder than intended.

Mom takes a step back, blinking as she looks down. Her voice deflates like a cheap blow-up mattress. "Well, then. I'll go."

I rub my forehead. "No, Mom, I don't want you to go—"

"It's okay. I have an entity lift scheduled, anyway." She points in the opposite direction. "I'm parked back that way."

I fold my arms over the ache in my chest. I don't want her to leave mad, but I'm too furious to talk to her right now. I need to calm down before I say anything else I regret. "Okay. I'll call you."

"Good luck with your promotion, Soph." She walks away, not looking back.

4

The Board Game

I'm the first one at the board meeting, greeting each executive as they arrive, one by one. A few minutes past the meeting start time, Missy Mulligan floats through the doors wearing a cherry-red jumpsuit and a confident smile.

I suppress a gasp. What is *she* doing here? She's not an executive or board member.

And I can't imagine showing up late to anything, let alone a board meeting.

Blood rushes to my cheeks when I say, "Hello, Missy."

"Sophie." Her spidery lashes reach the top of her eyebrows.

"I'm looking forward to working with you." I crack a tentative smile.

"You mean working *for* me."

My face twists. "I'm sorry?"

Missy puts a hand over her mouth, but the creases in her eyes give away her smirk. "I'm going for the VP position, Sophie."

"VP of Product Design, the same one I'm going for?" That can't be. I worked seventy-hour weeks to get Petjamas launched, and when it took off, they promised me this promotion. At that thought, a nasty chill darts up my spine. They *had* promised me, but then delayed it for this product pitch. I thought the holdup was for Lucas, but maybe not. My brain goes into overdrive.

"Veep of Product Design, that's right." She cocks her head.

It hits me like the smell of her perfume singeing my nose—the board wants to give Missy a shot to see how she performs before they promote me. I stand, blinking in stunned silence.

She moves her hand. "The department is desperate for my social networking."

Criminy, it's true. It takes everything in my power to keep my face expressionless. The board asked her because she's an influencer. They want the windfall of sales she can bring. I manage to say, "Best of luck."

"I don't need luck." She blinks again, and I wish I had a fly swatter so I could smack her eyelashes.

Hugh approaches the front of the room and waits for everyone to sit and the chatter to quiet before he begins with, "Welcome executives, members of the board, Sophie, Missy. I'm glad you could all join us here in Atlanta despite the friggin' heat." He raises his coffee mug. "Am I right? But I'm sure glad you did because we gotta select a new product line to announce at the industry's event of the year."

Hugh opens his palm toward Lucas. "And I'd like to take this opportunity to introduce Fur Bebé's new CEO, Lucas Nevarez. He may be my nephew and on the young side, but don't let that fool you. He's a Stanford alum and graduated Harvard b-school at the top of his class. For three years, he was on Wall Street, swinging multi-million-dollar deals. And for the past few weeks, he's been training at our Boston office. Lucas brings the wealth of experience Fur Bebé needs to grow." Hugh turns toward Lucas. "Welcome."

The room erupts in applause, and Lucas smiles, his face turning a light shade of pink. "Thanks everyone, glad to be here."

When Lucas meets my gaze, he scrubs his hand on his chin, and it appears he's struggling as much as I am to hold it together.

"Now, let's get to it." Hugh clasps his hands. "We're going to hear from Sophie Fox, our top product designer, and our brightest star from sales, Missy Mulligan. Welcome."

After we nod and smile, Hugh says, "Missy, why don't you go first?"

"Absolutely." She grabs her laptop and breezes to the front with an air of confidence that ratchets up my nerves. She sets up her computer to project onto the whiteboard before smoothing her crisply tailored jumpsuit. Even her smile looks bedazzled. "The latest, greatest thing for people is activewear. Everyone is sporting it, whether they're active or not. So, with that in mind, allow me to present Fur Bebé's new clothing line—Pet Sweats."

Pet Sweats? *Pet Sweats.* My insides constrict, like a snake is coiling around them. Indeed, it just might be. How did Missy come up with the *exact* same idea I did? My skin tingles as a numbness settles in. It takes everything in me to not show the shock on my face.

She continues, "A line of activewear for *all* dogs, whether they're active, inactive, or just wish to match their adopted parents. Given the research I did with *real* people, this trending clothing line has the potential to be a windfall for Fur Bebé."

Besides the phrase "real people," she's quoting my presentation, verbatim! I break into an instant cold sweat. She's a thief, and I have to call her out. Except VPs don't do that. VPs stay cool and handle curve balls. But what am I going to present now?

And my mother just made a big mess of things.

Missy advances the slides. "I sent out some samples to all my two-hundred thousand FaceSnap fans, and great news! They loved the idea." She shows images that her followers posted of their pets with her prototyped activewear on them. She says, "We need to make Pet

Sweats a *must-have* item." Her smile grows. "Translation: very high sales volume."

As I scan the room, almost every person has dollar signs in their eyes and hungry smiles on their faces. Lucas is the only one who looks skeptical.

And I can't even find enough feeling in my limbs to react. Missy continues, and although there isn't any hard data or research on what she says, she keeps bringing up all her social media followers.

If my brain were a circuit board, it would definitely be jammed.

There's just one thing I've managed to process.

Missy stole my idea. Unapologetically. In plain sight. I don't know how she did it, but she did.

"Where did you get this idea, Missy?" Lucas asks.

"Um." Her lip quivers. "I just got it while I was working out." Her voice is high. "The best news of all—I already have a long and growing list of those who want to preorder as soon as it's available." She pumps a fist. "So, let's do it!"

The room erupts in applause, Lucas the only person whose clapping is merely polite.

Hugh invites me to the front of the room, and I approach as I would the edge of a deadly cliff. I have to steady my trembling lips to say, "Okay, everyone, well, this is a bizarre coincidence..." I make eye contact with each person in the room, trying not to think about the looks on all their faces earlier when they met Mom. "But I have to say, I think pet activewear must truly be the latest, greatest thing because that's what I came up with too after doing extensive market research of my own." I let out a laugh that sounds more like a seal bark.

"I'll just skip past the introduction since Missy already covered that ground." My slides blink on the whiteboard as I feverishly advance to the few that are different. I stop and present my projected profitability charts, which show solid numbers, even in worst-case scenarios. I fly through the summary of all my research—graphs from numerous sources that show pet activewear is on an exponential rise.

When I glance around the room, everyone looks bored out of their minds. My throat goes dry as I skip further to a slide with Notorious D-O-G wearing a Flashdance-style pink headband and leg warmers. Reading it, I say, "There are so many viral marketing possibilities..." I trail off, finishing the sentence with, "but Missy already presented those."

"Yes," Hugh cuts in. "Do you have any other product ideas, Sophie?"

With all eyes on me and the weight of my career on my shoulders, the room blurs and the floor seems to shift under my feet. But I can't give up. I have to figure out something. Anything.

I have a ridiculously far-fetched idea that I can't fathom presenting—but I'm out of options.

I clear my throat and finally squeak out, "I do, actually."

"Let's hear it," Hugh says.

"Absolutely." I fake confidence as I open the messy PowerPoint slides of a brain dump I had last night after hearing Mom talk about Lulu and Yoda's wedding. I couldn't sleep after my run in with Lucas, so I started a presentation. Before I project the first slide, I hesitate in utter disbelief at myself. Then I click the mouse and say, "This is a pet bridal line." I swallow hard, preparing myself for the words that are about to come out of my mouth. With enthusiasm, no less. "From the veil to the tutu to the diamond engagement collar, all pet brides can have the wedding of their dreams."

When I scan the room, my stomach skydives. Everyone's mouths hang open as I say, "Along with formal wear, we can provide wedding decorations, pet-safe appetizers, and glamor photography services." I flip to a slide with my rough sketches. "With mix and match options, there's a perfect package for every taste and budget."

The only movement in the room is a few blinking eyes.

They are definitely looking at me like they looked at Mom a mere hour ago.

I muster the courage to look at Lucas. By his face, he's scrambling for words when he says, "It's a little out there, but do you have the numbers to show us that this idea could work?"

I swallow the lump in my throat. Lucas is probably trying to help me, but I have nothing. I hadn't gotten that far. "Not yet, but I can get it ASAP." I smile with quivering lips. "We can also bring another twist to the market with parent-pet matching bridal gowns." There's a long, pregnant pause before I croak, "Thank you."

I glance at Missy to see a smug look on her face. With scant applause and shocked faces around the room, I ache for the earth to split open and swallow me whole.

Perfect. I've officially crossed over—I *am* as bonkers as my mother. They, whoever they are, say we wake up one day and realize we've become our parents. It's just the circle of life. Mine's apparently complete.

And my career is toast.

5

Dog Eat Dog

Lucas had Missy and me email our presentations to the board, and now, he's asked us both to move into the hallway while they tally votes.

As soon as we're outside the conference room, I get up in Missy's face. "You stole my idea. And you're not getting away with it."

"Actually, you stole mine." Her voice is calm—too calm.

"Whatever. This scheme of yours isn't going to fly." They can check the metadata of the PowerPoint files we emailed them and see that I was the original creator.

"Sorry, Sophie, but I have work to do." She looks at her phone where a silenced cat video is playing.

I'm tempted to make a snarky remark, but I bite my tongue. I don't want to sink to her level.

When the voting ends, Lucas and Hugh usher me into one conference room while the rest of the board brings Missy to another.

My knees almost collapse when I take a seat opposite the two men at the large conference table. I keep my voice low when I say, "She stole my idea. Lucas, you *know* she did."

"Sophie—" Lucas puts up a palm. "That might be true, but we need proof."

"We have it. Check the metadata of our presentation files."

"Actually, we already did—that's why I asked you both to email them." Lucas flips his computer around. "Each file lists Missy Mulligan as the original creator."

I gasp, looking at his screen. I see her name there, but I can't believe my eyes. "That can't be." My hands shake as I open my own computer and access my presentation. When I launch it and check, sure enough, it lists Missy's name. I put a hand over my mouth. "She had to have broken into my computer." My voice is above a whisper.

"Do you have any evidence of that?" Hugh leans back, his brows furrowed.

I swallow the hard knot in my throat. "Not yet. But I'll get it."

Hugh inhales sharply, tapping his fingers together. "Look, Sophie. We want to be selected by Pet IQ."

"Pet IQ?" I parrot, my brain trying to catch up to his sudden topic shift. Pet IQ is the industry giant that makes or breaks pet companies. And right now, they're the talk of the pet world because in addition to Puuccí, their own clothing line, they want to carry another. They're in the process of selecting a second brand to sell in their online and retail stores nationwide.

Lucas's voice is croaky when he says, "As you probably know, Fur Bebé—with our affordable quality—would be a great choice for Pet IQ."

"But they've made it clear that contenders will have national brand recognition," Hugh adds. "Currently, we don't have that."

I lick my trembling lips, which have gone bone dry. "Okay."

Hugh's face goes hard. "The board favored Missy's presentation, and we elected to make her VP of Product Designs."

My breath freezes in my chest, as I feel like I just got socked in the jaw and kicked in the gut all at once. Speechless, I sit in silence, staring at Lucas with blurry vision. When I finally find my voice, I say, "But Missy broke into my computer, altered files, then stole them. She did a very bad thing."

"Without proof, there's nothing more we can do." Hugh's tone is clipped, cold.

"Then get proof." My voice sharpens. "Ask Missy to provide documentation of her nonexistent research. Or look at both of our search histories."

Lucas rakes a hand over his mouth. "I know you're emotional right now, Sophie, but none of those things are feasible."

"Are you serious?" When that gets no response from Hugh or Lucas, I compose myself before saying, "Getting the word out is not all the VP job entails. Missy will fail at all the other critical tasks the job requires. I'm the qualified and experienced person who can do the job—the *whole* job—right."

Lucas leans forward, guilt flickering in his eyes. "You're a brilliant product idea person, undoubtedly. But right now, brand exposure is our priority."

I don't have a rebuttal to that, so we sit in an awkward silence until another implication hits me. "So, I work for her now?"

Hugh avoids my gaze. "We can't keep someone on staff who appears to have stolen files. What message would that send to our employees, partners, and customers?" His face reddens as he hesitates. "I'm sorry, Sophie, but we're gonna have to let you go."

I can't draw enough air into my lungs to speak as I desperately blink back tears. My stomach knots, and suddenly, the room feels airless and hot, and it's shrinking by the second.

They're *firing* me? This cannot be happening!

With my pulse pounding in my ears, I manage to say, "But Missy stole from *me*. You can't let her get away with this."

Lucas's face pinches in guilt. "I'll do everything I can to get to the bottom of things, I promise. Until then, our hands are tied. I'm so sorry."

My misty eyes meet Hugh's hard gaze when I say, "But I've given this company everything I have, exceeding all goals. I've worked toward this for years, and it's *my* designs that are bestsellers. What about giving me a chance to get proof? What about keeping the promise you made to me?"

Hugh doesn't flinch. "This is a tough situation. We're no good to the rest of our other employees if we lose our stellar reputation. We're doing what we have to do. Missy has two-hundred thousand FaceSnap fans." His phone buzzes, and he taps his hand on the table before he stands. "I'm sorry, but I've gotta take this. Excuse me." He rushes out of the room.

I turn to Lucas, my voice desperate. "You *know* Pet Sweats was my idea."

"I will help you get the evidence to clear your name. But until then, I support the board's decision. Missy has the marketing reach we need." Lucas's voice now has an edge. "It's just business."

I blink as I process his harsh words. Finally, I grit, "Then you just sold your soul." I don't know why I'm surprised at his behavior. I spent some time chatting with him, so it's not like I really know him. And I don't. Not at all.

But why did I feel like I did?

My eyes narrow as I stand, slinging my computer bag over my shoulder. Leaning in, I lower my voice when I say, "Here's a lesson you surely didn't get at Harvard, on Wall Street, or from being the nephew of our founder. You're going to be sorry. You need experience. You need knowledge. You need me."

His expression matches mine. "Is that so?"

"Like a dinghy on the Titanic." I turn on my heels and march out of the room.

6

Hell on Wheels

I call Mom. No answer. I text her. No reply. For the first time ever, I'm the one entering a call-text-leave-a-voicemail frenzy. I send a final text—one I've never sent before. "911."

After snagging Notorious D-O-G and his crate from our PAW-CON booth, I reserve an Uber to take me to Fur Bebé's offices to pick up my personal things. I don't have a car; Riley always drove me to work when we lived together. I was going to get one after this conference.

So, in summary, I have no car, no home, and now, no job.

To say I'm screwed would be a whopping understatement.

During my trek to the Uber loading area, I see Mom sitting in the driver's seat of a Winnebago that's illegally parked. She rolls down the passenger window and hollers, "Sophie, over here!" as if I could miss her in that house on wheels. "You look weird," she says as I approach.

"What are you doing?"

"You don't have a car. I thought I'd pick you up." Mom eyes me. "Sorry I'm late." I make it to her window, fumbling with Mr. D's crate as she says, "I was doing an entity lift on Stalon and Nigel and couldn't stop halfway through. That pigheaded spirit refused to leave. I think it was really sad about being dead."

"I can't talk about this, Mom. They just screwed me over in there." I blink. "But who are Stalon and Nigel?"

"New clients and friends from a past life." She sighs. "Anyway, I figured you'd leave after they promoted Missy."

I inhale the warm late-summer air. "So, it was that obvious they were gonna pick her?"

"Actually, Missy already announced it on FaceSnap and Chirper. But isn't she more qualified?"

My jaw drops. "If more qualified means zero experience. Or thinking the S&P 500 is a NASCAR race."

"Oh." Mom's face goes blank. "I told you I had a bad feeling."

"Well, it's worse than you thought," I say, indignant. "Missy stole my presentation and made it look like I stole hers, so I got fired. Next time, use every gold candle in your stash."

"Don't be salty, Soph. My candles work. If the universe elevated you from this situation, it means you're meant for something else, something much greater."

"Of course. You have an explanation if it works and an explanation if it doesn't. How convenient." As I approach the passenger side, Mom's awful Shih Tzu, poodle-ish mutt, Gizzie, flings half his body out of the open window and starts yapping his head off. I adore animals, but not this one. Mr. D starts barking too, and I glance around to see if anyone is witnessing this scene—not that anything could top the one Mom made a few hours ago. Mercifully, the place is empty.

After I open the door, Gizzie leaps out and starts nipping at my ankles.

"Gizzie, no biting!" I hop around.

"Gizzie!" Mom points at the floor. "Inside."

The embodiment of evil jumps back in, leaving me to check my ankles for broken skin. I lucked out—for now. Besides the nipping, Gizzie growls nonstop and chews up everything, including walls. Unfortunately, this dog does *not* bother Mom's allergies, so she keeps him.

I step in and set Mr. D's crate by my feet before closing the door. "So, what are you doing in a Winnebago?"

"I brought it for the sting operation."

I exhale. "Back up. Where did you *get* a Winnebago?"

"Oh, this was Darryl's." Darryl is Mom's latest ex-husband, and her worst one to date, which is really saying something. She continues, "You know I caught him co-signing on a double wide with Dutchie while we were still married." Mom smacks the dashboard. "Anyway, because of that, I got Betsy here in the divorce."

"Oh." I didn't know that, and I realize it's been a while since I've visited Mom.

"Betsy's how I drove to Atlanta from Blue Vine. I've had her parked in Stone Mountain where Ernie, my neighbor there, has been taking care of Gizzie for me." She taps the steering wheel. "Now Betsy'll give us a home for a few days while we get you moved."

I can't break it to Mom that I have nowhere to go. Before I can say anything, Mom waves out the window, swooning, "Some luscious executive is giving me the eye."

Are you kidding me? "That's Lucas, our new CEO. And he's not so luscious when he opens his mouth." I groan, leaning forward to look out her window. Lucas is standing outside the revolving door of the hotel's entrance. We make eye contact, and I give him a death stare, fighting the urge not to slink down in my seat. "Can you pull away already?"

"You're not allowed to be embarrassed of me and the Gizz-ster."

"I'm not embarrassed because of you." I lower my voice. "I kinda told him off."

"What?" Mom turns and flashes me a proud smile. "Well, butter my butt and call me a biscuit. I'm proud of you, Soph. You did what I would've done."

And there it is. Ironclad proof that I screwed up royally.

Gizzie jumps to Mom's window and yaps his guts out. "Gizzie, don't be a nightmare," I scold.

"You know, Gizzie knows what you're saying." Mom grips him so he doesn't fly away. "That's why he's mean to you. If you want to get along with him, you need to stop talking trash. He's a wonderful dog."

Wonderful Gizzie turns and bares his snaggletooth at me as Mom tugs him back inside.

I buckle my seatbelt before saying, "Can we *please* go?"

"Fine, but Lucas is running over here. He must have it bad for you."

"No, he doesn't," I say, hating that I wish that were true.

Lucas calls out, "Hold up, Sophie. You can't take Notorious D-O-G." Lucas breaks into a sprint. "He's company property."

"See?" I huff.

Mom waves at Lucas and says, "Gotta run, bathroom emergency. Catch you later." She peels away, sending Gizzie through the air. Miraculously, I catch him.

"Mom, stop!" I yell. "I have to give the dog back. Mr. D belongs to Fur Bebé, and they can sue—"

Mom hits the breaks so hard they squeal before she guns it in reverse. After she stops and rolls down the window, I grip Gizzie while Mom takes Mr. D's crate and hands it to Lucas.

I shake a finger. "If I even get a whiff that Notorious D-O-G is not being treated like a prince, I'll come after you."

"He'll be well cared for."

"So, are you a Scorpio, Lucas?" Mom asks.

"Uh, yeah, actually." He goes wide-eyed.

"I got that. Determined. In control. Secretive. Donkey-stubborn."

I knead my forehead. "We can go now, Mom."

"Okay, bye, Lucas. We'll be in touch." She rolls up her window as he waves.

"Um, no we won't be," I grumble.

After she pulls out of the parking lot, she asks, "So, how bad did it end with him?"

"You don't wanna know." I put my face in my hands.

"Men are scoundrels," she says. Mom hates men. Her childhood was rough—so rough that she refuses to talk about it. She sighs, "But Lucas isn't."

"What?" I heard her, but I can't believe that last part.

"Lucas is one of the few good ones. I can tell. And he's definitely got it *bad* for you."

"Please."

Mom turns onto the road, running over the curb. Poor Gizzie goes airborne again, and I decide to hang onto him for good.

Driving, Mom lifts her chin in the way she does before she breaks into song. "I quit ma job I worked so hard to get. I lost ma place that I sublet. I lost ma dog that I'll never forget. Twang, twang, twang. And it isn't even noon yet." She stops singing, or more like howling.

I close my eyes. "I knew it was country song time. Do you know how predictable you are?"

"Just trying to cheer you up." She reaches over and pats my back.

Mom drops me at Fur Bebé's office, and when I arrive, Riley's there and she has everything packed up for me.

I approach her. "You heard? Already? And what are you doing back here?"

"I wanted to talk to you," she says in an uncharacteristically gentle tone. "I told my boss I had to return to the office to get some important paperwork. Anyway, Missy is the devil's mistress, and I'm going to make sure she pays dearly for what she's done." Riley pulls me into a hearty hug because she gives the best hugs ever. "I'm gonna miss you."

A wave of sadness hits. "We used to live together and work together. Now, nothing."

"This stinks. Keep me updated, okay?" She pulls away, wringing her hands. "Also, I should probably let you know. A lawyer—older guy—from Urban Productions came here looking for you." She flings up a palm. "But don't worry—I told him you'd left the company and I had no idea where you were."

"Urban Productions?" I rub my forehead. "The TV and film company? Why would they be looking for me?"

Riley gnaws on her cheek. "Um, that's the company that produces *Bridesmaid to Bride*."

My stomach turns into a pretzel. "Okay, so, something to do with Missy?"

"I dunno. Maybe defamation of character? Because of the presentation thing?"

A wave of dizziness clouds my vision, and I literally cannot take another hit. Shutting the thought down of anything Missy-lawsuit related, I say, "No way."

"They can't sue you if they can't serve you." Riley raises an eyebrow. "And I'm the only one who knows you're in a Winnebago. So, no worries."

"Thanks, Rye." I'm not a hundred percent sure she's right on that, but right now, I need to believe her. If nothing else, it'll cause enough of a delay for Missy to come to her senses.

I'm gathering the rest of my things when I see the decorations for the PAW-CON mixer tomorrow night sitting on the reception desk. Riley and I have been prepping for it, and she's counting on me. "Crap." I close my eyes. "Tomorrow's mixer."

"Don't worry about it. I got it."

I swallow hard, my stomach tightening. I can't go to that, but at the same time, I *can't* dump all the party prep on Riley. "No, no, no. I'll be there to help you." I feign a grin. "It'll be fun doing it and who knows—maybe I can network my way into another job."

"Are you sure?" She gasps. "What if the Urban Productions lawyer comes?"

I hesitate, thinking. "No one will expect me to be there." I can't *not* help Riley, no matter what. I bat a hand. "Absolutely. See you tomorrow night."

She raises a perfectly manicured brow. "Madame Puuccí is going to be there."

Madame Puuccí—Pet IQ's Founder and CEO and *Fortune Magazine's* most powerful woman of the year—is a *very* good person to know. My mouth curls up. "That's right. She *will* be there. Good thinking, Rye."

"It's why they pay me the big bucks."

I give her a wave and rush out the door.

Once Mom and I get back to the Starlite Inn near the conference in Midtown, she helps me throw clothes into my suitcase.

After we finish, Mom waves a hand. "Let's get outta this no-tell motel and get you to your Airbnb."

I bite my lip and hesitate before saying, "I can't really afford an Airbnb now. With no job, I need to hang onto my savings. I don't know how long I'll be unemployed. I shouldn't spend money until I have some sort of plan."

"Oh, Soph." Mom pulls me into a half hug with a weak pat, the best I'm going to get from her. "We'll figure something out."

When I step away, I recognize that look on Mom's face—she's about to dive off the deep end. I shake my head when I say, "Uh, oh. What?"

"I'll stay in Atlanta with the Winnebago. I'm divorced now, free from that ball-less chain. You can move in with me while you look for a job."

That sounds like a fiery ball of hell, but I'm too beaten down to argue. Mom is giving up everything to help me, something she's always done. "Okay, thank you."

7

Caught Pantie-Handed

At the Stone Mountain RV Park, we get the Winnebago hooked up to power and sewer. Once inside, I peer around the place, a sick feeling rolling through me when I see wall-to-wall junk. This brings back memories I've worked hard to forget—living in a packed trailer with Mom, barely scraping by after she couldn't pay the mortgage and we lost our house.

Separately, I think Mom might be a borderline hoarder disguised as an enthusiastic knick-knack collector.

Stepping through the mini-living room, I find the lopsided Popsicle stick house I made in second grade still intact on the tiny set of shelves. Of all my body of "art," I can't believe that's what Mom kept all these years. Beside it is the framed newspaper clipping of Lulu and Yoda's wedding, and I have to admit—Lulu looks stunning. Well, in an ugly pug sort of way. The picture makes me feel worse for Mom than I did when she'd first told me about Lulu's wedding. My eyes mist.

I miss Mr. D.

My tour of the place takes less than a minute with a peek into the airplane-sized bathroom with a tiny shower, and Mom's bedroom, a compartment above the cab of the vehicle. When I get back to the dining room/kitchenette/living room, I inhale a musty smell. "I think there's mold in here."

"That's just the scent of Betsy's aura. She's old, and that's her way of letting us know it."

"Are you kidding me? We're going to die of mold poisoning."

Mom ignores me, unfolding the kitchen table to make a flat surface. Then she slides the booth cushions down before opening a palm and saying, "Welcome to your new bed, Soph."

I swallow hard. Mom and I'd struggle being house-mates in a palace, let alone this micro-sized crap-hole. This has to be a one or two-night gig, tops. But I'll get to that later. Instead, I unpack as I fill her in on what happened during the presentation. Sitting on my new, hard bed, I say, "What now?"

"Don't worry, I've gotta plan. I have a spell that'll haunt Lucas for the rest of his life."

"No, Mother, you're a 'noble' witch, remember?" I wander three steps to the kitchen and lean on the counter.

"Hmmm." Another long pause. "How about just a teeny hex that'll make him impotent for a while?"

Although enticing, I'll deal with Lucas myself. "Don't do that either. I've got it," I say, meaning it. I'm going to handle this like a calm, rational adult. And if there are "cosmic boomerangs" as Mom says, Missy and the rest of Fur Bebé are going to get knocked into next week when the boomerang returns.

Mom rifles through her cabinets for food, pulling out a box of Count Chocula. "Dinner?"

"I'm not hungry now. Maybe later." I guess that's one perk of having a dining-table bed. I can bury my head under the pillow while I talk to Mom in the kitchen.

"So, that Hugh guy I met in the lobby. The President of the Board." Mom dumps the cereal into a large mixing bowl. "Is he married?"

I wince. Mom better not dare tell me she wants to date him. I get up and lean on the kitchenette island, hesitant when I say, "I'm pretty sure he's single. He just went through divorce number three."

"Huh." She grabs the milk from the refrigerator and pours it into her cereal. "I would've pegged him as the type who's been married a lot."

I roll my eyes. "Yeah, only three teensy times."

"Right? So, single, huh? Great—well, that means you can whip out the heavy artillery on him."

I scrunch my nose. "Artillery?"

"Do you think you could ask him out?" Chocula bits fly out of her mouth and onto my face.

"Seriously, Mom?" I wipe off my cheek.

"I'm just asking, jeez. You don't have to get your panties in a bunch."

At a loss for words, I glower at her.

"Soph, you want your job back or not?" Mom crunches her Count Chocula.

"Yes. But not like that. I want to earn it back, fair and square."

"There's that word again—the place with cotton candy and elephant ears." She sighs. "You should start your own pet clothing line. Forget those nitwits."

That's a nice thought, but that's nearly impossible without startup capital or investors. I plunge on. "I need to make myself more invaluable than Missy. Somehow."

Mom crunches away, which makes me bonkers. Finally, she says, "We'll just have to move in together."

"No!" I say, louder than intended. I can't have my mother mucking my life up worse than I've already done myself. And forget helicopter parenting—Mom is the hovering, UFO type. "I mean, that doesn't make sense. I'll get my job back."

"Mmm-hmm." She buzzes off to the bathroom.

What does that mean? I'll show her. After I get in my pjs and brush my teeth in the kitchenette sink, I turn on my laptop and email Brock about collecting my backup and research files. Then I brainstorm ways to impress Madame Puuccí tomorrow at the mixer. If Fur Bebé's board wants their clothing to be in Pet IQ stores, I'll go straight to the source and make that happen.

After Mom returns wearing her hot-pink robe, she sits on a counter stool. It hits me that I've been so preoccupied that I never asked her about her big undercover operation, so I say, "So how'd you catch your pantie-bandit cheater?"

She pulls out her computer from the case and makes a few clicks. "Log onto *The Grape Vine*. Look, it's right here."

I get up, lean over her to see her laptop, and start reading. Sure enough, there's a picture of Mayor Hayden with the headline: *Breaking News: Mayor Caught Cheating, Pantie-Handed*.

I'm surprised Mom pulled something like this off, but I'm still too annoyed about it to tell her she's done well. As I continue to watch the report, it flips to earlier amateur footage of the mayor marching in a parade with Mom behind him in a shopping cart being pushed by two guys wearing chaps—and absolutely nothing else.

"*Why* are you in a shopping cart?" I hold my hands over my face as if watching a slasher movie.

"My dogs were barkin'! Do you know how uncomfortable those boots were?" She points at the screen. "Oh, and that's Stalon and Nigel pushing me. Such nice young men—they're the ones I did an entity lift for this morning. They want me to meet them for beers this weekend."

"Sweet mercy."

"Anyway, I feel bad turning on Mayor Hayden like that." She rolls her neck. "But I think this is gonna be good for him. He'll be able to find someone who appreciates his fetish. He deserves freedom, and so does his wife, Susan. So, I want to bring him these after his divorce is final." She fetches a bag and pulls out a pair of edible underwear with a big padlock on the crotch. "Do you think he'll like these?"

I stare at the edible panties, wondering if the padlock is edible, too. "Well, I think those are a perfect way to tell someone you're sorry for busting them for cheating and exposing their private fetish to the world."

"I thought so." She ignores my sarcasm.

"So, how did you get involved with this, anyway? You sound like you know Mayor Hayden personally?"

"Yes, I do know Mayor Hayden. Very well, actually."

"How?"

"I can't say. Candle magic client privilege."

"Mayor Hayden is one of your clients?" I cock my head.

"I can't confirm or deny that."

"So, your client told you he collects panties after he sleeps around."

"Of course not! He's got a wandering eye, not a missing brain. I put two and two together and followed him around town for a while." Mom tightens her robe.

"Well, be careful." I return to my bed and sit. "That sounds dangerous."

As Mom turns and studies me, her eyes grow heavy. "You really never told people about me, Sophie?"

I knew she'd be hurt that my coworkers know so little about her, but I've come to dread the reactions I get when I try to explain her to people. Not able to tell her that, I reply, "You know it's difficult to explain what you do. Actually, I don't exactly know what you're doing now."

"I hate that we aren't as close anymore, Soph."

"I'm closer with you than anyone," I answer honestly.

"That's sad, honey. You can't keep everyone at arm's length forever. You drove all your ex-boyfriends away because you wouldn't let them in. That's no way to live."

I try to swallow, but my esophagus feels like it's in a vise. That's not true, is it? Maybe I struggle allowing myself to be vulnerable, but that's because I just haven't met the right guy yet. I remind myself that Mom knows how to play my heartstrings like a toy ukulele. After a brief argument with myself, I decide to extend an olive branch. I pat my hand on the mattress and say, "Let's catch up."

"Really?" She comes over and hops on the bed. "Well, for starters, the Mayor's wife, Susan, was ready to put a restraining order on me before she realized I was right about her husband." Mom continues to fill me in on all the details of this and her other undercover missions. Admittedly, it's interesting to hear how they all went down.

After that conversation ends, Mom says, "I think those fish blobs from that fancy hotel gave me gas. So, consider yourself warned."

"Perfect. Those were crab cakes." I slide under the covers. "Good night, Mother."

She clicks my lamp off. "Good night, Soph."

I try to sleep, but I toss and turn like I'm on the Twisted Cyclone at Six Flags.

It's not helping that Mom's screensaver is flashing. I get up to close her computer, but when I touch the screen, it wakes. I see a thumbnail of what looks like a picture of me as a toddler with someone, so I click to open it. It's definitely me, around two or three, standing on a stage with strawberry ice cream smeared all over my face and *Toy Story* T-shirt. With me is a hippie-looking guy with a mullet and long beard, and he's sitting in front of a set of drums and holding drumsticks. His eyes are the same shade of green as mine, and my stomach crashes to the floor.

That guy looks like he could be my father, Henry Winter, who Mom said was a drummer, except according to her, I've never met my dad. I blink as I try to process what I'm seeing. Why has Mom never shown me this picture?

I email it to myself before closing the application and snapping Mom's laptop shut. I don't know why I just did that—I can't deal with that picture right now—or ever. My father is dead.

Who cares if he and I met once, and Mom didn't want to dredge it up? She probably figured I'd be more hurt if I knew he'd met me. And with the nausea roiling in my gut right now, she might've been right.

8

Buzz Kill

After hanging twinkle lights, putting centerpieces on the cocktail tables, and finding a missing bartender, I head to the bathroom for a stint to freshen my makeup and pull myself together for tonight's PAW-CON mixer. Reminding myself I did nothing wrong, I stare into the mirror as I say, "You can do this."

I'm wearing my lucky gray Fendi long-tailed blazer with matching wedge heels—as if luck can save me tonight.

Upon returning to the ballroom, I find a bartender smiling and chatting with Riley. With her perfect curves, flawless fair skin, and thick auburn hair, nearly every straight, single man on the planet falls instantly in love with her. After she sits on a barstool, she turns to me and says, "Get over here, Soph. Sam's offering us drinks, on the house."

Of course. One benefit of our friendship is getting free drinks everywhere we go. Heading to the bar, I say, "Thanks, Sam." I look at Riley. "I think I might've earned this."

"Heck, yeah." She rests a hand on her rosy cheek, sprinkled with light freckles.

"The place looks awesome," Sam says. "You two did a great job."

"Thank you." It does look nice, but it helps that this space has square crystal chandeliers, mirrored pillars, and a skyline view of downtown Atlanta. I take in the luxury, reminding myself how fortunate I am to attend events like this. But it does nothing to raise my spirits.

I just have to face it: this evening is going to be a test of how thick my skin is, and I have no choice but to rise to the challenge.

And I made Mom promise every entity in her universe that she would never step foot inside this hotel again.

Sam is called away, and Riley turns to me, the usual sparkle in her big blue eyes dimmed. "You were going to be VP, and I was going to help you restructure the company." Riley is Fur Bebé's accounting manager—despite breaking every single stereotype about accountants—and she wants the donation program as much as I did.

"That's why you're the best, Rye. And we'll still do that because I'm going to introduce Madame Puuccí to the future of petwear and land Fur Bebé the Pet IQ opportunity." I wave my glass of wine in the air. "Imagine: RezQ—spelled R-E-Z-Q, petwear that fuses fashion and philanthropy. When you make a purchase, five percent of proceeds go to animal charities."

Riley slaps me on the shoulder. "I love the name—rescue animals with RezQ. Nice! Forget Fur Bebé's stingy board. They'll do it when Madame Puuccí wants it, which she will because it's brilliant." She winks, taking a sip of her clear, bubbly drink, which I know is a vodka tonic with a splash of lime juice.

"Thanks." I really hope she's right.

When PAW-CON attendees begin showing up, I'm surprised at how many people I don't know—this industry is growing like wildfire. And I'm glad because everyone from Fur Bebé is avoiding me. The caterers rush around with hors d'oeuvres and drinks, keeping all the attendees happy while Riley and I greet everyone at the door.

With the room full of bodies, clinking glasses, and chatter, Riley and I leave the entrance to mingle. I don't know if I'm being paranoid, but I swear people are looking at me and whispering.

I'm holding up reasonably well until Missy steps through the glass doors with Mr. D on a leash. He's dressed in bejeweled activewear, and he looks overheated.

The fire from my cheeks spreads to the tips of my ears, and I'm aching to snatch my Mr. D away before dumping my red wine down Missy's hot-pink spaghetti-strap silk number that looks like lingerie. Unfortunately, she pulls it off.

Mr. D doesn't even get a glimpse of me because everyone's offering Missy congratulations, hugs, and cheers. She floats through the room, her stilettos echoing on the marbled floor.

I take a big swig of my drink, my eyes still trained on her and Mr. D. When she talks to Hugh Nevarez, he's got dollar signs in his eyes, surely at her influential powers. Then she says something that makes Mark McCoy laugh, and he holds his drink up in an air-toast to Mr. D. When she brushes a crumb off Mark's lapel, nausea roils through me.

She fits the part—the look, the well-honed networking skills, and the air of confidence that comes from growing up with money.

I take deep breaths, regaining my composure. Forget them—*all* of them.

I just need to get Madame Puuccí interested in my idea so I can get my job back. Missy can only take away my dream if I let her.

When I spy Smithy Baldwin, the CEO of Whiffany & Co, I brush off my suit and square my shoulders. He's hiring designers, so he's on my networking list for tonight.

I lift my chin and approach him, extending my hand. "Hello, Mr. Baldwin. I'm Sophie—"

"Sophie Fox, I know," he says flatly.

"Oh, I'm flattered." My hand is still extended, but he doesn't shake it. I finally return it to my side, feigning an itch. "So, I know you're in search of designers, and I was hoping to run some ideas by you that I think you'll love."

He laughs derisively. "You've gotta be kidding me."

My throat goes dry. "Excuse me?"

He takes a big swig of his dirty martini before he whispers, "Look, I heard what happened. I can't hire someone who just got canned for stealing another's idea."

I tremble but stay standing tall. "That rumor's false, Mr. Baldwin. I have best-selling ideas, and I've never stolen anything in my life, which I'm about to prove." Brock emailed me back, promising to send all my backup files and search histories to the board.

"Sorry, kid. Whether it's true or not, Whiffany & Co can't bring on anyone who could tarnish our hard-earned reputation. You understand."

My stomach skydives, but I nod slowly. Did Missy just get me blackballed from the entire industry? "Sure."

Riley approaches me, and I don't like the look on her face. She leans in and whispers, "Sorry, Soph, but I just heard that Madame Puuccí isn't coming tonight. She's got called away to an emergency meeting."

I sigh so hard my shoulders sag. "Really?"

"Sorry, hon." She squeezes my arm.

"I'll get her next time." Except I don't know when that next time will be. It's not like I can just get a meeting with her. In fact, no one I know has ever gotten a meeting with her because they can't get past her gatekeeper, Frank Franklin, who's also *not* here tonight. And now, I look like a thief. Suddenly, a bone-deep exhaustion settles in.

I console myself by rationalizing that it's best I'm not pitching her tonight—the rumor mill has buried me alive, and all I have is an idea and a dream. That's not enough.

It's my party and apparently, I'll cry even if I don't want to. With tears threatening to burst, I race to the patio door. I can't embarrass myself in front of these people. *Again.*

# # #

After I step outside, I slide the glass door closed behind me. I've always found comfort outside at dusk, watching nature's show in the sky, and I hope it'll help tonight. But I can't tear my gaze from the roomful of happy, chattering people. Or at least the appearance of happiness—dazzling smiles, sparkling champagne and crisp, designer suits—not the real happiness of friends singing karaoke at closing time who don't care that you sound like a hyena attempting Adele.

"Hello?" An all-too-familiar voice behind me makes me jump so high that some of my wine splashes onto the glass door.

I whip my head around, and through glazed eyes, see Lucas standing at the patio railing. I frantically swipe the tears away and square my shoulders. "Are you everywhere?" I want to dart back inside but stop myself. Apparently, I'd rather be around this jerk than let the entire roomful of people see me cry.

"Beautiful evening." He nods to the sky.

My gaze flicks upward to see the horizon, which has started its transformation from bright blue to shades of orange and red, scattering magic across the sky. But tonight, the usual sparkles in the air seem to turn to ash when they settle around me.

I don't want guests to see my red-rimmed eyes through the door, so I walk over and sit on the teak patio chair.

After Lucas sits in the seat next to me—not a great sign that I'm getting rid of him soon—he smooths the dress shirt that stretches over his fireman calendar chest. The shirt's ivory color complements his bronze skin and whiskey eyes.

And... what am I thinking? Lucas is the enemy. It's clearly been too long since I've been with a man. Eight months and counting, but with work, I've had zero time.

That's not entirely true. I haven't felt much like dating since things with John crashed and burned. John said—surprise, surprise—I cared more about work than him, a common complaint of my exes. He was right, but deep down, I felt I had no choice. I was terrified that if I didn't hang onto the career reins tightly enough, they'd slip away.

Ironic. That happened anyway.

Lucas raises his plate of hors d'oeuvres. "Have you tried these bacon-wrapped dates? They're phenomenal. I don't know if you know this, but bacon solves every problem. Really."

The appetizer *does* look delicious, and I haven't had the chance to try any of the food.

He continues, "A peace offering?"

His gesture lifts some of the weight off my heavy heart. "Sure."

When he offers his plate, I take an hors d'oeuvre and bite into it, deciding that it is, indeed, phenomenal. I snatch two more, not caring that I look like I'm in a starved fury. As I chew, I notice that Lucas's khakis have hitched up his calves, revealing black socks with the red Spider Man logo on them.

"These bacon thingies are downright tasty," I mumble with a mouth full of food, a behavior usually reserved for drunken nights with my hometown friends.

"Told you." His lips split into a grin. "I gotta admit, I was shocked to see you here tonight."

"*I* was shocked to be here tonight. But I made a promise to my best friend that I'd help her. Unlike Fur Bebé, I honor my promises."

"Ouch. Regardless, you're gutsy."

"Thanks." My cheeks warm as I meet his gaze. "Glad to make a comeback. The last twenty-four hours haven't been my finest."

"Nor mine." His voice is firm when he says, "I'm not letting this go, Sophie. I've gotta fight to get the truth—but while earning the respect of the board and my employees as the young new CEO. And I didn't want..." he trails off, pointing inside to Missy, who's now all over Pet IQ's director of partnerships. "Wasn't she supposed to marry that Eben guy on live TV or something?"

"Didn't work out."

"Shocking," he deadpans.

"Shocking, indeed." I exhale, trying to wipe the visual of Missy from my mind. "So, why were you standing out here alone?"

"Just letting everyone recover from my killer one-liners." The corner of his mouth ticks up before he looks down. "Nah. I actually choked on a sip of sweet tea. I'd never had it before. Apparently, when they say sweet in the South, they aren't messing around."

"Welcome to Atlanta. And yeah, Southern sweet tea is sugar with a splash of tea."

"Noted. So, I decided to come out here and cough my lungs out in peace."

Against my better judgment, I laugh, not hesitating when I say, "You should've seen me when I first moved here from the sticks. Once, I tried to compliment a woman by telling her she smelled like Courvoisier. I thought it was a designer perfume."

Coming from the itty-bitty Georgia town of Blue Vine, the big city was a culture shock, to put it mildly. After community college, moving to Atlanta was baptism by fire. I made it my mission to become somewhat refined, learning enough about wine so that I could fake some sophistication. I've never gone wrong saying I tasted currants in a heavy red, for instance. Someday, I should probably try a currant to see if I'm right.

Lucas chuckles, and our eyes lock. The twinkle in his makes my brain buzz when I say, "Or worse, the time I admitted thinking escargot was a shipping company."

Lucas lets out a laugh, and it's the contagious kind, so I laugh along with him. I can't believe after what went down between us, we're having so much fun. Why is it impossible to stay angry with this guy?

"I would've liked to have met the old you." He sighs. "I guess I'll have to settle for meeting the new you."

"Yeah, just the new refined, regal me."

He grins along with me, but it falls off his face as he studies me, saying nothing. I cock my head and say, "Why are you looking at me like that? Are you going to tell me how when one door closes, another opens? Or how adversity creates opportunity?" I groan. "Or how someday I'll be grateful because all this drop-kicked me into a world where unicorns have rainbows streaming from their butts?"

He leans into me and squints. "Actually, I was about to tell you that you have a piece of bacon on your cheek." He reaches over and brushes it off with his forefinger.

"Oh." Blushing, I look down. When I finally glance back up at Lucas, I see that his eyes are trained on me. "You have a very expressive face. You're a terrible poker player, aren't you?"

He thinks he knows me already? "Maybe." I scowl, realizing I'm having way too much fun with someone who just turned my life upside down, so I stand and slide the glass door open. "I'd better get back inside. I might be needed for something."

"All right. But the sun's about to set, and it looks to be one for the books. You'll be sad if you miss it."

"True," I answer, then my arm hairs stand on end. "Wait, how did you know I loved—" I stop, looking at him wide-eyed. "Is it your Spidey-sense?"

He glances at his ankles. "I had no clean socks, so I was forced to make a quick detour to Kroger. These were the only black ones they had. But they did come with matching Underoos, so that's a bonus."

"I never buy my superhero socks without Underoos."

He smiles before nodding toward my phone. "How I know you loved sunsets—your wallpaper gave it away."

My lock screen has my favorite shot of a sunset over the vineyards of my hometown. "Observant."

"So, I've been told."

The way Lucas looks at me makes me feel really good… and really vulnerable. I want to share my treasured pastime with him, but it feels too intimate. I fold my arms tightly over my chest, deciding it's okay if I stand in the open doorway. Together, in silence, we watch the sun make its grand exit for the day. Before leaving, I turn to Lucas and say, "Well, you were right. I would've been sad if I'd missed that. It was auroral—the best kind."

"Auroral, huh. That's how I always describe my favorite sunsets."

My mouth curves, but my expression goes hard when I realize I can't leave without saying my peace. "I want my job back, Lucas."

He glances away before meeting my gaze. His lips twitch, as though he's carefully selecting his words before he says, "I wish more than anything that I could give you that. But I can't. Not yet, anyway."

I nod slowly, my heart pinching. "Then I'll just have to do everything in my power to make you sorry."

"For what it's worth, I'm already sorry."

His words kick up my pulse, and when my eyes meet his, they linger a second longer than they should. It sparks feelings—feelings *not* okay for this particular man.

Time to go. "Bye, Lucas Nevarez."

9

Cheeto Combat

Each morning, a crowing rooster wakes me. Literally. Today is no exception.

Mom's neighbor, Ernie, has a rooster that's up at the crack of dawn. In a daze, I don't remember where I am. Ah, those blissful seconds when I forget what my life has become. And who brings a rooster to an RV park?

It's been three days here, and the only thing that's kept me sane is that I've spent a few hours each day volunteering at the animal shelter, cleaning cages and bathing the pets to prepare them for their new families. It's definitely not a cushy job, but I love being with animals.

Yesterday, I also hit up the driving range to inflict my pain and frustration on innocent golf balls.

I'm trying to stay positive, but I really miss working at Fur Bebé. My creativity was put to good use with new pet product ideas, and I was in a good position to give my clothing exposure.

And I miss Mr. D something awful. Suffice to say, if I scrub the baseboards of this Winnebago one more time, the cheap paint is going to come clean off. I need to get busy finding another career job.

"I'm not doing enough," I mumble, pulling up the covers that fell off my shoulder.

"Oh, believe me, you're doing more than enough," Mom says, and I look up to see she's standing at the kitchenette counter like a quiet, eerie huntress, sipping coffee.

I scowl. "What does that mean?"

"You keep 'cleaning and organizing.' In other words, you're moving or throwing out all my stuff that I need. I can't find anything."

"How did you find it before? The place is nuclear." I get out of bed to change into a blouse and jeans.

"I have a system."

Once I'm dressed, I head to the coffeepot. After I have a cup in hand, I return to the bed/dining table where I sit. "Anyway, I meant that I'm not doing enough for my career. I thought that working for a rescue shelter would be rewarding. Which it is. But…" I trail off in thought.

"You're only helping one or two animals at a time, and you have the brains and the power to help thousands of animals." Mom doesn't look up from stirring her coffee.

"Yeah, maybe that's it."

"Of course that's it, Soph." Mom shoots me a "duh" look. "You're smart. Really smart. And driven, and talented, and caring. You're never going to be happy at a job cleaning cages. That's why you worked your way up at Fur Bebé."

"Right." I trace the bohemian pattern on the bedspread with my finger. "That plan went to crap, didn't it?"

"Yeah, so?"

"So, now what?" I tug a loose thread.

"Get a new plan." She takes the trash bag out of the can before stepping outside.

Gizzie jumps up on my lap, and his breath is so bad I swear it makes my eyes water. I have a sack of pet product samples from the conference in my suitcase, so I get up and dig them out. I find some Yum Breath chews, which are supposed to work miracles. I give one to Gizzie, hoping it works immediately. But then it doesn't matter because he jumps down.

I grab my laptop and get to work on creating a FaceSnap account of my own—Missy's not the only one who can get two-hundred thousand FaceSnap fans. I'm going to raise awareness for RezQ—the petwear idea I came up with for Madame Puuccí that I'm now designing, sewing, and knitting myself. If I can get enough followers, Fur Bebé will realize they need this new line... then they'll realize they need me.

Before I can do anything, Gizzie paws my leg. I look down, and he actually has a sweet look on his face as he tilts his head and gazes up at me. Mom's probably right, I could make more of an effort with him. So, I bend down, pick him up and set him on my lap. Amazingly, he stays put.

When he gags, I jump up to move him off me, but it's too late. Something neon orange splats all over my pajama top.

I look down to see that it's also on my pj bottoms, too. When Mom steps back inside, I say, "Gizzie just threw up all over me."

"Gizzie's sick?" Mom buzzes over. "He never barfs up his Cheetos."

"Right." I run my hands in front of my puke-stained blouse. "I made this up as some vendetta against him."

"Where is he?"

I scan the Winnebago, spying a half-empty bag of Cheetos on Gizzie's dog bed, but no Gizzie. Mom and I go into her bedroom and find Satan there. The dog returned to the comfy haven of her bed after yakking on me.

Mom cuddles Gizzie. "Poor, sick baby. Did you give him anything, Soph?"

I stand on the stairs to her room, shifting on my feet. "I gave him a chew for his breath."

Mom goes wide-eyed. "What was it?"

"A Yum Breath. They're supposed to be great—"

"Oh, no. No, no, no!" Mom's face crumples.

"What?" My voice is screechy. "What's wrong?"

"I have some clients that gave those to their older dogs, and one had a seizure and the other died."

"Just because some dogs happened to get sick doesn't mean they were caused by the Yum Breaths."

Mom's face pinches into a tormented frown. "Whatever. Now you might've killed poor Gizzie."

Great. We've been living together for approximately sixty-one hours, and we're already at war. I start to argue with her, but then I see her eyes misting up. Although I think she's being overboard, I feel terrible that she's so worried. My tone is gentle when I reply, "They gave out Yum Breaths at the conference. All the dogs were fine. And I saw Gizzie eating grass earlier. That'll make dogs throw up."

"It was definitely the Yum Breaths. Those things are poison. You can feel the toxicity when you touch one."

"I'm sorry. I'll throw them out." I still don't believe Mom, but if she feels this strongly, it's definitely not worth battling her over some silly breath chews. And, on the off chance she's right, I'd never want to make Gizzie sick.

Mom keeps babying him while she ignores me. Living with her is going to be intolerable.

Why does Satan get more affection than me? And he's acting completely fine. Not able to stand smelling like death, I squeak, "Is there somewhere to rinse these clothes out?"

She points at the door. "Go outside and walk to the top of the row and turn left. Past the luxury triple slidout RVs are the porta potties. You'll find a hose hookup there."

"Swell."

"Oh!" She holds up a finger. "Check out the brand new WindWorm 2000, second from the left. It's a real beauty—my dream triple slideout Winnebago."

"Will do."

When I get back, Mom's taken Gizzie and left... somewhere.

Not sure what to do with myself next, I pull up my horoscope on my iPhone, hoping it will perk me up. Reading it aloud, I say, "Watch out. Heartache is in store for the sensitive Cancer crab as Mercury and Venus move into alignment." I close the browser. "Whatever." I don't even have a boyfriend. Why do I read this crap?

I change into fresh pjs, even though it's nine a.m. Spying the half bag of Cheetos still on the floor, I pick it up to throw it away.

But I don't. Instead, I shovel the orange crumbs in my mouth as I crawl back into bed.

10

The Bling Machine

This week, I've been working a minimum-wage job at the shelter, which is definitely a step up from volunteering. Since it's Friday, I don't have to be there until noon, so I wake up late to the smell of coffee, but an empty Winnebago. I get dressed, then grab my laptop and a cup of coffee before stepping out the front door. Mom isn't outside either.

Where'd she go? I try to call her, but she doesn't answer. Ugh, I hate that I have to worry if she's in one piece.

I place my mug in the netted holder of one of Mom's collapsible lawn chairs that are under the retractable awning. It's weird to have a front porch view of the freeway. It is quite convenient, though, as far as catching an Uber.

Then, I take a seat and open my laptop, as I need to get busy working on my FaceSnap account because it *has* to get me my job back at Fur Bebé. There, I can continue doing what I love *and* fighting to make a difference.

But so far, I've garnered about 0.1% of the followers I need. To torture myself, I click on Missy's account to see that her posts about Pet Sweats have thousands of likes and comments. There's no doubt about it—she's definitely getting the word out about the product line—*my* product line.

Returning focus to myself and my goals, I start going through the photos I took of some of the shelter dogs yesterday. I have some great shots of the two most cooperative dog models, Wonton and Sushi, wearing RezQ's fall sweaters. I've realized my own FaceSnap account can give RezQ exposure *and* get these shelter dogs adopted—a win-win.

My phone buzzes, and I exhale when I see that it's Mom. Accepting the call, I say, "Where are you?"

"Can't say." From the background noise, it sounds like she's in a wind tunnel.

I shake my head. "Okie doke. Are you hang gliding?"

"I wish. You sound down."

"No kidding." I slump into my chair.

"You're not a quitter, Soph. Work harder to get your FaceSnap account to blow up."

I look at my hand to see if I have any fingernails left to pick at. I don't. "I have two-hundred followers. I need two-hundred *thousand* followers. I have yet to get one adoption from it."

"It's cute, but there's nothing really unique about it. You need something more bold, different."

I poke a finger through a rip in the arm of the canvas chair. "If I were like Missy, I could make niche things become big things. But so far, I don't have that kind of influence. Or any influence."

"So think of a way you can demand attention."

I blink. For that, I need to channel my mother, the master of notoriety. "Well, celebrities get attention."

"Now you're thinking."

"Right. Trying to convince a famous person to dress their dog in my clothing could prove humiliating." I cock my head. "That's where you thrive."

"Exactly." She disconnects.

I study the phone, wondering if Mom was cut off or simply made the executive decision that our conversation was over.

Hearing the beep of an unfamiliar horn, I flip around to see my mother's head hanging out of the driver-side window of a black clunker. "Sophie, check this out!" she yells, pulling up in the gravel driveway beside me.

I approach the Toyota Tercel hatchback, a car that's been souped up, albeit a long time ago. It's accessorized with rusted-out ninja throwing star spinning rims, a large tail wing with one fin—the other has fallen off—plus a sweet lightning bolt body sticker that's peeled off in spots. "What is this?"

"Surprise!" She hops out. "This is your new car. It's *way* faster than it looks."

"Holy crap, thank you." I rub my eyes. Studying the car and taking a minute to process the situation, I ask, "Where did you get it?"

"One of my new clients wanted to sell it, so I traded it for six-months' worth of astro-traveling sessions."

I gasp. Mom got a car in exchange for universe-hopping sorcery? "Who gave it to you? You've been here less than two weeks. It isn't stolen, is it?"

"Vorian-5 would never steal. He's an evolved soul."

"*Vorian-5*? Who's that?"

"He's Kepling, from Kepler-186f. I met him at the gas station. We hit it off, and he needs my help visiting his home planet." She tugs my arm. "Anyway, you need a car for sting ops. So, come look inside. It's mid-nineties, but it's got all new tires, and Vorian-5 said it's never been in an accident."

As I walk around the car, I spy another surprise. "What're those black boxes in the back?"

"Surround-sound speakers. Since they short out here and there, Vorian-5 threw them in."

Mom hands me the key. "You're gonna want to take it for a test spin, Soph."

"Really?" Although I hate the car, I'm really grateful. Now that Mom's done… whatever it was she did with Vorian-5, I don't have to Uber to work anymore. "Thank you so much, really." I give her a hug.

She gives my back a hefty pat before pulling away and saying, "Yup. Now let's go."

"Okay." I jump into the turd on wheels. I am curious about the "*way* faster" point Mom made.

Looking around, I say, "It's not bad," before turning the key. "As long as it doesn't bounce when I drive it."

"Oh wait, Soph, we can't leave yet. I need to go back inside the Winnebago. I forgot to blow out my candles."

What? "You're gonna burn that Winnebago to the ground someday." After I say those words, I realize I slept with flames unattended.

Comforting.

When curiosity replaces shock, I ask, "What spell are you doing now?"

"An animal attraction one. I lit a blue one for Lucas and a pink one for you. Every few days, I move them closer. You two are going to have a sexy encounter soon."

"I don't even want to know what that means." I narrow my eyes. "I'm never even going to see him again. It's not happening, Mother."

"Just wait for it," she says before jumping out of the car and running inside. When she comes back out and gets in, she yells, "Yeehaw. Let's do this!"

When I press the gas pedal, the thing accelerates from zero to warp speed in a few seconds flat. "Woah!"

"Vorian-5 put in a custom rocket launcher engine for fast getaways." Mom pumps a fist. "Burn rubber, baby!"

Several turns later, we're merging onto the interstate, and I'm about to find out just how fast this rusty old car can go. When I hit the gas, our necks jolt as we speed up from thirty to ninety at a stomach-dropping pace.

With wind whipping my hair and blood surging through my veins, the rush of adrenaline kicks in, and I feel happier and freer than I have in a long while.

But I am a little nervous about how this clinker got its hypersonic speed.

I look back at the speakers. "Maybe we should check behind those for drugs. Or dead bodies."

11

Coffee Kitten

Riley and I are meeting today because she's looking for proof that Missy stole then altered my Powerpoint slides. As one of Fur Bebé's accountants, she has access to company files, and I have yet to hear back from Brock.

So, I'm counting on Riley because I want Missy to face consequences for what she did, but mostly, I *really* want my job back at Fur Bebé. I'm missing it more by the minute.

It's Sunday, and since Riley has to work, I'm here at the Coffee Kitten, a new cafe on the ground floor of Fur Bebé's office building.

I *really* don't want to see any of my ex-coworkers, but since Riley's helping me, I thought I should come to her and buy her coffee.

I'm standing outside waiting when I hear a familiar voice say, "Sophie, is that you?"

I turn around to see Ted, my buddy, who's usually in Fur Bebé's parking lot with his treasure-filled shopping cart. I always brought him a sandwich after getting one of my own. As Ted approaches me, he puts his hand up in a wave. "Hey, Sophie!"

I walk over to him. "Hi, Ted, sorry I haven't been bringing you dinner. I'm no longer working at one of the companies in your building."

"Don't worry about it. But I wanted to ask if that man found you?"

"What man?"

"I dunno. He just said he was here looking for you. I told him I hadn't seen you this week."

"That's weird." My stomach knots. Please tell me it wasn't the lawyer from Urban Productions again. "Was he an older gentleman in a suit?"

"Nope. Ragged jeans and gray T-shirt. Handsome young fella. About your age."

My face twists. I don't know of anyone looking for me besides the lawyer, but Ted has been confused before. I think this might be one of those times, so I just say, "Well, if he comes asking again, tell him I'm now working at the Fulton County Animal Shelter, okay?"

"Will do. You take care of yourself, now."

"You too." I feel a bit sad as I watch him saunter away. I miss him, and I can't help him anymore.

"Soph, over here." It's Riley, and I turn to see her standing outside the doors of the Coffee Kitten. I rush over and give her a hug before we make our way through the place, which has white kittens painted on walls and tail-shaped chairs. We exit the back door to the patio and step up to the kiosk. Since I insist on getting the coffees, Riley snags us a table in the shade, which is a score because the place is packed. Hoping to be incognito, I slide my sunglasses on.

The young, pony-tailed barista ignores me when I try to order, and after I finally get her attention, she acts like I'm asking for mochas with edible gold.

After finally making it to our table, I hand Riley her pistachio latte and she takes a sip. Then she blinks before setting her cup down, speechless.

"What? Is it terrible?" I take a seat beside her.

As I put my stirrer stick through the sip hole, Riley says, "I already forgot how weird you are."

I ignore her as I suck at the tiny straw. When my raspberry mocha is bitter sludge mixed with berry Popsicle, my face puckers. "This tastes like I made it."

"No kidding. Screwing up coffee this badly takes skill." Riley scowls. "And I'm going to be a prisoner here."

"Right, because of its proximity to Fur Bebé's office." I finish her thought.

When she takes off her jacket, I can't help but notice her T-shirt. It says, "Kiss me, I'm schnockered."

I nod to it. "It's casual Sunday at work, I see."

"I got this during an undergrad semester abroad in Amsterdam, and it still works." She gives it a tug.

"I have a feeling it isn't the T-shirt, Riles."

"It's definitely the shirt." She removes her coffee lid and peers inside as though she's half-expecting it to blow like a rotted sewage pipe. "And I'm keeping it until it falls apart."

"Right on." I fist bump her. "I may need to borrow it someday. In the very far and distant future. When I'm not living with my mother in a Winnebago."

"At least your mom's cool. I don't know what's gonna happen when my momster gets back from the Bahamas." Riley groans. "So, tell me how you're doing—really?"

"I'm okay. The shelter's been a growing experience." She flashes me a "cut the crap" look, but I don't want to get into it all right now. Transitioning the topic away from my feelings, I say, "Do you think you can come by the shelter and take some shots of the dogs I'm featuring on my FaceSnap account? Your pictures will be so much better than mine."

"Sure, no problem. Just let me know when you're ready."

"Tomorrow? I made two plaid Sherpa petticoats for fall, and they're fantastic. I can't wait to see how they turn out."

"Sure!" She smiles. "That's a great idea, Soph. You always have such great ideas."

"Thanks." I pick a nail. "I just have a looong way to go before I have enough followers for it to make a difference. But it's a start."

As we chat, Riley gets caught up watching the "fine human specimens" passing by. She's not wrong—all the hotties of Buckhead are out for their Sunday coffee fix. She lowers her voice. "I need to order one of those to go."

"Do it. *All* of it," I say knowing her MO is to kiss and run.

"Hey, I just might." Riley does a hip wiggle. "I could really use a fine little somethin' somethin' in my bed."

"Come on, you can't stop yourself, Kissing Bandit."

"Yeah, why do I do that?" She flutters out an exhale. "I probably need therapy. Or a good hypnotist. I should talk to your mom."

"Please don't."

She grins, but it falls off her face when she clicks her computer. "I can't find any backups of your Powerpoint files yet, so I'm going to call my cousin, West. He's a computer programmer. Maybe he'll know something I don't."

"Thanks, Riles."

She puts a finger up. "But I did find Lucas's schedule. He's meeting Frank Franklin at Novu Villa's driving range two weeks from today."

"No way." Frank Franklin is the Vice President of Products at Pet IQ. I've met him before, and he doesn't impress easily. That's a big problem because to get a meeting with Madame Puuccí, you *must* convince him first.

So, Lucas is making progress with Pet IQ. It's not a meeting with Madame Puuccí, but Frank Franklin is the gatekeeper who can make that happen.

"Speaking of the devil." Riley juts her chin forward, and I shift my eyes to see Lucas approaching.

I slump in my chair. "He actually *is* the devil," I snarl in a whisper, even though I know that's not really true. Lucas has transformed into his casual weekend gear, apparently, wearing a brown vintage cowboy shirt with pearly snaps and a pair of wrinkled cargo shorts. Birkenstocks finish the look. "And why is he dressed like a tech dork? He's an uptight Harvard alum."

"Stanford undergrad, remember?"

"Oh, right."

"He's so hot. Think he's taken?" she asks before Lucas comes within earshot.

"Hey." Lucas smiles, hesitation in his voice. "Working today too, Riley?"

"Yup, fun times."

Lucas gives Riley a polite smile before turning to me. He shifts on his feet before he tugs at his shirt. "This is my Sunday outfit for work."

"Yeah, on a dude ranch."

"Yippee ki yay," Lucas deadpans.

Riley holds back a laugh.

Lucas jabs a thumb over his shoulder. "I'm gonna grab a coffee. I'll be right back," he says before heading to the kiosk.

I point to Riley's computer. "My backup data, Riles. Focus."

"Bow chika bow wow." Riley put both palms in the air.

"What?"

"That answers that. He's definitely taken." She twirls her body in an awkward dance motion. "And you better watch out, or you two are gonna be doing the horizontal mambo on his big fat CEO desk."

I scold her with my eyes. "He *fired* me."

"Hugh fired you," Riley mumbles, distracted. She's busy watching Lucas place his order. "Did you see that? The betty barista's being totally nice to him."

"Here, we have some banana nut ones, too." The excited squeal of the barista rings out. "I made these myself."

Riley's face pinches. "She's giving Lucas free muffin samples! She didn't offer you any."

I drag my head back up.

"Delicious." Lucas takes another bite. "You did a fine job with these." I see him sneak a glance my way.

The barista cackles. "They were made with love, like all my coffees."

"There was no love when she made our drinks." Riley's lip curls. "They taste like she spit in them."

I crack a smile. Lucas is still looking at me.

Riley pokes me. "He is totally checking you out. Lucky lady."

"He's probably hiding something."

"Yeah, like an eight pack under that rough-riding shirt." Riley fans herself.

I scowl, but it's for show. I'm so happy to see Riley again. "Lucas looks like he just rolled out of bed and threw on some clothes that he found on the floor."

"Don't you get it? It's a style. It's a Cali, retro, I-don't-care, non-style style. And it's sexy. Way sexier than men who try too hard."

"Hmm, I'm not so sure about that. And I do fashion."

"*Dog* fashion. And Lucas is *so* cool that he's above trying to be cool. I think *you* should come to his office today and ride him like a quarter-slot bull."

"The devil, Riles."

She opens her mouth to say something else, but then has to zip it because Lucas is heading back.

When he gets to our table, Riley stares at her computer, looking hard at work.

Lucas has a nervous look on his face when he says, "Sophie, can we talk? Please?"

"I can't right now, sorry. Riley's helping me—"

"I'm going to return these coffees. They are totally unacceptable." She stands and zips away.

He looks at me, his eyes contrite. "So, I've been working with Brock to try and recover your files. Sophie, it's not good news. Brock said your computer wasn't backing anything up or recording histories. He looked everywhere."

"That can't be." So, that's why I haven't heard back from Brock. With a familiar ache returning to my chest, I say, "Isn't it odd that nothing's there?"

"It is, and it all should be. But Brock thinks it might've just been a random error. He doesn't think Missy would have the kind of expertise it would take to hack into the Fur Bebé system."

It takes my brain a moment to process what Lucas is saying. So, there's *no* trace of what she did? That cannot be a random accident, but Brock is right. We're talking about *Missy* here. "I'm with him on that one. But that just means she had help."

"I figured that too, so I asked Brock about it." Lucas swallows hard. "He said there's not much more we can do. There's no way to catch Missy or her accomplice when there's no trail. The only way would be to set up a system to track them if they try it again, but since you're no longer at Fur Bebé, that can't happen. I'm sorry."

I rub my forehead as the exhaustion that's been plaguing me returns. "I just can't believe this." My voice is weak. And has anyone thought to question Brock—the new IT guy who probably has a crush on Missy—about his role in this whole mess?

So, that's it? Missy's really getting away with this? And I'm really not getting my job back?

I cannot accept that. Because if I do, it means I have to accept that everything I've done for the past three years of my life, and, more importantly, everything I've given up—relationships, parties, trips, time back home in Blue Vine—is gone because someone unjustly took it from me.

My mind spins back to my sophomore year in high school when, somehow, I'd made it on the ballot for homecoming queen. I couldn't believe that enough people had nominated *me*, the bookworm from the single-wide trailer on the outskirts of town. Then, my friend, Amy, who was on the homecoming committee, told me that I'd won! I couldn't believe it—it was too good to be true.

As it turns out, it was. When the announcement came on the loudspeaker, Sonoma Presley was the winner. Amy told me that Sonoma's cheerleader friends—who were doing the final tally—had to have stuffed the ballot box. Since Amy couldn't prove what happened, I was out, and Sonoma was crowned at the homecoming game's halftime show.

I guess I should be used to this kind of thing happening to me by now, but it's clearly not the kind of thing one ever gets used to, especially when I've worked myself to the bone to rise above it.

It feels like I'm always trying to pull myself up by my bootstraps, but that doesn't work when one doesn't even have boots.

Lucas touches my shoulder. "I'll keep working on it. In the meantime, is there anything else I can do to help make up for what happened?"

My stomach tumbles as I swallow back the bile rising in my throat. I can't drink any more coffee now, and I just want to go home. I'm angry at Lucas, even though logically, I know he's just the messenger. And his gesture is nice, but I can't accept it.

As I'm opening my mouth to say, "No," an idea pops into my head. "There *is* something, actually. There's a man pushing a shopping cart that lives in this building's parking lot. His name's Ted, and I used to bring him sandwiches. Can you make sure he has food every day? Preferably from the Crunch Munch?"

Lucas stares at me for a beat, deep in thought. "Okay, I promise to bring him *something* every day, and I'll go to the Crunch Munch once a week. Does that work?"

His offer eases the sting in my heart a bit. "That'd be great, thank you."

Riley returns to the table, and Lucas puts a hand up in a wave. "I need to get back to the grind. Sophie, let me know if there's anything else I can do. Riley, I'm going to plant myself in my office, so if you need anything, that's where I'll be."

Riley shoots me a concerned glance before she looks at Lucas and says, "Sure, thanks."

Lucas's words remind me that Riley's heading back to work and I'm not, and my eyes gloss.

Not that I want to be in the office on a Sunday, but more than anything, I wish I was back working at Fur Bebé with her. Thinking about all the fun times we had, I realize those are the "good old days" because now they're gone. At least for now.

12

The Sweet Pad

I slogged through the week, which was much better now that I had my own car to get to the shelter, and now that it's Friday, Mom says she's got a surprise for me.

She directs me to pull off the freeway and into the parking lot of a ritzy apartment complex in Buckhead. I say, "What are we doing here?"

Mom smiles conspiratorially, and I'm scared. She raises her arms. "I found your sister!"

"I don't have a sister."

"Eva's your sister."

"Eva?" I squint in thought. "Oh, as in Eva, my ex-stepsister? And if you're counting her, what about her twin, Paige? Anyway, you were married to their dad for like, two months. Twenty years ago."

"And your point?"

"My point is that I hardly know her. Well, anymore. And neither do you." Eva and I stayed friends after our parents' divorce, and she and I got along great as pre-teens, but that was so long ago now. I never hit it off with her sister, Paige, and actually, neither did Eva. Paige was the literal evil twin.

Mom steps out of the car. "Well, Eva's your sister and my daughter. And I called her father, Richard. He put me in touch. She lives here."

"You still talk to Richard?" I hop out of the car and follow behind Mom, who's walking... somewhere.

"I talk to all my exes but Darryl. Since he tried to kill me."

"What?" I stop walking.

Mom turns back. "Darryl left the gas and the lighter on in the oven. When I opened the door, it blew up in my face. Burned my eyebrows off. He was hoping it would be the end of me, I could tell."

"I'm sure it was an accident."

She scowls. "Humph. Accident, my saggy ass! He had a guilty look on his face when he told me to check the oven for the missing casserole dish."

I step in closer to examine her brows. I hadn't noticed before, but they're penciled in. "Anyway, Eva lives in this complex that Richard owns." Mom points ahead. "Look!"

I follow her finger to see that through the iron fence ahead, there's a crystal-clear pool with lounge chairs and even a tiki bar. "It's really nice."

"Glad you like it—" She throws up her hands "—because this is our new home!"

"What? How?" I scan the building, thrilled at the idea of escaping the Winnebago. "Really?"

"Yup. Richard said you and I can park the Winnebago in the back of this parking lot for a great price. There's an electrical hookup and sewage connection there since they've had visitors with RVs before. I wanted to bring you here to meet Eva, but also for you to see where we're going to live."

I gasp.

Her face glows. "You're welcome."

"Wow," I murmur, closing my eyes. So, I'm still living with Mom in a Winnebago. Just now in a parking lot.

But... there *is* a pool.

Mom takes out her phone and hits a few buttons before putting it to her ear. After a pause, she says, "Hey Eva, we're here."

After Eva comes out of the building to meet us, I realize how happy I am to see her. She's always been gorgeous, and she still is with her thick black hair wrapped into a loose bun, which compliments her black turtleneck dress and boots.

She pulls me into a tight hug, saying, "Sophie, I'm so glad you're here."

"Me too."

She waves a hand. "Come inside. I'm working from home today, but I'm between Zoom meetings."

I say, "You look great. And dressed for success."

"She's a divorce lawyer." Mom follows Eva. "A real shark from what I've heard."

Eva sighs. "That's me. A shark on the job. And a guppy with men."

"Yeah, tell me about it." I shake my head. "Remember that no boys pact we made?"

"That's right!" She points at me. "Okay—I would've been much better off if I'd stuck to that."

"Me too. Well, at least you've got the career part right. I guess I blew that too."

Eva scrunches her button nose. "I kind of hate my job, to be honest. As soon as I get my finances in order, I want to start my own restaurant. I've been doing catering on the side."

I remember how much Eva loved to cook and how good her food was. "That sounds like you. I'm sure you'd do an amazing job with it."

"Aw, thanks, Sophie." She touches my arm as we reach her front door. "Come inside, and I'll get you both some coffee. Or do you want espresso?"

Mom barges inside. "Both."

I nod. "Espresso sounds great."

Eva's apartment has the sleek, modern vibe with a two-sided gas fireplace and an open kitchen with quartz countertops. She has two massive bedrooms and bathrooms, and a large covered patio with a peaceful view of trees and foliage.

We spend a while sitting on her velour couch, drinking espresso, and catching up, and I can't believe she and I have both lived in the same city and never reconnected. When we talk, it's as if we've never been apart.

Eva heads to the kitchen, then returns and gives Mom and me slices of biscotti to go with our espresso. After Mom munches hers down in two bites, she says, "So, Eva, do you still have to marry a Jewish guy? Because that really limits your prospects."

Eva laughs, groaning. "Dad cares about that far more than I do, but it is my heritage. There are some traditions I want to pass on to my kids."

I glance at Mom with furrowed brows. "But Richard married you, and you're not Jewish."

"And we're divorced now, Soph." She gives me a "duh" look. "We lasted three months, remember?"

"Yup, I remember." I was actually wondering how they got married in the first place, but whatever.

"Eva, see if you can get Sophie to open up about her problems." Mom reaches for my biscotti. "She's so bottled up, she's gonna blow."

I slap away Mom's grabby hand, scolding her with my eyes. "Overshare."

Eva chuckles. "Let's hang out. I have a pool... wait, no! Now, *we* have a pool, and I make mean margaritas."

"It's definitely a date." I put half the biscotti in my mouth before Mom attempts another steal. And it's rich, crumbly perfection.

"Sophie needs friends, Eva," Mom says. "She hasn't got any now."

"That's not true—I have Riley." I brush my cheek with my napkin. "But I can always use more friends, especially you, Eva," I say, meaning it. Riley works at Fur Bebé, so I won't be around her as much now. As I talk, I tell Eva about RezQ, its FaceSnap account, and getting shelter animals adopted. I try not to sound too discouraged when I say, "I'm brainstorming ways to get more followers." The account's following is still abysmal, although since I'm not getting my job back, I'm not sure how to proceed with it all, anyway.

Eva wrings her hands. "Skye told me. And, actually, I want to help."

"Really? How?"

"I'm a member of the Novu Villa Country Club." Eva's voice is hesitant. "I've done several catering events for them."

"Okayyy." I drag the word out, glancing at Mom. I'm not sure I like where this is going.

Mom bubbles over. "Raven Monroe's having a birthday party for her dog there this weekend!"

Raven Monroe is a famous fitness guru whose husband is the tech billionaire, Thomas Zaine. My stomach does a somersault. "I don't understand."

Eva sips her coffee. "I'm invited to the party. It's Lady Paw Paw's third birthday. She's a bulldog, and she has her own FaceSnap account."

"Still not following."

"If *your* clothing were on this famous birthday girl, it might get you noticed by Pet IQ's CEO," Eva says, a nervous flutter in her voice.

"That it would," I squeak as my breath catches. What did Mom strong-arm Eva into planning?

Eva bites her lip. "I can get you in."

"Get ready to sew your butt off for the next week, Soph." Mom lifts her chin. "We've got a plan."

When I see the look on my mother's face, my palms go clammy.

Whatever she's got up her sleeve, it's not going to be pretty.

13

Birthday Bash

This past week, I did as Mom ordered and sewed until my fingertips were raw. Riley and I had our photoshoot, and it turned out really well—the coats looked amazing on Wonton and Sushi. I was a bit disappointed when the posts only generated about fifty more FaceSnap followers, which is now 0.12% of what Missy has. At this rate, I'll be a century dead in the ground before I have enough to matter. I wanted to try and implement some viral marketing ideas yesterday, but I was cut short when I had a box of kittens come in.

And since I'm no longer getting my job back at Fur Bebé, or possibly anywhere else since I've been blackballed, I have to get this RezQ going well enough to convince someone to hire me despite my "checkered past."

So, yeah. Today's plan of getting a RezQ dress on a celebrity birthday dog has to work.

Mom, Riley, Eva, and I have about twenty minutes to accomplish our mission: crashing a party at the most sought-after venue in metro Atlanta: Buckhead's Novu Villa Country Club. The place boasts over three acres of gardens and ponds and is swarming with staff.

Thanks to Eva, we're all dressed like Novu Villa caterers and arriving as a part of the Club's "exceptional customer service."

The hope for today: get the birthday girl, Lady Paw Paw, into the dress I made for her instead of the one she's wearing now, and it'll make it on Raven's FaceSnap account. Then my RezQ line will rocket to fame. A tall order, no doubt.

And it involves making a bit of a mess at this five-star venue.

"They can't see your license plate, Soph," Mom says as we round the corner. "We have to find a place to hide the little speed demon."

"At least it's not the Winnebago." I flop my head back.

Down the street from the Novu Villa, Mom parks in an alley so we can run back and blow out of here, sight unseen.

I get Lady Paw Paw's dress selections ready. There's one I hope Raven picks—chiffon with pearls and gold roses sewn into the bodice.

Riley runs a finger over it. "This is amazing, Sophie."

"This will really make Lady Paw Paw's features pop, won't it?" Mom's smile is proud.

"Thanks, y'all. I loved creating it, too."

I'm also proud of the silk hats I made—they've got a British royalty vibe with pearled netting.

When I have the doggie dresses, hats, and bow ties hidden in a cabinet of one of the two collapsible server's carts I ordered on Amazon. Mom looks at her phone. "Eva says our window of time is now. Ready?"

"I think so," I mumble, jealous that Riley gets to stay in the car as our "backup" and "getaway driver." I adjust my dark-haired wig that's pulled into a tight bun.

"Let's crash a birthday party." Mom has her game face on, along with a red-haired wig.

"On it." I lift our server carts out of the car and expand them. When Mom and I start to roll away, Riley says, "Wait. How do I take the emergency brake off?"

Oh, jeez.

Riley is already a lousy driver. Now she's operating a rocket-launcher of a vehicle?

After showing Riley, Mom turns to me and says, "So, do you feel ready?"

I shudder. "I think so."

"Remember what I taught you. Stay calm, say no more than you absolutely have to, and make eye contact when you're lying. And trust *no one.*" Mom takes a deep breath.

"We're just servers, Mom. Chill."

But I'm talking a big game because my legs shake as we make our way to the Novu Villa Country Club.

The venue looks even better than I'd imagined—it's a pristine garden party with a million twinkling lights on the trellis above an island patio, which is surrounded by a moat with a drawbridge. Lanterns float in the water, which is all breathtaking in the dusky light.

It's a hard pill to swallow that some people can't afford food and clothing where others have the kind of money to do all this for a *dog* birthday party. It makes me even more determined for RezQ to take off, so there's at least one designer petwear line that donates to animals in need.

Mom and I roll onto the scene and start serving pre-party cocktails, like we know what we're doing.

Raven is with the birthday girl, fluffing Lady Paw Paw's dress and making sure that her hat stays on. "Stay next to Mommy," she says, giving the dog a treat.

All the guests, along with their pets, are decked out in elegant attire. My favorite is a handsome Scottie who's rocking a yellow paisley bow tie. It should look ridiculous, but he pulls it off.

Eva, who's mingling in the crowd, gives us a discreet thumbs-up as Mom works her way to the drawbridge and under the trellis where the birthday girl sits. Mom rolls her cart with a hidden fish past the dogs.

Sure enough, Lady Paw Paw takes the bait, sniffing the cart and following Mom, who's serving drinks to the family of the birthday girl. When no one is looking, Mom removes the hidden fish and kicks it into the pond.

My heart races as Lady Paw Paw darts off the drawbridge and leaps into the water, landing with an epic splash.

Gasps fill the air as Raven lets out a wail before yelling, "Lady Paw Paw, no!"

Following his buddy, Duke of Sausage takes a leap into the pond too.

Lady Paw Paw is underwater for a nerve-wracking amount of time before popping back up with the fish clenched in her jaws.

Butterflies explode in my stomach as I hope no one suspects foul play. *Mom selected the bright orange carp fish found in the pond*, I remind myself. That should cover our tracks.

After Raven and her family surround the pond to grab the dogs, they manage to capture The Duke of Sausage, but Lady Paw Paw escapes their grip and tears off toward the garden with her catch.

All the guests stare, spellbound, as Lady Paw Paw disembodies her fish before rolling around in it.

When the birthday girl emerges from the garden, her face and once silky rose-gold gown, is crusted in reddish-brown mud and fish guts.

Check.

Raven bursts into tears as she watches on, crying out, "What are we gonna do now?"

That's my cue. I head over to the distressed mother of the birthday girl and touch her shoulder. "Ma'am," I say softly. "I know it's not ideal, but we do have backup clothing for times like this."

With mascara running down her face, she meets my gaze. "You do?"

I smile. "Yes. This has happened before."

"Oh. Yeah… I guess it would happen." She exhales. "Can I see them?"

"Of course."

Eva follows behind as I usher Raven inside the mansion and to a closet where I hid the RezQ clothing to look like a selection of backups.

Raven takes out my chiffon dress of golden roses. Because I had to make it look like it was designed to fit multiple types of dogs, the underbelly is stretchy spandex with hooks. "This is gorgeous!" Raven flashes a dazzling smile. "I can't believe you have these ready to go."

"We do our best."

"You really do." Thumbing through them, she pulls at the label. "I've never heard of RezQ before."

I clear my throat, ready to give my prepared speech. "It's a fantastic new socially conscious petwear company, and it's right here in Atlanta. At Novu Villa, we prefer to support local talent with a cause."

"That's fabulous!" She turns the dress over in her hand. "And this is gorgeous. I'll be proud to say I'm supporting a local designer as well." After a beat, she says, "I'll have to check out the website."

I exhale a silent stream of breath, as I just got that up and running last night. "You definitely should."

"And I'm going to let my photographer know about this new designer. It makes for a phenomenal story on my FaceSnap account."

My heart leaps in my chest, but I keep my voice even when I say, "Everybody wins."

After Raven selects the embroidered gown, the infinity-shaped hat, and the double-breasted tuxedo for Duke of Sausage, she pays before heading off to get the dogs cleaned up and changed.

A man who looks like the manager of the place with a suit and name tag on approaches me, a puzzled look on his face. "Who are you?" I don't like his tone. Before I can answer, he points to the selection and says, "How did these get here? I didn't approve them."

Eva steps over and says, "Hello, Mr. Clayton. I had these ordered the last time I catered here. We'd run into an issue, so I wanted to make sure this was available."

"Wow. Great thinking, Eva. Thank you."

I rush away before he can get a close look at my face and possibly realize that he didn't hire me. Once the dogs are cleaned up and dressed, Mom and I go back to serving champagne while Raven and her mother ready the birthday girl.

It's the perfect scene, Lady Paw Paw sitting under the twinkling lights with lanterns glowing in the pond behind her, an expression of bliss in her face as she peers at the treats in Raven's bag.

The photographer positions the birthday girl to look like she's gazing off into the sunset above the gardens.

It's stunning.

But with the manager now approaching Mom with a nasty scowl, it's time to go.

Mom and I lock gazes before abandoning our carts to head into the mansion and collect my pet clothing.

Then we beat it out of here.

Once we get into my car and jump inside, Riley says, "What happened?"

"Mission accomplished," Mom barks. "But step on it—we can't let them see our escape vehicle."

Riley floors it, and we all go flying as the bling machine peels onto the road.

"We did it!" I cry out.

Holy crap, we actually did it!

"Way to go." Riley tears around the corner, and I think my stomach actually gets sucked into my throat as my life flashes on supersonic loop through my mind.

Riley says, "Let's celebrate at Eating Nemo. Little dead fishies are calling my name."

I just had an amazing thing happen, and I don't want to tragically die immediately after. So, I give her a nod as I grip onto my seat so hard all the blood drains from my knuckles. "Dead fishies it is."

14

Tangled Up in Blue

Eva and I are two peas in lounge pods in the toasty fall weather, and her blue "electric" margaritas are a little too delicious. This is just the mental break I need on a Sunday afternoon, getting away from the rescue shelter, Mom's Winnebago, and well, Mom, for a stint.

We ate at Eating Nemo yesterday, then decided we earned another celebration today after our huge victory—*Buckhead Lifestyle Magazine* plans to run a feature story on RezQ! They're even interviewing me. Riley's headed out of town this morning, as her parents are forcing her to meet them in New York for some networking engagement for their firm, and I wish she were here at the pool with us.

Because it's so nice...

Until the gate swings open and Mom comes marching in wearing a pair of sunglasses that are so big and round, they look like a set of bug eyes.

"Jeez, Soph, you're looking too thin. You need to eat," she says as she passes by.

I hold back a groan. "I thought you had a client appointment."

"Hi, Skye," Eva chirps, waving. "I'm so glad you're here."

"I *did* have a client appointment, and now there's a big emergency." Mom grabs another patio chair and puts it between Eva and me. "I did a candle love prayer for Stormy to get this guy she's wild about, and now it's turned her into a total stalker. I knew I should be careful doing a prayer when the moon is in Aquarius, it's way too powerful." Mom adjusts my umbrella to shade herself before she sits back and kicks her feet up.

"*That's* the big emergency?" I fight to keep my voice calm. "You can't be responsible for a stalker just because you did a love prayer for her." I twist the umbrella back to shade me.

"Sophie, didn't you hear me? Stormy could be arrested."

Eva studies Mom like she's a reptilian shapeshifter, a common initial reaction to Mom's work problems.

Great. My mother's going to scare off Eva, who doesn't appear to remember how eccentric Mom gets.

"Wait, what?" Eva's bronzing face twists in confusion.

"So, my client, Stormy," Mom says, starting over. "I'm afraid she's about to be served a restraining order. I did an emergency reverse stalker prayer, but so far, it's not working."

I rest my head back on the lounge chair and close my eyes. "If your prayers work, which you believe they will, then she should stop stalking him."

"I know that, Sophie," Mom snaps. "But I also feel really guilty. Stormy paid me three hundred bucks to help her, and I had to reverse it without her knowledge."

"Did you give her a money-back guarantee?" Eva says.

"No way. I'd never do that with Stormy. I'd go broke."

Mom starts to adjust the umbrella again, and I put my hand over hers. "Leave it alone, please. I was here first."

"Then offer her a discount on something else." Eva holds up a palm. "Keep her away from love prayers."

"Give her a free past life regression," I offer, remembering Mom mentioning that service before.

"That's good." Mom waggles a finger. "Then Stormy can't harm anyone from it because any guy she meets there will be long since dead. Yeah, I'll do that."

Time for another electric margarita. I refill my cup as Mom tells Eva about the different love spells. I'm officially drunk by the time Mom says, "Eva, we need to burn dragon's blood resin through your apartment and cleanse it from evil spirits."

"*Please*, Mother." I can't hide the irritation in my voice. "We were relaxing."

"Sophie." Mom scowls. "Stop trying to control the things I do and say. Eva can tell me if she wants her apartment cleansed or not."

"Fine." Somewhere inside, I know she's right, I shouldn't do that, but I'm drunk and tired of her barging into my life.

"I'd like to burn dragon's blood resin through the apartment, Skye." Eva's voice is soft. "That sounds fun."

"Great, let's go, Eva." Mom stands and waves her up.

Eva flashes me a guilty look so I say, "Go." I swing my wrist. "You two have fun."

As they walk away, Mom teaches Eva the dragon's blood resin prayer and how it rids a place of all negativity.

Once they're gone, I mumble, "Evil spirits," wondering again how Mom always seems to infiltrate my life. "Well, Mom and Eva aren't the only ones who can have a good time," I say to the pitcher of margaritas on the table.

I pour myself another glass, drinking it and making big plans. To do what, I'm not exactly sure. I don't want to swim. I don't feel like reading. Lying here alone is kinda boring. When Eva texts me to tell me that she and Mom are going to the witch store, whatever that is, I decide to call it a day. When I stand, I conk my head on the silly umbrella that's now hanging over me. "Son of a biscuit." I put my hand to my head.

It's throbbing, and something wet trails down my face. When I take my hand away, my palm is streaked in red. The sight of my own blood makes me woozy while I walk, listing slightly, over to the pool's gate.

But as I take each staggering step, I realize the margaritas are launching a vicious revolt in my stomach. I suck in the cool evening air, attempting to persuade the beverages to stay put.

When I stumble out of the gate, I hear, "Sophie? Is that you? Are you okay?"

I spin around so quickly I lose my balance, toppling over a bush. My world spinning, I stand and close one eye to regain focus. Lucas is standing on the grass, wearing his cargo shorts and Birkenstocks and carrying his laptop case.

I freeze. Why is Lucas outside my pool? At my new apartment complex? Even injured, I manage to croak, "You again?" How is he *always* around to witness me at my worst?

He runs over and puts his arm around me. "Yes, me again. You're hurt." He pulls me toward the curb. "You need to sit."

My skin flushes and my stomach sounds a warning gurgle, but I can't admit I feel sick. Lucas probably saw me conk my head. "I'm okay," I lie, trying to escape.

"Sophie, I'm not sure you're aware of how much you're bleeding." He squats down to look at my wound. "Let me help you."

And that's that. I try to jump up, but a projectile of reincarnated electric blue margarita shoots out of my mouth and all over Lucas's T-shirt. He holds up his hands and looks down. "Nice shot."

I want to apologize, but I can't speak. Lucas holds my hair and leans me over the bush. When I finish, he snatches a pool towel, wiping me off before getting to himself. Then he peels off his puke-stained T-shirt, revealing a set of washboard abs.

"I drunk too much," I slur, blinking. "Drank. Whatever." I pat his knee. "So, sorry."

I'm pretty sure I see the briefest of smiles flash across his face before he says, "Hold on." He runs and snatches the first aid kit hanging on the pool fence. He gently cleans my wound, taking great care not to miss anything before saying, "This kit is out of Band-Aids." Lucas reaches into his wallet and says, "I have some from when I was babysitting my uncle's grandson."

When I see what he pulls out, I say, "You're putting a Transformers one on me?"

"You're not really in a place to be picky right now." His amused eyes contradict his words. "But did you have something better in mind?"

"Trolls Band-Aids make the pain go away faster. They sparkle."

"I'll remember that for next time."

"Next time?" I immediately feel better, but it's more likely because of Lucas's statuesque body reflecting in the dusk light than his doctoring. It's short-lived, though. Glancing down, I see that in the kerfuffle, I had a nip slip. This stupid tiny bikini! I try to be discreet as I poke it back inside, and Lucas is a champ, pretending not to notice.

When I'm steady on my feet, Lucas comes up with a hose and rinses me off before spraying off his arms.

Once I've swished a mouthful of hose water, Lucas holds me up as he says, "Let's go to my place. It's in this complex, just one building over."

"Wait, you live here?" I stop walking and start my inquisition. "Did you know I live here? And do you wear Birkenstocks on a regular basis? So many questions."

Lucas cracks a grin. "Yes, I do wear Birkenstocks when I'm not required to be in a suit. As far as the apartment, I needed a place, and your mom found me something here I can rent month-to-month. And no, I had no idea you lived here too." He winks. "If I had, though, I would've come sooner."

Wow, he's sure flirty when he's not my boss. And I'm not having it. I scowl. "My mom got this place for you?"

He purses his lips. "Yes."

"How did she get your number?" I study his face.

"Not sure on that one. I thought she'd gotten it from you."

"I don't have your number."

His brows dive. "Oh. Anyway, your mom thinks I'm an old soul she knew in another life. I asked her for some advice and, well, we kind of bonded." He pauses, looking at me sheepishly. "I don't like that face. Was that bad?"

I fold my arms. I want to lecture Lucas *and* Mom. Lucas seems to charm people to get things, and I won't allow him to do that to Mom. And Mom has managed to worm her way into yet *another* acquaintance in my life. I'm too frustrated to answer, so I try to walk away. But I stumble.

"Let's get you some water you can drink, okay?" He grabs his briefcase before putting his hand on my back.

"Okay." I cave, letting Lucas wrap an arm around me as we walk. I'm curious why he has his briefcase on a Sunday, but I don't have the strength to ask. Instead, I say, "Let's go to my place so I can shower and change." My being sick and injured doesn't stop my breath from quickening when my bikini-clad body presses up against his bare chest.

This is bad. Very bad. A "sexy encounter" indeed. Mom's dang candles!

When Lucas walks in the Winnebago, he goes wide-eyed but quickly fixes his face, which I appreciate. At least Mom took Gizzie.

"Don't mind the mess." I bat my bras and underwear off the bed. "There's not enough space for my clothes, but that's a shelving problem I'm in the process of fixing right now."

Lucas chuckles. "There's no question in my mind that you have a great idea on how to fix it."

I smile and nod, leaving Lucas in the living room while I shower, change into jeans, and brush my teeth in the micro-bathroom at record speed. I return to the kitchenette and soak his shirt in the sink, insisting on cleaning it. Then I give Lucas the only oversized T-shirt I can find—a baby pink one of Mom's that has *Broads on Hot Rods* printed across the chest. When he puts it on, the shirt stretches thin across his pecs and shoulders. It looks absurd with the cargo shorts and tattered Birkenstocks he has on.

But he still looks smokin'.

After we sit on the couch, I say, "So, how are things at work?"

"Good," he says, an octave too high. "Missy's a bit of a challenge to work with but—"

"All her FaceSnap followers, I know."

"Yeah."

"Well, then. I definitely ended up with the better end of the deal." I move my palm around the Winnebago. "Living here in paradise."

"It is." He chuckles. "So, where's Skye?"

"She's at the witch store with my ex-stepsister." Now that I have Lucas in front of me, it's time to kick off negotiations. I smooth my

T-shirt before saying, "Look, I want Notorious D-O-G back." I lift my chin. "You've ripped him away from his adoptive parent, which is emotionally destabilizing. I'll bring him to any Fur Bebé PR events."

Lucas taps his fingers together. "I want to help you, Sophie, but Notorious D-O-G is in the office every day. Can you really drive him there and pick him up?" When he looks at me, his eyes are contrite. "And he's with Deborah. He loves her."

I groan. I miss Mr. D so much, but if anyone would spoil him to death, it would be Deborah. She's Fur Bebé's administrative assistant and one of the nicest humans ever. Although, I hope she doesn't overfeed him like she does everyone else at the company.

"And your home life is in transition now," he says gently.

I shoot him a glare before exhaling. "Fine." I look around, my mind spinning. "Then I at least deserve visitation rights."

"That I can do. I'll talk to Deborah and see if something can be arranged."

"Great, thank you." I bite my lip. "Make sure Deborah knows how much Mr. D loves taking in the views of the city."

"Will country views work?"

"That's not funny. Mr. D loves the glow of the evening lights, the moving cars, and the skyscrapers against the sky. Watching the city is his happy place."

"City views it is." He shakes his head before saying, "You're difficult. I like difficult." The smile fades as his gaze intensifies.

I don't respond. I feel myself being drawn closer to the edge of the magnetic black hole that is Lucas Nevarez. But fraternizing with the enemy is *not* okay. And now, he's just trying to be nice to me because he feels guilty. The fact that he's tempting me makes me wonder just how hard I conked my head. I look toward the door and stand. "I better get to sleep. I have an early morning."

"Yeah, I have to get to work. On a Sunday evening. Again."

"I understand how that is."

"I know you do." He steps toward the door. "So, where are you headed early tomorrow?"

A change of subject. Of course. "The animal shelter where I work." I'm not telling him about RezQ. He can find out for himself when I crash his driving range meeting with Frank Franklin next week, or from *Buckhead Lifestyle Magazine* when my article is published.

"You really love animals, don't you?"

"It's why I initially took a job at Fur Bebé. I wanted to expand the company's donation program. Which I couldn't do because I wasn't a voting member of the board, so..." I trail off. "So, now, while I wait for you to beg me to come back and take a board position at Fur Bebé, I'm doing something to make a difference."

He nods before saying, "Goodnight, Sophie Fox," with a twinkle in his eyes.

.

15

Swingers

Ah, my happy place—the driving range. I'm standing here, driver in hand, a bucket of balls at my feet, and the morning breeze feathering my skin. Imagining Missy's face on the golf ball I'd placed on the tee, I take my Big Bertha driver and set out to obliterate it. After the loud crack of a solid connection, the ball sails past the 180-yard mark. This is always what the doctor orders.

I arrived here good and early so I could score the spot beside the two Lucas reserved for himself and Frank Franklin, Pet IQ's VP of Products. I'm wearing the required collared shirt, but it's not buttoned. My golf skort just clears my bum cheeks, and its built-in briefs are so tight they're practically painted on. I'm not proud of my outfit, but Mom insisted.

"Look at you." Lucas's voice rings out behind me.

Drat! He's here early too. I should know that about him by now. I turn around, preparing myself for a scolding.

"Nice swing." Lucas's gaze darts up and down. "Nice attire."

"Thanks." Heat crawls up my cheeks—he looks so sleek and sexy in a golf tee, the thin material showing his carved physique.

Mom needs to do a hard stop on her "animal attraction" spell.

"So, what are you doing here, Sophie?" Attitude drips from his tone.

"Seemed like a fine day to perfect my stroke."

"Right." He rubs his temple. "Riley got her hands on my schedule, I see. I don't even want to know what you're planning on saying to Mr. Franklin."

"Mr. Franklin? As in Frank Franklin?"

"No, Benjamin Franklin." Lucas shakes his head as he approaches. "How's the pool injury?" He leans in and studies the cut on my head.

I absently brush my hand over it. "It's better. Except for the voices."

Lucas lets out a full-bellied laugh that almost makes me forget he's the enemy. Then he heads over to his bag, takes out his driver, and tees up a ball.

I say nothing as I turn and pretend to focus on my target, eyeing him in my periphery. When he takes his first swing, I can't help but get distracted by how effortlessly he drives the ball past the 250-yard mark. I give him a chin nod. "You've got a pretty smooth stroke yourself."

Well, then. My brain reels through a scene involving a naked Lucas entangled in sheets.

He flashes a knowing half-smile, but then says, "I was a little scared you were going to out-drive me for a minute. But then I pretty much crushed it."

"I have a jelly jar that won't open, tough guy," I blurt, still flustered. "Grape. At home. That's *stuck*-stuck, even after hitting it against the counter and using a jar gripper on it." I blink, realizing I still needed to clarify. "That you can muscle open if you need to flare your manly peacock feathers."

Flare your manly peacock feathers? I've never said that before in my entire life. Who says that?

His half-smile becomes a heart-melting one. "I am highly skilled with jelly jars. Grape especially."

Nope. I'm not getting sucked into *that* verbal land mine, so I zip it and focus on the ball.

I note a chink in Lucas's golf armor when he begins shanking his drives. I can't let him get away with that. "You should switch places with me, Mr. Nevarez. You seem to have a draft that's blowing your shots to the left."

"Don't think I didn't see that worm-burner of yours."

I lift my chin. "I was experimenting with my grip."

"Experimenting. Right."

I return to punishing my golf balls until I see Lucas in my periphery, smiling at me again. "What?" I ask, wondering if I'd actually said, "Die, Missy," out loud during my last swing.

"I don't think I've ever had this much fun at a driving range, especially with my swing so off."

My face flushes. What happened to that morning breeze? I wipe my brow. "Agreed on the fun part. But not on the off part, obviously. My swing's a work of art. In fact, it should be in a museum."

When that earns a chuckle out of Lucas, our eyes meet, and neither of us look away. My body temperature rises a degree, and I can't blame the weather.

"Hello, Mr. Nevarez?" a voice calls out.

Lucas and I turn to see Frank Franklin approaching, and he's wearing a white golf tee that matches his hair. As soon as Frank sets down his designer bag carrying shiny, Titleist golf clubs, Lucas extends his hand. "Mr. Franklin. So glad you could make it."

"As am I." I jump in and shake Frank's hand too, flashing him my best smile.

"Sophie Fox?" Frank's gaze flashes to my chest before he blinks and meets my eyes. "I thought you left Fur Bebé?"

"I did. I'm just here practicing. Bizarre coincidence, huh?"

"Yeah..." Frank's face puzzles.

"It's great to see you," I chirp. "How are the twins doing in their piano recitals?"

Frank's eyes brighten. "That's great you remember that. Jenny's doing really well, but Penny's struggling a bit. She doesn't like it as much as her sister does. She wants to play the guitar instead."

I lean on my club. "Maybe you can compromise with the cello? Another string instrument?"

He waggles his finger. "That's a great idea. I'll run that by Penny." He studies me, a smile spreading across his face that shows the deep creases around his eyes. "I'm actually glad you're here. I know you designed Petjamas, and I'd love to pick your brain."

Inside, I squeal. "Absolutely."

Frank takes his driver out of the bag. "When we're done here, why don't I treat both you and Lucas to a drink in the clubhouse?"

A barely audible growl seeps out of Lucas before he forces his mouth into something of a smile. "Well. That sounds great."

"It does, doesn't it?" I flash Lucas a proud grin, and he shoots me eye daggers.

Frank begins hitting balls—smooth as butter. He's probably on the course almost daily.

For about forty-five minutes, the three of us practice mostly silent, focusing on our swings. After finishing our session, we make our way inside the clubhouse and into the bar, which has mahogany everything and smells of unlit cigars, leather, and old money.

After we take a seat at a high-top table and get served three glasses of top-shelf scotch on ice, Frank turns to me and says, "So, give me what you've got."

I square my shoulders. "I have an opportunity for you to jump on the latest trend in petwear, Mr. Franklin."

"Please. Call me Frank."

In my peripheral vision, I see Lucas rolling his eyes when I say, "Sure. You can be the first to get the hottest item on your shelves, Frank."

"I'm listening."

I reach in my bag and slide over a copy of *Buckhead Lifestyle Magazine*—which has Lady Paw Paw on the cover. "Featured here is RezQ, my new petwear line that donates five percent of proceeds to animal charities." I pat the magazine. "And this copy is for you, so be sure to check out the article where they interviewed me."

"Wow!" Frank studies the cover. "This is really something." He flips to the earmarked page, which shows a picture from my FaceSnap account. It's of one of the shelter dogs, Zip, wearing only booties while modeling summer wear, which was taken to raise awareness about paw injuries caused by walking dogs on hot pavement. Frank taps his finger on the page and says, "I love to see a brand that's socially conscious."

My proud smile spreads. "RezQ has also helped get four shelter animals adopted."

Lucas rubs his temples as I give Frank my well-practiced pitch on RezQ, and why it's a must-have brand for his stores. I appreciate Lucas not interrupting, especially since his face is reddening with each passing moment.

When I finish, Lucas jumps in with, "We'd be honored to have Petjamas on your shelves, Mr. Franklin. A *proven* best-selling product. I'm thrilled to hear you like them. And now we have a fantastic new pet activewear line—Pet Sweats."

His words about *my* clothing lines twist the knife in my gut.

"I do like Petjamas, Lucas. A lot. And the pet activewear sounds great as well." Frank swirls the ice in his drink before taking a sip.

Lucas taps his fingers together, leaning forward. He's going in for the kill. "We also have all the distribution channels that'll get you whatever amount you need, and quickly."

Distribution. Ugh. I knew Lucas was moving in on my weakness. I don't have that. Yet.

"Right." Franklin sets his glass down. "But here's my problem—and this goes for both of you. I need more than a few successful lines before I can even approach Madame Puuccí about carrying either of your brands in our stores. She runs a tight ship—and she's seeking a designer who provides top-selling shirts, coats, collars, pajamas, activewear, and formalwear. We want our customers to have whatever they need with the brand they'll grow to love."

My stomach plummets right along with Lucas's face. We both blink, and a long silence drags out before both Lucas and I vow to get Frank what he needs so we can score a meeting with Madame Puuccí.

When we're both done practically begging, inside, I'm smiling. Lucas is going to realize that with Missy, it'll be nearly impossible to create more designs in a big hurry.

He's going to realize he needs me.

After Frank takes the last swig of his drink, he stands. "I've got an eleven o'clock tee time, so I need to git. But Lucas, we'll be in touch about the fashion show."

I gulp. "Le Chienne Couture Fashion Show?" That's *the* annual fashion show for petwear in New York City, which this year, will be aired on the Bravo channel.

"Yes," Frank says. "Fur Bebé is being considered for a last-minute spot. I'm sorry, Sophie, but RezQ just isn't established enough for me to put you on the roster."

"I understand," I say, but I don't mean it. We'll just have to see about that.

Lucas and I bid Frank farewell, then watch him leave the bar before we let scowls crease our faces.

Lucas's eyes narrow. "Penny should play the cello—really?"

I fold my arms. "Bragging about Petjamas and Pet Sweats, both *my* ideas, right in front of me? Do you have any shame?"

"A little bit, actually. Yeah."

His honesty catches me off guard, and my lips curve upward against my will. When I catch a glimpse of his sheepish grin, our eyes lock.

He doesn't look away when he says, "I can't believe you came here."

"I can't believe you fired me and picked Missy. But it's a dog-eat-dog world, apparently."

He lets out a laugh, and a spark flies through the air as our gazes continue to linger.

Finally, he shifts his eyes and says, "We should putt."

"What?"

"Putting." He points to the putting green outside. "The most important part of the game."

"I'm not really the putting type." I don't want to admit I can't putt worth a darn. That's the problem with using the driving range as an anger management system. It hasn't taught me how to put the ball in the hole.

Lucas stands. "We need to make sure these drinks are out of our systems before we drive home. And a good golfer has to be the putting type."

I groan, but cave. He makes an excellent point.

Once we're on the green, I manage to putt the ball further from the hole than where I'd started, and I become legitimately frustrated at myself. I'm bad, but not this bad. Lucas is screwing with my focus.

When I bend over to fetch my ball, I hear a ripping sound. It seems my unnaturally stretched skort briefs are starting to give, so I recompose myself before going into an awkward plié.

Lucas holds back a laugh. "Need some help?"

"No." As I continue easing myself down, I hear another rip. "Fine. Yes." I definitely need to stay upright, or my bum is going to soon be exposed under the pleats.

Lucas steps over and fetches my ball before placing it back on the green for me.

"Thank you," I grit, lining up my putter.

"Wait." He puts a hand on my shoulder. My next shot flies off the green, past the rough and into lost ball territory. He sucks air through his teeth. "Sorry. I was gonna give you some tips. No offense, but your putting stroke is no Sistine Chapel."

"Watch it, Shankapotomus." I fling a hand on my hip. "But yeah, it's not 'finely tuned' like yours. Clearly you get more practice with all the brown-nosing you do on the course." I prepare to hit another ball. "I wish you'd use your position for good instead of evil."

Yup, I went there.

"You know, Sophie, I'm trying. In fact, I just implemented a new policy on any donations Fur Bebé receives. It ensures the most pets get the funds."

"Most pets?" Although I agree with him, I can't stop myself from playing the devil's advocate. "That's very logical. But what if it's one pet that needs all the resources? Then being spread thin isn't so great."

"Why save one animal when you can save several?"

"Because that *one* animal might be adored by a child who can't wait to get home from school every afternoon to see them. If I had a thousand dollars and needed it to save Mr. D or save five dogs, I would save Mr. D because I love him." I stop, wiping my forehead. "Haven't you ever had an animal you loved like that?"

"Not exactly. My uncle loves animals, as you know, but…" he hesitates. "Well, my dad's allergic. So, we never had pets at home."

"Oh." I study Lucas, wondering what that would be like. I grew up surrounded with animals and can't imagine life without them. "I guess you won't know until you find *that* pet. The one you'll do anything to save. When that happens, you'll understand."

"Fair enough." He nods his chin toward me. "How about you let me use my skills gained from my brown-nosing to help you putt."

"Fine."

"You gotta steady your wrists," he says.

My wrists aren't my problem, he is.

Which worsens when he steps behind me and puts his strong arms over mine. I send a silent thank you to my brief seams for hanging on by a literal thread.

Deep breaths. Lucas's body is flush against me, and I never want to move. The electricity running through me is making my skin buzz, and good heavens, he feels like a solid wall of heat.

Gooseflesh appears on my arms where he touches them, and I'm pretty sure none of this is going to help my precision golf game.

Together, we swing a practice stroke. Then he says, "See, like a pendulum. You need the control."

Oh, definitely.

When he steps away, I try again on my own, keeping my wrists solid. When I whiz a "gimme" shot past the hole, I fight the urge to launch my putter airborne as I walk toward my wayward ball.

"Easy, slugger." Lucas approaches me, the corners of his mouth lifting. "Control and finesse make *all* my strokes smooth."

"Please." I give him a disapproving head tilt, but that same X-rated scene from earlier flips back on in my head. Golf is decidedly a bad sport to play with the sexy enemy.

A buzz from Lucas's pocket makes him stop what he's doing and pull out his phone. He texts for a while with his brows furrowed, then looks up. "Soph, you need to—" He stops speaking as he starts texting again. "Just a sec."

I place my putter back in my bag. I'm done with this torture for today, especially in this skort with ripped briefs.

"Your mom needs you to stop by the grocery store for milk," he says, putting his cell back in his pocket. "She's texting me since your phone's off."

"Seriously?" I groan, deciding it's beyond time to make my case. I sniff. "Look, Lucas, neither of us is going to land the Pet IQ opportunity without each other. You need my formalwear and socially conscious image, and I need your distribution and suite of products. That I designed, by the way."

"Man, you're like the serial killer in those corny 80s horror flicks. You never die."

I point to myself. "I bounce back. Like Rubbermaid."

A chuckle escapes his lips. "I admire you, Sophie." He rubs his forehead, sighing. "But let's be honest—you need Fur Bebé a lot more than Fur Bebé needs you. If I ask the board to bring you back, they're going to say that we can design our own formalwear, and that being socially conscious won't make or break the Pet IQ deal."

My stomach sinks, again, but I'm starting to get accustomed to this feeling. It rolls off a lot easier these days, and I shrug before I say, "And, as usual, the board would be wrong. Missy can't design a potato sack, let alone formalwear. But all right. If you're not with me, you're against me."

Lucas takes a step toward me. "So, you're saying we're going head-to-head for this Pet IQ opportunity?"

Yes, I guess that *is* what I'm saying. Apparently, I'm taking Mom's advice—I *am* starting my own line, without any upfront capital or investors. I hold up my fist for a bump. "To fighting it out."

"Okay." His fist meets mine. "May the best brand win."

16

Eating Nemo

After working two solid days on a pressure campaign to get Madame Puuccí's attention, I'm meeting the crew at Eating Nemo for Tuesday Happy Hour to celebrate. Our campaign worked! *Love Buzz Magazine* ran an article on RezQ.

Eva, Mom, and I make our way past the exotic fish tank to find a private table in the back where Riley's waiting for us. We slide into the cherry-red velvet booth with Japanese writing watermarked into the fabric.

"Thanks for getting us our spot, Riles." I settle into the seat beside her. Seeing edamame and sake cups in front of each of us, I say, "Nice!"

Riley flips her hair and smiles. "And the sake's the good stuff. I worked the bartender over for it. You're welcome."

"Thank you, Master Flirter." I bow my head. "Everything else is on me tonight, okay? I have to thank y'all."

"I can't believe you made it into *Love Buzz*," Eva says with a squeal as soon as she sits.

"*We* made it." I grab my phone, and we all go quiet as we get sucked into the article for the hundredth time. It talks about how Puuccí isn't raising money for animal organizations like RezQ, and urges people to make the switch.

Eva reads the headline aloud. "*RezQ or Puucci?*"

"I still can't believe you're being compared to *Puucci*. This is epic." Riley doesn't look up from her phone. "What we did worked."

"I know," I squeak. "It's beyond what I'd even imagined." We sent our hot pavement awareness photos to some dog loving FaceSnap accounts with big followings, and they shared them with our message about how the big retailers should be doing more. RezQ's FaceSnap account started picking up the pace this afternoon. *Finally*. "And I have all of you to thank for it."

"It's fine, just make it rain. Then pay up," Eva says.

"Definitely." I click onto my FaceSnap account. "The number of our followers is ticking up by the second." RezQ's up over twenty thousand now, still woefully short of the two-hundred-thousand goal, but I do have preorders for Lady Paw Paw's dress and hat. I've now specked those out for mass production, and I'm on the hunt for outsourcing companies. And it looks like after this *Love Buzz* article, things are going to get busier.

Then I see something surprising. One of my followers looks like Ted, but Ted doesn't have a phone. When I click on his picture, it's definitely him with those startling green eyes and ragged wool coat. I can't believe Ted got a phone. That had to be Lucas, right?

Wow. Ted's now a fan, and that makes me beyond happy.

"Did you see all your followers demanding RezQ be included in Puucci's runway show?" Mom is glowing.

"I know, that's incredible, right?" Riley looks up from her phone. "They've been at it since the *Buckhead Lifestyle Magazine* article came out."

"RezQ could become a cult classic." Eva rubs her hands together.

I say, "I highly doubt Madame Puuccí will actually let RezQ in. She only invites top designers."

"Yeah, but social media pressure is a powerful thing. Madame Puuccí also cares about her image." Eva gnaws on her edamame.

"But Soph…" Riley frowns. "I hate to rain on this happy parade, but I ran the numbers. Even with all these sales, you're only just breaking even with the costs of materials and outsourcing."

A new email message pops up on my phone. When I see who it's from, I almost stop breathing. "Hold that thought, Riley." I put up a finger, pausing to compose myself. "Y'all aren't gonna believe this—I just got an email from Frank Franklin."

"What?" Riley goes bug-eyed.

"Are y'all ready?" A waitress materializes in front of our booth holding a pen and pad.

Riley and I rush to order our standard dragon and Philadelphia rolls so we can read the email.

"What they're having plus Tuna nigiri and edamame," Eva says. I'd forgotten she can eat everyone under the table and never gain an ounce. "Oh, and more sake too. It's on special."

"Make that another round for the whole table," Mom adds. Then she stares at her menu for a while until she says, "That tempura is still half-priced too, right?"

"Yes, for another fifteen minutes," the waitress says.

Mom feigns to be deep in thought, which is all for show. She'd be getting tempura even if it wasn't on special. She never eats raw fish because she says she "isn't a fan of Salmon or Salmonella." Truthfully, she lives for fried food.

"Tempura's fine," she says hesitantly, and I roll my eyes.

The second the waitress walks away, Riley says, "Spill it, Soph."

After reading the email, I'm buzzing with euphoria when I say, "You're right, Eva. Frank says Madame Puuccí wants to discuss showcasing RezQ in her Le Chienne Couture show! Forget Frank—Madame Puuccí *herself* wants me to meet me at the Loft Lounge this Friday."

"Holy schmoly." Riley closes her eyes. "It worked—she's caving to the pressure!"

Eva breaks into a bright smile. "This is the big one. *Madame Puuccí*. In the flesh."

"And I'm friends with Roach!" Mom cries out.

I look at Mom, blinking, as I wait for her to make any sort of logical connection as to how that relates to my meeting with Madame Puuccí. Instead, Eva cuts in with, "Who's Roach?"

Mom waves her chopsticks, still in their wrappers. "He manages the bar at the Loft Lounge. I made friends with him that morning of PAW-CON when I was looking everywhere for you, Soph. We instantly hit it off—he's a Pisces like me. When we talked, I felt he wanted a baby. Sure enough, his wife was having a hard time getting pregnant, so I did my fertility dance for him. That maneuver's like the stork."

"Oh, wow." I fight to keep my face from pinching.

"Anyway, I'll come in as your backup, working as a bartender. I have a few alternate identities." She winks.

I close my eyes. "Okie doke."

"And we need new dog models. And get ones that don't have the worst breath ever." Mom curls her lip. "Like that Giant Poodle, Munch."

"Ohhh, yeah." Riley sticks out her tongue.

I groan. "You know what, she can't help it. Don't get all judgy on Munch."

"Soph, you should give her Yum Breaths," Riley says. "They're supposed to really work on bad breath."

"No!" Mom's face contorts.

I cut in. "Mom thinks Yum Breaths are toxic."

"Promise me you guys won't give those to any animals. *Ever*." Mom puts a hand over her heart.

"We promise." Eva nods like a bobblehead.

"Good." Mom exhales.

"So, Sophie, since you're actually working for yourself now…" Riley's face puckers as she bites her lip. "I found some office space in Fur Bebé's building that you can use for *free*. We could work together again! Well, sort of."

"Wow Riley, that's great. And so nice." I raise a brow. "But what's with that face?"

She hesitates, clearly struggling to get the words out. "It's very cozy…" She puts up a palm.

I cock my head.

"Okay, it's a supply closet, but if you're working in there, you can help the building manager track when the ceiling drips so he can figure out the source of the leak."

"Riley."

"It's free office space! And you'd be by me."

I close my eyes. As bad as it sounds, it would be a break from the Winnebago where there is zero room and constant interruptions from Mom. It sounds like either way I go, I'm stuck with mold. But then I have a thought. "Wait, has that lawyer been back looking for me?"

"Nope. There's been nothing or no one from Urban Productions."

"Good," I say. "I'll think about it. And thank you for looking out for me… I think."

"It's what we do for each other." Riley holds up her sake cup, and after the four of us clink our cups together, she says, "And cheers to you. You'll land this runway gig."

"Thank you." I do jazz hands and eke out another squeal. "And I have something that's going to be a show-stopper." I go on to tell them about my latest idea.

"Wow!" Riley's voice goes up. "That sounds amazing. I don't really like over-the-top things, but that's gonna kill."

"Take that, Lucas." Eva has a proud smile as she holds another piece of edamame to her mouth.

"Yeah." My tone deflates as I put my phone away and lean my head back against the padded booth. Things are getting complicated with Lucas. I feel guilty because I clearly like him, which is why I have to *stop* liking him. Guilt cannot stand in the way of what I have to do. He's forced me to be his competition, and this is my shot to accomplish my dream and do something big for myself *and* the animals.

I didn't expect something this big to happen, but now that it is, I have to ride the wave.

"Um, hello?" Riley side-eyes me. "What happened between you and Lucas?"

"Nothing. We just hung out at the driving range after Frank Franklin left."

Eva scolds me with her eyes. "And he helped you home after you hit your head on the pool umbrella and puked on him."

"*What?*" Riley's jaw hits the floor. "You're so dead for not telling me any of this."

"You were out of town."

"Don't worry, Riley—" Eva sniffs, "—we had to beat it out of her after seeing the gash on her head."

"I told you that you two would be doing the pickle tickle soon," Riley deadpans.

"We're friends," I say, not believing my own words.

"Okay." Riley rolls her eyes so hard it looks painful.

Eva turns to Riley. "I'm always just friends with the brilliant and gorgeous guy who bandages my wounds."

Mom's eyes twinkle. "Soph, you know your mom roots for knocking boots."

"I'm eating, Mother."

"And trust me, more than anyone, you're looong overdue." Mom picks up a carrot tempura. "But do to Lucas what you do to the rest of us—stay the mysterious type. No spilling secrets in the sheets. Kapeesh?"

"My lips are sealed. Promise."

17

Dolly Llama

Returning home from working at the shelter, I see a Harley parked in front of the Winnebago. Mom's wearing her biking jacket and unpacking something out of the back storage case.

Stepping out of my car, I say, "So, where'd the Harley come from?" even though I'm not sure if I want the answer.

"Roach loaned it to me for a bit. I needed it for work, but he said I could keep this beauty for a while." She smacks the seat.

"So, what happened today?"

A proud grin peeks over her lips. "You know how I made friends with Shannon, the manager of the animal shelter?"

"No, I didn't know that. How did you meet her?"

"She's the *manager where you work*, Sophie," Mom says in her "duh" tone.

Although that answer shouldn't be sufficient, it somehow is with my mother. "So, what did Shannon need from you?"

"Well, since I've helped her so much, she recommended me to the police. They called her because the state senator got his dog stolen, and they were looking for his Boston Terrier pup, Jimmy Chew, spelled C-H-E-W. Shannon didn't have him, so the police asked for my help to rescue him." Mom holds up her phone that displays a picture of an adorable gray Boston Terrier puppy with spots on his ears. "He was snagged by a pup hoarder in a biker gang, which we knew because Jimmy Chew had a GPS tracker in his collar. But they needed me to find the dog after the hoarder took the collar off."

"So, you got Mr. Chew back?"

"Sure did! The perp caved as soon as we got to his house. Didn't even put up a fight. He knew he'd gotten himself in too deep this time."

I gasp. "That sounds dangerous. You can't do stuff like that alone."

"I didn't."

My face twists in confusion.

Mom nods to the door. "Go inside the Winnebago."

I step in the door, going wide-eyed when I see Lucas at the kitchenette sink, washing his hands. "Hey," he says, cool and casual.

I'm anything but as I grapple with images of me pressed up against shirtless Lucas the last time we were in this Winnebago together. Unsurprisingly, like Topless and Suit Lucas, Bad Boy Lucas is smoldering. He's wearing a long-sleeved thermal that's tight enough to show his muscles, faded jeans, and black boots. And his hair is tussled, wild. "Hey," I manage to say.

He dries his hands on the dish towel before approaching me. "So, your mom tell you?"

"Yeah. You two did good today." I study him, puzzled. Why is he doing all this? It's surpassed whatever guilt he had over giving my promotion to Missy.

He runs a hand through his helmet hair. "It was awesome." His cheeks are flushed, and he looks fresh and revived. "That was my first time on a motorcycle."

"Pretty cool, huh? So, you didn't have to work? It's Wednesday, and you're the guy who works weekends. In ranch wear."

The corner of his mouth ticks up. "I told them I'm taking the day for pet philanthropy. And I was not lying."

"No, you weren't."

Well, didn't Mom and Lucas just have a bomb-diggity day saving puppies. Without me!

"Maybe you're rubbing off on me," he says. "Saving animals is awesome."

On second thought, maybe this day was a good thing. "It is, isn't it?"

"It makes the concept of RezQ—which I always knew was good—take on a new meaning. And it's inspiring." He shrugs. "And I might like the off-the-wall photos of your awareness campaigns."

A warmth rushes through me, and somehow, Lucas becomes even more beautiful to me than he already was, which I didn't think was possible. His dark eyes sparkle with flecks of amber, and his golden skin radiates—like he just became more alive. Maybe he did. "I'm so glad."

When Mom comes back inside, I try to hold back the hurt in my voice when I say, "I would've helped you too, Mom."

"You had to work, Soph." She won't meet my gaze. "And no offense, but I needed muscles." She shoots Lucas a wink.

I fight off an eye roll—I can't allow myself to be jealous of Lucas. "Well, I'm proud of both of you—" I stop speaking because I hear whimpering sounds. When I peer around, I see a tiny pink dog crate sitting on the floor beside us. "Oh, no!" I choke out. "No, no, no."

"Yes, yes, yes!" Mom sings, opening the crate and letting two itty-bitty Yorkie puppies run free on the floor.

"You didn't!" I put a hand over my mouth. "From the puppy hoarder?"

"Yup." Mom's glowing so much, she could be radioactive. "He admitted he had too much on his hands with the other eleven dogs, so he let me adopt these two precious babies."

"What about Gizzie?"

"What about Gizzie? Now he has two baby sisters to love."

"In this Winnebago? We're going to become a fertilizer farm." I shake my head. "On top of the mold we're farming in here."

"There's no mold. That's Betsy, I told you, Soph. Anyway, I had to rescue these babies," she says as she chases one down. The pup's about to commit hara-kiri by leaping into her heating vent. "It's my moral obligation as a licensed pet psychic to take them in and rehabilitate them."

"Where did you get *that* license?" I ask.

"Well, not Harvard or Stanford." Mom flashes Lucas a knowing look.

"Join the club." I study the puppies. "Why do they need rehabilitation? They look fine."

"I can hear their thoughts. They have emotional baggage, feeling neglected and abandoned." She takes a tiny bowl from her cabinet and fills it with micro-sized pellets.

I go after the other puppy and pick it up. It's adorable, sporting an aqua sweater that has "Dolly" crocheted on the back. "How do they already have personalized sweaters?"

"There's a knitting kiosk at Pet IQ. Lucas and I stopped there on the way home."

"I did not know they had that."

"Lucas did." Mom's lips curve in a conspiratorial grin.

I eye Lucas, wondering how he knows so much about Pet IQ services. Is he making secret progress with Madame Puuccí? Is he scoping out stores to brown-nose? And if he is, that's not a bad idea.

I set Dolly at the bowl, and she scarfs down the food. Mom puts down her sister, but she's not interested in the grub. Instead, she takes off running. I chase after her, not wanting Mom's carpet to become a toilet. When I snatch up the other pup, her sweater says, "Llama."

I let out a chuckle as I carry Llama back to the food before setting her on the floor. "Mom, you spelled their names wrong if you were naming them after the Dalai Lama."

"I certainly did not. Dolly is named for the Dalai Lama *and* the best country singer of all time. Llama is named for the Dalai Lama *and* the animal, which represents tolerance and perseverance." She looks at the floor to see them both running off this time. "Get back here Dolly and Llama!"

Mom captures the twins, who are not living up to either of their namesakes by jumping, squirming, and squealing. She puts the puppies back in their crate. "I'm taking them on a walk to see if they'll potty for their Mama."

As she heads to the door, I watch her. She closes her eyes and yawns, and it hits me how worn out she looks. I worry about her doing this stuff—it's difficult and not safe.

When she's outside, Lucas cuts into my thoughts. "Your Mom can take care of herself, Soph. She'll be okay."

I refuse to meet his gaze, as if that'll stop his uncanny ability to know what I'm thinking. The feeling is both warm and disconcerting, and I don't know what to do with it. So all I say is, "I'm glad you went with her today."

"Sure. Your mom's tough." His mouth tugs to one side in a half smile. "I know where you get it."

"I guess that's true, isn't it?" I shrug, playing it cool, but my heart almost forgets to beat.

"Come to my apartment this Saturday?" He shuffles his feet. "I have a surprise for you."

I *really* can't get involved with Lucas, even if he is helping me and Mom. Besides everything that's happening, now is not the time to roll the dice on a bet I always lose.

He reaches over and strokes my hair, his gentle touch sending a shiver down my spine. And I can't help noticing how his flexed bicep looks in that thermal.

Okay, maybe hanging out with him at his place isn't the worst idea? He could slip and tell me dirt on Fur Bebé. I nod slowly. "Sure."

After he leaves, it hits me that I'm alone, a rarity in this tiny house on wheels. I decide to do something I haven't been able to put out of my mind since finding that photo of me and Dad having ice cream together.

I rush to the new cabinets I installed under the stairs leading to Mom's bedroom and pull out a box I ordered from OriginLinx.com, a site for tracking ancestry. I tear it open, and the brochure reads, "Find the family you didn't know you had. Learn about the possible royalty in your lineage. Once you trace your origins, find *linx* to lost relatives through OriginLinx!"

The words ratchet up my excitement to take the test. I know my father's dead, but I could still learn about my relatives on his side. Clearly, a part of me needs to understand more about where I came from. Yearning for family is weaved into our genes.

I follow the instructions and complete the kit as quickly as possible before packaging it back up. Then I rush to drop it in the building's outgoing mailbox before Mom can see what I've done.

She can't know about this because she'll be over the moon, and I don't want to let her down if I change my mind about seeing the results.

When I get back to the Winnebago, Mom's home with the puppies, so I make sure Gizzie is locked away in her room before letting Dolly and Llama play. Of course, Gizzie growls and snarls every time he sees them. I have the puppies running around on my bed with me as Mom pours herself a wine in the kitchen, grumbling about where I "hid" the wine glasses.

I walk to the new cabinets and point to them. "Did you see what I did?"

"Yes." She flings a hand on her hip. "Now *that* was actually helpful. Thank you."

"You're welcome."

I study Mom, seeing her differently than I did just five weeks ago when my entire life got flipped on its head.

I never really appreciated just how brave she is, or how she faces tough times, head-on. We couldn't afford much, but she always made sure I had what I needed—buying quality thrift clothing—and going out of her way so I could experience new things. A resort vacation was out of the question, but camping and lakes were dirt cheap, and she and I always loved hiking. Just being herself, she'd make friends at the lake, so I'd end up getting boat rides, waterskiing, and once, even a ride on a jet ski. Mom took on hard jobs to pay the bills—once she even worked as a night janitor—and she never complained or seemed afraid. I study her when I say, "Were you scared today?"

"A little, I guess. But this is something I have to do. The world should be a better place than it was for me growing up."

I blink, something needling my chest. That answer was impressively self-aware, and it provokes an overwhelming desire to know something

Mom's always refused to talk about. "Can you tell me more about your childhood? You never talk about it."

"There's a reason for that."

"Please." I approach her before touching her hand. "I really want to know."

"It wasn't a good one, and I don't like to think about it."

"It'd mean the world to me if you'd let me in. I need that right now."

She sighs, taking a long pause before saying, "Sit."

After I transform the dining table into my bed, I snatch Dolly as she darts by and I give her a good belly rub. Her little leg taps like Thumper when I hit a particular spot, so I do it over and over, chuckling.

Mom sits beside me before taking a sip of her wine. "My dad abandoned us when I was five. Mom and I lived in a ratty apartment above the Teacup Tavern, and its sign used to flash in my window. It kept me up nights. I still have nightmares about a big flashing neon teacup. Anyway, Mom would go down to the bar a lot, and I was forced to figure out my own dinner and put myself to bed. Sometimes, I'd hide in the laundry basket because I feared the drunks who wandered around outside our apartment. I always took my favorite doll, Timmy, in with me because I thought he'd protect me."

It's hard to believe she'd never told me that before. It's even harder to believe I've always been too self-involved to push her for an answer. The profound sadness I feel for her seeps into my being. "Left all alone? At five?" My heart hurts when I think about how tough that must've been on her. She managed to do so well for herself given her upbringing.

She doesn't say anything more about it as she puts her glass down and starts running her fingers through my hair. Soon she's giving me a braid, something she used to do to comfort me when I was little.

After a rough childhood, Mom then had to become every role to me—the nurturer, the protector, the disciplinarian, the supporter, the chauffeur, the friend. If parenting is the toughest job in the world, then what is single parenting?

A handful of times at my grade school's open houses, some well-intended person would ask where my dad was, or if he was coming. Mom would joke that I didn't need a father because she could shapeshift, but I could always see the pain in her tired eyes.

Llama comes over and I lay her beside Dolly before rubbing both their tummies at the same time. "So, you and Lucas really are friends."

"He called me, Sophie." Mom tugs at my braid.

I lean in closer to her, realizing how much I miss having her play with my hair. "Fair enough, but didn't you think that's kind of weird?"

"He wants help honing his extrasensory perceptions. He's got some sort of psychic gift if you ask me."

"I've noticed," I say reflexively. "I mean, he's got some great people-reading skills."

"It's too bad you don't believe in psychic abilities, but maybe you will when your third eye opens."

Dolly and Llama have already fallen asleep, belly up, so I brush my fingertips over them. "All righty, then. I'm gonna close all three eyes. I'm totally beat."

"Rest up, Soph. You're gonna need it for Friday's meeting with Madame Puuccí." Mom reaches over and rubs Dolly's ears before scooping her and her sister up.

"Goodnight, Mom."

"Night, hon." Mom stands holding the pups, and when I climb under the covers, she checks that the Winnebago's locked, two eyes on me and one always making sure I'm safe.

And I'm grateful.

18

The Sting

Sucking in deep breaths, I have to pull myself together for cocktails with Madame Puuccí in a few hours. I'm cranked up on a jumbo Supremely Bean raspberry mocha, and nerves vibrate through me. This is far more than business—I'm meeting my hero.

I slip on my trusted midnight cocktail dress, which is professional, but the off-the-shoulder sleeves give it flair. Once my pair of red Prada pointy-toed heels are on, I'm ready to execute Operation "Get RezQ into Le Chienne Couture."

Here's the plan: Mom's going to be a bartender, a widow who owns nine dogs. She'll listen in on my conversation with Madame Puuccí, then step in and fawn over my designs if needed.

Researching Madame Puuccí on FaceSnap, I discovered her favorite cocktail is rose water and gin. With that in mind, Mom's bringing rose water to serve her.

When Mom ducks out of her short bedroom door, I do a double take. Somehow, she's done it again. A black suede cocktail dress hugs her figure and a gold fringe necklace tumbles into her cleavage. Her penciled-in lips make her look like she'd had enhancement injections.

She wears green contacts, a flowing red wig and long, fake eyelashes. Mom looks... well, kinda hot.

I gently broach the subject of how she's instantly smaller. "You look so svelte."

To my horror, she pulls up her dress to show me her Spanx. "I jammed these on, and they're two sizes too small!"

"You're wearing Spanx?" I blink in awe at my mother.

"Yes, and don't ever say I don't love you. This thing makes me feel like I've been swallowed by a snake."

"Then why are you wearing it?"

"I had to fit into this cocktail dress—I wasn't about to buy a new one," she says. "I can't believe women do this for men. If a man doesn't like me, *all* of me, he can go bungee jumping off a fifty-foot cliff with a sixty-foot rope."

I love that attitude. "That's great. Every woman should feel the same." There goes Mom—being wise again.

She tugs at the waistband. "Anyway, Spanx are highway robbery. These are Spunx."

And maybe not.

Mom makes us put in hidden earbuds and microphones in our bras. As I'm readjusting my strap, I say, "Is all this necessary?"

"Absolutely. I have to admit, I'm a little scared. I feel an unwelcome energy blowing in."

"I hope you're wrong." I bite my thumbnail, realizing that when it comes to gut instincts, Mom has yet to be wrong. And I should tell her so. "You were right to encourage me to pursue the RezQ line. It's the best thing I've ever done."

Mom smiles, but it fades quickly. "Glad to help."

I know her indifference is a facade, but I appreciate her skipping the "I told you so." Still, she deserves credit where credit's due. "You did good."

She rolls her neck. "Great. Now let's focus. We've got a job to do."

"I'm ready." I sigh. "I hope."

With that, Mom grabs her "sting op" purse, which is the size of a beach bag, before we hop in the bling machine to make our way to the hotel. As soon as I pull onto the road, my stomach starts doing gymnastics. "So, Roach is cool with you bartending?"

"He was more than happy to head home and let me finish his shift. I think he knew I'm up to something more, but he didn't ask. He's meeting us in the alley behind the bar."

"All right."

We park a couple of blocks from The Loft, then walk to the back of the hotel. There, Roach is waiting for us by the dumpster. With no neck, Terminator shades, and gnarly tats on his pale biceps, he lives up to his name. Or appears to. Mom takes the apron he gives her, then she follows him through the back door.

I make sure my earbuds are hidden in my ear, and my bra microphone is working before I walk around to the front and enter the swanky lounge, which is packed on a Friday night. But I immediately see Madame Puuccí sitting on a tufted velvet chair because she's impossible to miss.

She looks like she does on a billboard, except now, she's real.

Her white hair is pulled into two-strand twists, gold flower pins placed in a work of art. A white dress with gold petals fits her like it was made for her—which it surely was.

Her umber fingers are adorned in rings of various stones, which match her neckwear.

I work my way past the two-sided fireplace, which flickers in the dim atmosphere. After approaching, I smile and extend my hand. "I'm Sophie Fox. It's an honor to meet you, Ms. Puuccí."

"*Madame* Puuccí." She gives my hand a squeeze. "Sit, darling."

I can't believe I messed that up—I'm clearly nervous. "Madame Puuccí. It's a pleasure."

After I take a seat across from her, I'm ready to ask if I can go get her a drink, but she cuts in with, "So. Tell me one reason why you deserve to be in Le Chienne Couture."

I inhale to steady my breath. "Well, people love my designs."

"*Some* people certainly do." She taps her long, pointy fingernails together. "Some people also like SpaghettiOs."

So, then. She thinks I'm the SpaghettiOs of fashion. I keep my voice from deflating when I say, "Raven Monroe picked my dress for her dog, Lady Paw Paw."

"Raven Monroe *had* to pick your dress."

"Novu Villa Country Club selected my brand as a backup," I squeak.

"To support a local apprentice designer who claims to have a little cause." Her tone is emotionless, yet somehow, it cuts through me like a straight razor.

I swallow hard, my brain reeling through things I can say next.

"Madame Puuccí?" Lucas's voice rings out. "Sophie?"

I flip around to see him looking handsome as ever in a sleek collared shirt and dress pants. My stomach plummets.

How is *he* here?

"What a coincidence—bumping into you both." His lips curve into a guilty smile.

"Well, what's your name, Mr. Handsome?" Madame Puuccí holds out her hand to be kissed.

Lucas obliges before saying, "Lucas Nevarez. I'm the CEO of Fur Bebé."

"Oh, yes, I've heard *all* about you." Her ruby red lips stretch into a smile. "You're really getting that company some fabulous press."

Please.

Lucas motions to the bar. "So, Madame Puuccí, may I get you a drink?"

Oh, no, no, no. That's my trick.

Madame Puuccí flutters out a laugh. "I'd love to see you try. I doubt they have rose water."

I stand. "Actually, let me see what I can do. May I get you any food, Madame Puuccí?"

"I don't eat bar food, Ms. Fox."

"Right." They say never meet your heroes, and I'm starting to see why.

As soon as Lucas and I are out of Madame's earshot, I snarl, "How did you know about this meeting?"

Lucas shrugs.

Through my earbud, I hear Mom say, "Oops, it might've slipped. I didn't know he'd pull this."

I gasp. "Seriously? After your lecture about me spilling secrets in the sheets?"

"Sorry."

Walking next to Lucas, I suppress the urge to feel… whatever it is I feel when I'm next to him. He and I fight through the crowd of bodies and round the corner to the packed bar, squirreling our way into the freshly vacated Jetsons' style stools. "I can't believe you did this," I say.

"Really, Sophie?" His eyebrow quirks. "Dog-eat-dog world, remember?"

"Humph. What if this ruins both our chances?"

"From what I heard of your conversation with Madame Puuccí, the only place you have to go is up." He holds up his finger to get the bartender's attention.

"I just needed more time to win her over. Now I'm hosed, Mr. *Handsome*." As I try to place our drink orders, a woman elbows her way in and cuts me off.

Mom is at the other end of the bar, and I don't know why she's not serving me—I'm the whole reason she's here. I wave at her, but she doesn't look in my direction. I turn to another bartender, a hipster with a goatee, and flash him my best smile. He takes my order after I point to the rose water.

As we wait, Lucas says, "There's room for both of us in the show, Sophie."

"Oh, no. I don't *want* you there." Actually, that's not entirely true. I don't want Missy and Fur Bebé there, but details.

"Come on. We've both earned it, fair and square. Even-steven."

"I bet you were popular in preschool," I say with a fleck of condescension, but boy, how I *do* like fair and square. After another elbow from behind, I hop off my stool.

"Not to brag, but I shared my toys like a champ. Or so my mom told me." This is the first time he's mentioned his mother, and I find myself curious about her. But I don't ask anything because something in his eyes shuts down before he blinks it away. "I went back to the driving range the other day, and I got scolded for wearing my cowboy shirt."

I succumb to laughter, noting he changed the subject. "Speaking of your miserable choice of attire, you must be beside yourself right now, separated from your Birkenstocks. Did you tell them you'll be blissfully reunited by tomorrow?"

Lucas's eyes dance with amusement before he looks down at my feet. "At least I don't have tourniquets around my toes."

"These are quite comfortable," I lie, secretly trying to move my toes. I can't because they're numb.

A guy who's been trying to get to the packed bar decides to shove his way in behind me, and my finger scrapes against something sharp on the counter before I'm knocked straight into Lucas's chest.

Lucas instinctively flexes, and my breath hitches as I rediscover just how hard his body is. And his smell—it's so lovely, it fogs my brain. Lucas pulls me into a hug to keep me from falling to the floor, and every inch of me reacts to him, as usual.

Logic gnaws its way into my head, screaming, *Danger!* Lucas is messing with my runway show.

"Hey, watch it, man," Lucas says to the guy.

"Sorry." I hear from behind.

I try to pull out of the hug, but I can't move because the crowd has me pinned. When I realize I'm straddling Lucas's leg, *I* mind, but my body doesn't. My body loves it.

My body is a traitor.

I put my face into Lucas's neck so we aren't nose-to-nose. I stare at his ear in front of me, just sitting there, so kissable and sexy. I lean in, making sure my lips touch his lobe when I whisper, "Sorry."

He turns, and I feel his breath on my cheek when he replies, "No problem, Sophie Fox."

The electricity between us short-circuits my brain, and my hands brush over his neck. Before I know it, we are now, indeed, nose-to-nose. I can barely focus on my words when I say, "Does addressing women by their full name get you anywhere?" Although I try to speak with disgust, the croak in my voice makes my words sound like a beg.

"You tell me." Lucas's strong hands move down my back.

I have no answer. Or not one I want to share, anyway. My thoughts scatter like marbles, and I'm not the only one having a reaction because pressed up against him, I can feel his shallow breaths.

For goodness' sake, my body needs to start listening to my mind. Lucas is off-limits. *Period*.

The pushy guy leaves the bar, and I finally have space to move. I pull away, breaking the spell. When I look at my smarting finger, it's bleeding. "Oh, no." I wrap a cocktail napkin around it.

Lucas immediately reaches for his wallet and pulls out another Transformers Band-Aid. I hold my finger out while he gently bandages it, saying, "Now, this is my last Band-Aid. So, no more getting hurt."

"Ten-four."

When I glance over at Madame Puuccí, Mom is there, serving her a drink and chatting her up.

When Lucas follows my gaze, he goes bug-eyed before saying, "Gotta go." He rushes away, and I smooth out my skirt before darting to catch up.

I take off, leaving the drink behind. Madame Puuccí has one now, and I'm sure Mom can swing by and pick this other one up for her shortly.

Okay, so my hormones had taken over a bit, but overall, I'd done a good job of staying in control. Right?

\# \# \#

As soon as Lucas and I make it back to Madame Puuccí's table, Mom looks at me and gasps. "Oh, no way. Are you the RezQ designer? Raven Monroe's dog wore your dress!"

"Oh, please," Lucas grumbles under his breath.

I smile, feigning humility. "Yes, I am." This Raven Monroe thing is getting beaten to death. Maybe Madame Puuccí has a point—I'm a one hit wonder.

Mom shows Madame Puuccí her phone full of pictures of "her" babies, who are all wearing my designs. "These are the best-fitting dog clothes I've ever found. And each one captures their unique, individual personalities. I'm telling you, RezQ is the best." Mom keeps swiping left on her phone as she goes through her portfolio.

I smile, shooting mom a "dial it back" look. She takes the hint and puts her phone away. Then she says, "I'll be back around if you need anything else."

After Mom's gone, I wring my hands, waiting for Lucas to rat Mom and me out. But he stays silent as Madame Puuccí studies me, putting a fingertip on her chin. "People *do* seem to like your designs, Sophie. Maybe it wouldn't be so bad having a rags to riches story. A socially conscious designer for the commoner."

"Yes." I nod enthusiastically, my stomach flip-flopping.

Madame Puuccí's phone buzzes from a text, and she puts up a finger. "Hold on, this is from Frank." After studying her phone, she scowls at me. "Missy Mulligan just posted a picture of someone she's claiming is your mother." Madame Puuccí shows me her screen.

It's Missy's FaceSnap account, and on it, is a picture of Mom in her dominatrix outfit from that morning at PAW-CON. The caption reads, "Does this look like a responsible pet parent? Here's RezQ's founder's mother—who put her 'beloved' pet Lulu up for adoption because the poor thing had breathing issues."

I gasp, and I think I might actually be seeing red. I can't stop the tremble in my voice when I say, "Mom *fostered* Lulu, a shedding pug who set off my mother's allergies. *Mom* couldn't breathe, that's why she placed Lulu for adoption." I point to the screen. "This is a lie."

"But this *is* your mother." Madame Puuccí groans. "In that unspeakable outfit?"

"Yes, and she's an amazing woman—"

Madame Puuccí's palm goes up. "Enough. I don't want to hear another word."

"If I may, Madame Puuccí." Lucas raises his hand like a schoolboy.

"Yes, Lucas."

"That outfit Sophie's mother's wearing is one of her crime-fighting undercover personas. In fact, just two days ago, Skye went on a dangerous undercover mission to rescue the state senator's dog, Jimmy Chew. She's a real-life superhero."

I can tell by his tone that he means his words, and it subdues my anger. Lucas truly does care about Mom, and that means everything to me.

"*She* rescued Jimmy Chew?" Madame Puuccí puts a delicate hand over her heart.

"Yup. That was her." Lucas's face lights up in a smile, and it's genuine.

Wow. Lucas turned that around right quick. Now I'm wondering if I should thank Missy.

Then Lucas makes his going-in-for-the-kill face. "Madame Puuccí, you definitely need up-and-coming designers at Le Chienne Couture. Why not choose brands that are making a splash? Clearly, RezQ's becoming a threat for Missy Mulligan to go after Sophie with this post. It'll make for quite a show to watch Fur Bebé and RezQ go head-to-head."

She leans in toward Lucas and smiles. "Hard to argue with that, isn't it, Mr. Handsome? Okay, let's do it. It's going to be a tight fit, but I'll make room for both of you."

My eyes lock with Lucas's, and a spark flies between us.

He's making it *really* hard for me to hate him.

19

Rooftop Reunion

"Mr. Nevarez, welcome." The balding doorman ushers Lucas and me inside Lucas's apartment building. In Eva's dad's suite of complexes, this place is definitely next level. Actually, next, *next* level.

The doorman turns to me. "Welcome, miss. I'm Sydney."

"Hi, Sydney, I'm Sophie." I smile politely, glancing around the exquisite marble-tiled lobby before we get on the elevator and make our way to the top floor. Lucas enters a code that takes us to the penthouse suite.

Un-freaking-believable.

We step inside, and I stand in silence, taking in the vast two-story grand room. A wall of windows frames a breathtaking skyline view of downtown Buckhead. French doors led to a wraparound patio. This place is a stark reminder of who Lucas and his family are. While he makes a hefty salary as a CEO, this place surpasses that and heads into old money territory.

I manage to finally blink. "What a dump."

Lucas's lips crack into a grin. "I'll be right back."

Lucas said he had a surprise for me, and I force myself to stop fidgeting with my phone while I wait.

He disappears into what appears to be his bedroom before returning with a crate. When Lucas unzips it, Mr. D comes running out and toward me.

"Mr. D!" I cry. His tail is wagging so fast it's a blur, and he jumps into my arms. I break into tears, saying, "Who's the best boy in the whole wide world?"

After hugging and cuddling Mr. D, I put him down so he can run circles on the floor. When I finally look at Lucas, he has a contented smile.

Wiping away a tear, I say, "Thank you. Thank you so much."

Lucas's eyes gloss over, and he nods slowly. "You're most definitely welcome." After he swallows, he points to the window. "You said that Mr. D loves city views."

"Yes."

"You and Mr. D should come with me." He holds up a finger. "After I grab us some wine." Lucas goes into his open-concept kitchen with huge stainless-steel appliances and quartz countertops.

"And after I take Mr. D out." I grab his leash and take him downstairs for a quick walk. When I return, I snuggle Mr. D as I continue to scan Lucas's place.

On the foyer table is a picture of Lucas and a man who appears to be his dad on a sailboat looking tanned, rich, and happy. Through the glass doors of Lucas's office, there's a desk stacked high with paperwork.

After getting us a bottle and two glasses, Lucas grabs a duffel and takes me to the stairwell where we climb to what has to be the roof. Sure enough, when he opens the door, I see a bird's-eye view of downtown Buckhead set against the backdrop of Georgia's rusty foliage of fall.

Lucas nods to a pergola where two chairs sit. "Great place for sunset viewing."

"I'd say." Apparently, he really does love views as much as I do. I hold Mr. D in my arms, letting the light breeze rustle his fur while he peers at the view, his tongue hanging out sideways.

We take a seat in the folding chairs, and Lucas hands me a turkey cranberry wrap from The Crunch Munch. "No way." I squeal, my jaw going slack. "This is amazing, and I'm starving. Thank you so much." I break off a bite of my turkey and feed it to Mr. D. "How did you know this was my favorite?"

"I asked Birdie from The Crunch Munch. She and I are friends now since I go there once a week for Ted."

"Thank you. To the moon and back. I've missed this." I chew in pure bliss. After I swallow, I say, "That reminds me. Ted has a new phone. Did you have something to do with that, perhaps?"

"Perhaps."

"Then, perhaps, thank you." My mouth curves as a warmth rushes through me. Then when I take another bite, it's so delicious, I close my eyes.

When I open them, I see Lucas gazing at me in the same way he did the night of the PAW-CON mixer when he says, "You're welcome." And it pulls me that much closer to the edge of his black hole. Fighting it, I look up at the sky. I can't let his thoughtfulness and supernova hotness turn me into a puddle. So far, I've done a decent job of staying cool cat. Well, minus last night with Madame Puuccí, which I'm not proud of.

After taking another bite of sandwich, I say, "So, tell me about growing up in Boston."

Lucas has a peaceful look when he answers, "It's cold. And it has the best cannolis on earth—or more specifically, the espresso with cinnamon cannoli. How about you? Where are you from?"

"Nice try—don't think I didn't catch that pivot. I'll talk about me first if you promise to talk about you afterward."

He hesitates before he says, "Deal."

"Good. So, my hometown is Blue Vine, Georgia, population 12,231."

"And what was that like?"

"Hayrides, barn dances, not being able to get fired from Squeezy Cheese without the whole town talking about it."

His mouth tilts up. "And how does one manage to get fired from Squeezy Cheese?"

I pet Mr. D's head as he stares at the view. "As it turns out, if you accidentally set yourself on fire wearing the sacred Squeezy Cheese costume, you'll find yourself out of a job in record time."

"Good to know. I mean if I'm ever gainfully employed as the Squeezy Cheese mascot."

"I'd strongly advise against it. The costume's a cooker." I shake my head. "Not to mention the kids who pee on your lap."

He nods, his smile fading. "So, you like Bob Dylan."

My face puzzles. "Yes."

Before I can ask him how he knows that, he says, "You had him playing at the PAW-CON mixer."

"Oh, right. My mom made it her life mission to make sure I loved Bob Dylan."

"Good call." Lucas's eyes skim my face. "I think Dylan's music is like blue cheese. You hate it at first, but if you keep eating it, you'll like it and have no idea why."

"You might be right about that."

"What about Billy Road?" Lucas studies me as he waits for my answer.

"Love him too, and Mom didn't even have to force feed me that one." Billy Road is a more modern Bob Dylan with a twist.

"He's so incredibly talented. And he's had a hard life too."

I sigh. "Don't all the most talented artists?"

"That's definitely true. It's a curse."

After a silence, Lucas clears his throat. "So, there's something I want you to know."

"Okay."

He taps his fingers together. "Work relationships are business. Personal relationships are different... I don't compromise them."

"Meaning you shouldn't date those you work with. Or against."

"Right. And I never have." He looks up in thought. "But with you, it started personal. Well, accidentally personal. Then it went to work, worsened by the fact that I was your boss, then back to personal."

"Right. The second personal was worsened by you not punishing my coworker for stealing my presentation." I flip a wrist. "But bygones."

He reaches over and gives my hand a squeeze. "Give me time, Sophie. I haven't forgotten about you or what was done to you. I promise, I'm working on it." He wags a finger. This must be difficult for him to spit out because he's acting like he doesn't have it together. And Lucas always has it together. He must read my thoughts again, because he says, "I'm getting to my point, I promise."

"Okay, good."

"I know you're the competition I have to crush, but I'm finding it difficult."

"Is that so?" My heart rate accelerates.

"Yeah, which means I should *not* tell you what I'm about to tell you." He closes his eyes, then opens them. "Madame Puuccí is planning to select which brand will be in her stores from the designers that air on Bravo."

"Oh, wow." The gesture kicks up my pulse another notch as my mind whirs. Madame Puuccí is smart—it makes sense that she'd dovetail off the big PR the brands will get if televised. "*Why* are you telling me this?"

He takes his hand away and eats the last bite of his sandwich, wiping his fingers on his napkin before leaning back. "It didn't seem fair that I knew that and you didn't." The corner of his mouth ticks up. "When I beat you, I want it to be fair and square."

There's that phrase again—the one I love, and my breath hitches. This man really does have the odd-shaped key to my heart.

I laugh. "That sounds like a challenge more than a threat. So, challenge accepted."

"All right. But just so you know—I never lose."

"And I never quit."

My tone is light, but my mind kicks into overdrive. I'd planned on using one of my runway walks to make a socially conscious statement, as it is a part of my brand. But now, I'm wondering if that's not such a good idea. Madame Puuccí is infamous for keeping things classy, and she loathes anything controversial, as demonstrated by her reaction to Mom's dominatrix outfit.

I can't take any chances on my shot with Pet IQ. Doing what's best for business is a compromise I made all the time at Fur Bebé. But I'm tired of saying I'm designing petwear to help the animals, then not following through and *doing* it.

But what's more important—landing the Pet IQ deal and staying in business, or staying true to my brand?

It has to be staying in business because without it, my brand ceases to exist.

Right?

Lucas turns his gaze to the sky and sinks into his chair. "This is the part I've been waiting for." We watch the setting sun color the sky, a tangerine glow outlining the scattered clouds over the sky rises. He stares into the distance when he says, "This is definitely one for the books."

"For sure." I snap a series of shots with my phone before holding up Mr. D so he can get a good look. Then I say, "I can't believe I've found someone who likes sunsets as much as I do."

"Why do you love them so much?"

I think about what I say to people when they ask me that question. I tell Lucas a lot of things, but I'm not ready to tell him or anyone the real reason I love sunsets. "They're the best art in the world, and they're free. Or so everyone says."

"Sounds like there's a story there."

"Yeah. I'll tell you someday, but not today."

"Fair enough." He gets up and wanders to the rooftop ledge. I stand and put Mr. D in the chair, and he curls into a ball. After following Lucas, I inhale as the fresh breeze hits my face.

"So, is your family still in Blue Vine?" he says.

"My mom's here in Atlanta right now, as you know, and I'm an only child." I bite my lip. I'm not mentioning my dead sperm-donor of a father, nor the fact that I have no living grandparents that I know of. "Do you get to see your folks much?"

"Not as much as I should. I spend too much time working, that's for sure. And maybe a little too much time golfing." He flashes a guilty smile. "Which reminds me. I can lend you my putter if you want to practice your short game."

"I'll take you up on that, thanks. And nice try, but we were talking about you. Or at least I was *trying* to get you to talk about you."

"You caught that. Again." Lucas glances down. "I just like hearing about other people. My life isn't very interesting. All I do is work."

"I don't believe that." I recognize his redirections because I've been known to do that myself a time or two. Or ten. "There's much more to you than meets the eye, Lucas Nevarez." I don't know if it was wise to be so direct, but my words have already flown through the air like missiles.

Missiles that, by color draining from Lucas's face, do more damage than intended. He glimpses at me before returning his gaze to the setting sun. After he stands quietly for a long moment, a pained expression haunts his face when he says, "My mom was a lot like yours." He smiles, but it's forced, and even in the dimming light, I see his Adam's apple bob with the effort he makes to control his emotions. It's as though his iron shell cracks, revealing a glimpse of vulnerability.

My breath catches with the sharp lance to my heart. "You said, 'was.'"

"Yes."

"I'm sorry." I swallow back the hard knot in my throat. When I think about all the complaining I've done about my mother, I grow hot with shame. Fumbling for words, I blurt, "I should go easier on my mom."

"You could." His voice is smooth, gentle. "But she knows you love her."

"I'm glad you two are friends," I say, meaning it.

"Me too."

I open my mouth to ask him what happened to his mother, but I stop myself. It's too much, and I already feel like he's told me far more than he was comfortable sharing. So many things flash through my head: him not having a dog growing up. His closeness with my mom. The picture on the foyer table with just him and his dad. I don't know what it's like for a parent to die, not really. Yes, my father's dead, but I never knew him. I have pain, but it's different. It's one of rejection, an emptiness where innately, I know something is supposed to be there, but because I've never had it, I don't know exactly what that something is.

Lucas lost someone who adored him, who would've done anything for him, which makes my soul hurt, and I'm out of words. I close my mouth and look down.

Lucas puts a finger on my chin and coaxes my head up. When our eyes meet, he says, "My mom. Someday, I'll tell you that story when you tell me the real reason you love sunsets. Deal?"

My heart stumbles around in my chest. There he goes, reading my mind again. And he said, "Someday." I return the gaze, whispering, "Deal."

Our eyes lock, and I take in all the features of his face. The face that held so much pain just now when he told me about his mother. The same face that made me laugh with his Spidey socks and Transformer Band-Aids.

"You amaze me." His voice is low and husky. He leans closer, and heat sparks through my body when he brings his lips to my ear instead. "I'm fighting it, but it's impossible to stay away from you, Sophie Fox," he rasps.

I bring my lips a breath away from his. "You should do something about it."

His eyes darken before he slowly brings his lips to mine. His mouth moves gently, sweetly, before I feel the lightest brush of his tongue.

And this—all of it—is better than I'd imagined a thousand times since the moment I met him.

I'm officially sucked into Lucas's magnetic black hole, and I may never escape.

20

The Office

I took Riley up on her offer to use the supply closet in Fur Bebé's building for office space. If I had to work one more second in the Winnebago with Mom and her three dogs, the claws were going to come out—and I'm not referring to the dogs.

My new "office" has two walls of shelves packed ceiling-high with paper, files, and cleaning supplies. With great care, I tiptoe through the tiny room to the back corner where a plastic chair's tucked under a folding table.

Over it, a fluorescent light with no panel radiates approximately a zillion watts. This could be where criminals are brought for questioning.

With a big mug of coffee, I get to work, but it's hard to focus in this chilly, windowless closet that smells of Pine-Sol and musty rot. There's a buzz that fills the room every time the air conditioner clicks on, which I will my ears to tune out because I have four days to prepare for the runway show. Then, Mom and I are hopping on a plane to New York.

I don't hear any drips or smell mold, so that's a definite plus.

Taking a break, I check my horoscope, thinking it'll give me a boost. It reads, "Recent turning points in your life have taught you strength. You'll need it as the days ahead are going to be challenging. Do not attempt any romantic relationships right now. Embrace your life today, as tomorrow isn't guaranteed."

"Are you *kidding* me?" I close the browser. "I'm *so* done with this garbage."

Against my will, my body takes me back to what happened on Lucas's rooftop, reacting the same as if we're kissing all over again. A bolt of electricity zips down my spine, and I touch my lips. They feel soft, changed.

But the horoscope is right—just because our kiss was amazing doesn't mean any relationship can come out of it. Because I know good and well it can't.

I force myself to focus back on work, but for some reason, I've never felt so alone as I do in this supply closet.

That's until I realize I'm not. Wall shavings scattered around a hole in the bottom corner of the room are a sure sign a mouse is in here with me. Leaning back in my chair, I make a mental note to buy a potent air freshener, a light fixture, and a humane contraption to trap and release my four-legged office mate.

If this was a fairytale, I'd chat with the mouse, and he'd impart deep words of wisdom while cheering me on. But it's real life, and I doubt he's going to bring in his birdie friends and make me a fabulous dress.

# # #

After a knock, I say, "Come in," assuming it's Riley. I have her pistachio latte here waiting.

When the door opens, Lucas stands there holding his briefcase, and my breath hitches. "What are you doing here?"

A vision of his lips pressed against mine rushes into my head again, and my skin turns to gooseflesh. At the mere sight of him, heat coils through my body, and I want to run into his arms and feel his soft lips against mine, all over again.

I force myself to blink the thought away. Again. Things are definitely more complicated now.

"A little birdie told me you'd started working in the building." He nods at the plastic chair in front of my folding table desk. "May I?"

"Of course."

As he approaches, his broad shoulder knocks a bottle of Windex off the shelf. He stops to pick it up before carefully putting it back, label facing forward. Once he's made it to my guest chair, he sits before reaching into his briefcase and saying, "I have something for you."

He cups his hands over his eyes to shade them from the fluorescent sun above me while he digs through his case.

"Thank you, but I don't do gifts." I shift in my seat. I'm terrible at accepting presents, especially from men.

"It was only three dollars and thirty-eight cents." Lucas pulls out a small box wrapped in aluminum foil and dressed in a foil bow.

I study the box. "Unique packaging."

"I didn't have any tape or wrapping paper at my apartment. Then I had a thought—aluminum foil."

My lips split into a grin. "The bow you made looks real."

"I'm not really the origami type. So I was pretty impressed with myself."

"I'm pretty impressed with yourself." I unwrap the gift, unveiling a box of Trolls Band-Aids, which earns a full-bellied laugh.

Lucas's proud smile widens. "I figured this was a worthwhile investment for you."

"Thank you. Unfortunately, these will get put to good use." This is the type of gift I can accept, and somehow, Lucas innately knows this. This shouldn't surprise me by now, and it doesn't, exactly, but it's more than that. To say he reads me like a book would be an understatement. It's more like he sees my soul, transparent and bare, with all its secrets, quirks, and innermost workings—something no one else is privy to, not even me.

He purses his lips. "So, in full disclosure, I was hoping this would be a 'Welcome Back' gift."

I respond with a raised brow.

"How about we call off this competition and you come back to Fur Bebé?"

My breath snags. "Excuse me?"

"I'm offering you your job back." His lips twitch, as they do when it's clear his brain's searching for just the right words. "Missy's great for exposure, but she isn't creating acceptable new designs. In fact, I've actually been doing some designing myself. She also doesn't have solutions to problems like you do." He swallows hard before he says, "It was a mistake letting you go."

I hold the corners of my mouth even. "Are you saying I was right?"

"Yes. You were right. The board needs you. I need you." He flashes that heart melting half-smile of his. "I believe your exact words were, 'Like a dinghy on the Titanic.'"

"I believe they were." I'm glowing, and it's not just because I'm under a floodlight.

"Until I find proof of what Missy did, I can't ask her to resign. But I can offer you a co-VP position, working laterally with her."

"Co-VP," I yap. "You just said Missy sucks."

"That's not what I said... exactly. She's not great with ideas, but she is at marketing. This is the best I can do, but if you come back, it allows us to set something up to catch Missy."

The gears of my mind whir to life. What Missy did to me is like a pebble in my shoe that I can never shake out, no matter what I do. "Okay, that's enticing. But until then, what about me tarnishing Fur Bebé's reputation?"

"I told the board that it's painfully clear she stole your idea based on the fact that without you, she hasn't had another good one. And if anyone questions us about it, we can simply say that we're moving forward after you were reprimanded."

Reprimanded?

But Lucas went to bat for me, and this might be my only chance to get my career back on track. This makes something flutter in my chest. I meet his gaze, and that all too familiar tingling affliction I get around him returns. Except now, my body knows what it's like to have his breath on my ear, his warm, gentle kisses on my skin, and his strong hands on my back—which makes the feeling electrifying.

It doesn't hurt that he just made me the offer of my dreams. Or it *was* the offer of my dreams—for some reason, right now, I'm not so sure.

But I'm being silly. This *is* the job of my dreams. I go to answer yes, but my mouth says, "I think so."

He tilts his head. "You think so?"

I hesitate, trying to clear the fog in my brain whenever Lucas is around. Settling on a mind with scattered clouds, I wring my hands and say, "Yes, but contingent on Fur Bebé donating five percent of proceeds to animal charities. At least for the RezQ line."

"Wait. What?" His eyes go round.

"My price went up." I can't bring myself to work for a place that doesn't help animals in need. After everything I've been through, I've worked myself to the bone to ensure I'm doing that now—or I will be as soon as RezQ starts making money. I can't lose that. "With all the branding on social issues I've done, it's the only thing that makes sense."

He flutters out an exhale. "You drive a hard bargain, Ms. Fox. I can't promise it'll pass, but I'll bring the measure to a vote at the next board meeting. And since we're in a financially tough spot, I can ask for three percent. If I do that, given everything, I can't imagine it being voted down."

Okay. This is a good offer. Possibly even a great one. But I still can't force my mouth to say yes. Maybe it's because if I come back, Lucas will be my boss, and whatever this is between us has to end?

But if I *don't* come back to Fur Bebé, we're still competitors. Lucas and I can never be together, regardless.

So, it's done. I just need to shake it off. This is what I've been waiting so long for, so I fill my lungs and squaring my shoulders. "Okay, I'll do it."

"Wonderful. Can you start this afternoon?" He's using *that* tone, the one that's nearly impossible to say no to.

"Works for me."

Neither of us is able to fully extend our hands due to lack of space, so we shake on it as if we both have rabbit paws.

A loud knock precedes the closet door flinging open, then Riley prances in. "Oh, sorry, Lucas. I didn't know you were in here."

"It's okay. I was just leaving." He stands.

Riley gives Lucas a raised brow as he shimmies past her toward the exit. As soon as Lucas closes the door, she rushes to my desk and snatches the Trolls Band-Aids. "Holy. Crappity. He gave you these?"

"Yeah."

"It's love. I know it. I'm going to be your maid of honor, right?"

"Of course, Riles. When I actually get married. Which will *not* be to Lucas." I hand over her latte.

"You're the best." She takes it.

I'm about to tell her the big news when she says, "I have someone I want you to meet." She heads out the door and returns with a cute guy.

"Sophie, this is my cousin, West. West, Sophie," she says.

"Nice to meet you, West." I smile at him, realizing that now she's mentioned it, I do see a familial resemblance.

His wavy brown hair is wild but still looks good, which isn't remotely fair. Riley said he's a computer scientist, and he pulls off the standard attire—hoodie, jeans, and tennis shoes.

I say, "So, Riley dragged you here awfully early in the morning."

"Yeah. You wanna know how?" Riley says. "Donuts. Deborah brought them."

"Of course Deborah did."

Riley's eyes perk up. "So, I helped get him a job as a computer scientist at one of the other companies in our building. Isn't that great?"

"It is! And welcome." I lift my palm.

"Thanks."

Riley plunges on. "Knowing West, with all the food Deborah brings, he'll be mulling around Fur Bebé's like an adopted cat."

The corner of his mouth quirks. "Sounds like me."

I chuckle.

He swipes a hand through his hair. "Let me know if I can help you with anything, okay, Sophie? Since the computer equipment room is right across the hall, I'll be here all the time." He scans my supply closet. "Is there food in here?"

"Nope, none, sorry. Not even water—the cooler doesn't work." I sip my coffee, which is now cold.

Riley puts a hand on her hip. "You better stop drinking your coffee through a straw when you hit it big. You don't want your minions thinking you're a little out there."

"Yeah, about that." When I tell her I'm returning to Fur Bebé, she jumps and throws her arms up, splashing her coffee and taking out the entire section of Lemon Dust Pledges.

21

Conflict of Interest

I'm glad I dressed the part today as I smooth out my all-black Versace suit with red buttons, which match my red high heels.

The very red high heels that Gizzie sunk his teeth into, which means one is barely holding on with super-glue.

As I walk into the Fur Bebé's office, Deborah is at the front desk, and her kind face is riddled with guilt. "Hi, Sophie. It's wonderful to have you back." Her voice is always soft, but right now, it's luxury toilet paper soft.

"Great to see you, Deborah," I say hesitantly, studying her face. What is she so worried about? Mr. D is tucked away under her desk, and he doesn't move from his comfortable spot. He used to come to me immediately, and that stings a bit. It shouldn't—he's happy—but it does.

"Let me walk you to your office." She stands, interlacing her fingers.

"That would be lovely." I readjust my box of things on my hip.

Deborah ushers me back to the place I've missed so much, and I take in the fresh scent of new carpet and cedar.

Wow, I'm really back here. My office that's ergonomic, spacious, and has a panoramic view of downtown Buckhead.

After I set my box down, she pulls me into a hug. I realize how much I missed her—she was my office mom.

"Thank you." I pat her back before she steps away. "You give the best hugs."

"Aw, thanks, darling. Now. The board wants you to meet with them in the conference room tomorrow, one-thirty sharp."

"No problem."

She clears her throat, her voice whisper-light again when she says, "With RezQ's new launch plan ready to go."

"The *entire* launch plan?"

"They need you to hit the ground running, hon. I'll get you more coffee, okay?" She reaches and grabs the mug I just set down on my desk.

"You're a lifesaver, Deborah."

She waves a hand before leaning in and whispering, "Fur Bebé has struggled without all your amazing ideas."

"Thank you."

"Show them who's boss," she says.

I give her a salute, a warmth rushing through me before she turns and leaves.

I work nonstop until seven-thirty, happy that I've pulled together RezQ's market data and pricing strategy. When I hear a knock at the door, I'm expecting Lucas, but Missy steps inside. My body tenses.

"What are you working on, Sophie?" She darts over to my desk and peers over my shoulder.

"My launch plan for tomorrow." I snap my laptop shut even though I have no plans to leave anytime soon.

She flashes me her big, Cheshire Cat smile. "Can you brief me on RezQ? So I'm prepared for tomorrow?"

I blink. "You're kidding me, right?"

She bats her eyelashes, but I don't flinch as I stare her down. "You'll see my ideas in the boardroom, but that's the *only* place you'll ever see them. You and I both know the truth—you're a thief. Now get out of my office."

# # #

Lucas blazes through my door the next day, intensity replacing yesterday's casual enthusiasm. "Sophie, board room. Now."

"What? My presentation isn't until one-thirty."

"Sorry. It's been moved to eleven—"

He stops speaking because as I jump up, the heel of my shoe gives out, and I grab his shoulder to keep from falling. When I slip the shoe off, the heel swings back and forth.

I decided to wear my red heels again today since they'd brought me luck yesterday. "Gizzie," I say.

Lucas furrows his brows. "He's awesome—he wouldn't do that. Would he?"

"Um, that's *all* he does." Superb—another Gizzie fan. "Anyway, my launch plan isn't finished." My voice turns desperate. "You haven't even seen it yet."

"Just present what you've got." He adjusts his tie. "The board has another lunch meeting at noon. Okay, let's go."

Ripping off the heel and tossing it into the trash, I say, "I'll stand on my toes. And why do they want RezQ's plan so fast?"

"They're going to introduce the line after the big PR push from the runway show." Lucas speaks as he speed-walks.

"That's good. I think." I say as I hop-run.

We rush into the meeting where the C-level executives and board members are standing and talking. A tenseness permeates through the casual chatter.

"Well, Ms. Fox," a voice says in a Boston drawl. I turn toward Hugh Nevarez as he extends his hand. "Welcome back."

"Hello, Mr. Nevarez. Thank you." I force a smile, fighting to return the firm handshake. He looks different to me now. There's no admiration, no jittery nerves that come with the need to impress him, no respect. There's just... nothing.

Hugh introduces me to two new board members, and I'm glad to have a reason to avoid Missy by engaging in small talk with them.

After Hugh calls me to the front of the room, I kick off my presentation by introducing different options of my RezQ line, showing the variety of collars made from Swarovski crystals of various cuts and colors. "We need a premier marketing strategy, which I've outlined. But before we go into that, we have to discuss pricing. There's a higher cost of producing these products, but they have sky-high profit margins."

Surprised murmurs echo around the room, and a pit grows in my stomach as I advance to the next slide. "We can take advantage of the price break from buying the crystals in bulk."

"I need to stop you, Sophie." Mark McCoy, our CFO, raises a finger. "Those prices are simply too high. I was under the impression you'd have less expensive options."

Lucas gets a nervous look on his face. "Since Sophie just returned to Fur Bebé, she and I haven't had the chance to spec out RezQ's new pricing."

I paint on a smile. "The RezQ line targets the top one percent, and with that group, the price point works."

"Why can't we just use cubic zirconia?" Brock barks out a laugh that shows all his teeth, which look even whiter since I saw him last. "I mean, these are just animals."

Just animals? I know what Brock meant, and he probably has a point, but that comment always strikes a nerve. To me, animals are family, and I'd hope those working at a pet company would feel the same. Also, I have an issue with Brock because I'm not so sure he didn't help Missy cover her digital trail. Who else could it be?

I smooth my skirt when I say, "Unfortunately, that simply won't work with RezQ's market, Brock. Our high-end clientele prefers exclusive things, so an affordable line with fake diamonds won't fly."

"That's an ironic statement." Brock's condescending smile widens. "Coming from the person with a missing heel."

"At least I'm not missing a proper analysis." There must be steam pouring out of my ears, but I hold my face expressionless as I say, "If we lose our market, we lose our high profit margins, which we need to donate three percent to animal charities—the cornerstone of the brand, as indicated in the name."

Hugh leans forward. "Sophie. I'm not sure we want to target the wealthy."

Now, *this* argument I expected. "I used to feel that way as well, Hugh. But since launching RezQ, I've started thinking of it like a Robin Hood model—selling exclusive, high-end products to the rich in order to take the profits and donate them to those in need." I shrug. "Otherwise, the rich are buying someone else's pet products, and none of that gold mine is being used to help rescue animals."

"Fair point." Hugh's voice has an edge. "*If* we want to donate to charity. I don't think that's something Fur Bebé's interested in."

"Let's table the pricing and donation conversation for next week, everybody," Lucas blurts, his face beet red. "We don't need that yet, as we're just introducing the line. Sophie, let's meet and work on this together this afternoon."

I knew the three-percent-to-charity part of the deal had to be voted on, but Lucas made it sound like it would easily pass. But he and I can talk about that separately.

"Sure." I exhale, trying to loosen my jaw. "Let's talk about which petwear I'm planning to showcase on the runway at Le Chienne Couture." I flip to the slide showing my cashmere sweaters on Wonton and Sushi. "I have these models trained, and I'm all ready to go with this look."

Hugh puts his palm up. "I'm sorry, Sophie, I'm gonna have to stop you again. Here at Fur Bebé, our spokesperson is Missy. She's the face of this company, so it's going to be her doing all our runway walks."

My eyes move to see her wearing her signature smug smile.

I blink as fury bubbles inside me, and I'm not sure if I'm angrier at Fur Bebé's board or myself. Why did I think they would be any different? These are the same people who tossed me away like a candy wrapper when they got a sweeter offer, and they didn't take any steps to help me when I'd been so clearly and blatantly wronged.

And now, this is so far beyond unacceptable, it takes every ounce of self-control I have to keep my voice even when I say, "I'm sorry, Hugh, but this is *my* line—I designed it, sewed it, and brought it notoriety through a successful FaceSnap account. I should be the one to do the walks for it."

Lucas's face shoots past red and moves to purple. "Sophie makes an excellent point. It *should* be her to do the runway show for RezQ. Absolutely."

Hugh's eyes skim the others at the table, who look skeptical. Finally, he shakes his head before he says, "That's not going to happen, Lucas, Sophie." He regards me with heavy eyes. "You have to understand. We can't put ourselves in that position. It's too risky with the bad press associated with you since the uh... incident."

Lucas leans forward, a vein bulging on his forehead. "We talked about this, Hugh. There is no reason why Sophie can't speak publicly about a product she developed. Having her face on RezQ hasn't stopped its sales—quite the opposite, actually. People relate to her, and her FaceSnap followers are die hard." Lucas's eyes dart around, his nose flaring. "Even *after* Missy shared that unflattering picture of her mother."

Hugh balls his hands into fists, his tone acid. "Lucas, the board has already addressed this with you. You're either with us or you're not." He punctuates each word when he grits, "Do you understand?"

Lucas exhales sharply, swallowing hard, vibrating with anger as he sits in silent defiance.

With all eyes on him, the tension thickens in the air, and my adrenaline kicks into overdrive. My jaw quivers as I desperately try to think of something, anything, that can make this all okay.

Except there's nothing. It's *not* okay, none of it.

This meeting is ridiculous. This *company* is ridiculous. Why did they bring me back? They don't want to donate to animals in need, which is the entire purpose of the RezQ line. We'd have to change the name. And they don't want to negotiate with me, or make sure I'm given a fair shake. They just brought me here because they're desperate for the ideas that Missy isn't bringing them.

I deserve better than to be a company's last choice. I deserve better than to be used and tossed aside.

"Stop," I cut in, my tone surprisingly emotionless. "If you thought I'd come back and let the person who stole from me and turn my life upside down present yet *another* one of my lines—the line I created from nothing but my own blood, sweat, and tears—then you underestimated me. Again." The words rush out, easy, and I already feel lighter on my feet. Well, foot. "It doesn't matter which side Lucas chooses because this discussion is over." I gaze around at the shocked faces at the table before I say, "I quit." Without a trace of regret, I disconnect my computer and limp out of the room, my head held high.

Once I'm in my office, I collect my box, which is still packed because since I've been here, I've worked so hard, I've had no time for anything else.

After taking off my heels, I march down the hall of the building and return to my supply closet where the cement floor is chilly against my bare feet.

I stare at the mouse hole, almost wishing my office mate would make an appearance. I'm ready to... cry? Celebrate? Scream? Whatever it is, I want company *that* badly.

22

Man's Best Friend

Lucas wanted to apologize for everything that happened in the meeting earlier today by inviting me over and making peanut butter and jelly sandwiches for dinner. Against my better judgment, I said yes.

He stood up for me. He put his job on the line for me, and had I not intervened, he might've *lost* his job for me.

I also have an espresso with cinnamon cannoli to give him.

So, yeah, I'm on my way to his place.

I fiddle with the jelly jar in my hands, suddenly feeling entirely out of place and intimidated, coming back to Lucas's apartment. The last time, I'd let my feelings get out of hand.

But I haven't had a date make me dinner in years, even if it is just PB&Js. A man in the kitchen is sexy, plain and simple.

Sydney enters the code in the elevator so I'm able to take it all the way to the penthouse suite.

Exiting the elevator, I approach Lucas's door, which he opens. I hold up the jar. "Here it is. The stuck lid that stands between us and killer PB&Js."

Lucas grins. "We can't have that."

He takes the jar from me, and two seconds later it pops open. When he hands it back, I tighten it so I don't end up a sticky purple mess. "Thank you. I have to say, that was pretty manly."

"Glad to flare my peacock feathers." Lucas gives his sexy half-smile. "You know what's even more manly than opening lids?"

"I can think of a lot of things."

"Bacon."

"Bacon," I parrot.

"Yes." Lucas points to the kitchen. "I'm making us mean BLTs. *Way* better than a PB&Js."

"That's what you're making us for dinner?" I feign disappointment, even though I'm thrilled about the major upgrade.

"Just wait." He ushers me into the kitchen where I set down my jelly jar. He's cooking crepe-style wraps for the bread, which look crispy and buttery. He has Billy Road playing softly in the background—a sign he wants this to be a romantic meal. Right? Which I'm totally on board with, apparently, because excitement tingles through me.

Hey, he's not my boss anymore. Or again.

"This is impressive." I peer around to see a cooking war zone: flour, a dough cutter, sizzling bacon, perfectly ripe tomatoes, avocados, a block of white cheddar, and freshly fine-shredded lettuce. He's making a BLT unlike any I've seen before. "You really think bacon solves everything, don't you?"

"It does, empirically."

I reach into my purse and pull the small box of two cannolis. "I have another problem solver—dessert."

He shoots me a puzzled look before opening the box. When he sees what's inside, his eyes go brighter than the light in my supply closet. "No way—you remembered! And where did you find these?"

"There's an authentic Italian pastry shop just north of here." I don't tell him that it's actually a half-hour north.

"This is so awesome, thank you." He gazes at me adoringly. "Why don't I get you some wine so you can sit and relax? I just need a few more minutes."

Now that's service. "Sure." After he hands me a glass, I head to his grand room where I kick off my heels, sit on his black leather sectional couch and run my feet through the plush rug. I turn on the seat heater to try it out, and wow. So this is luxury. I can see why people get used to it in a mighty hurry.

As Lucas comes into the room carrying the bottle, I hold up my glass. "This is divine."

"It's one of my favorites." Lucas studies the label. "I can give you one to take home if you want."

"Um, yeah."

He heads to his wine refrigerator and returns with a bottle labeled, "Vigne d'or Reserve Malbec."

"Thank you," I say, before setting it on his coffee table that doubles as a modern art piece. It looks like a blob of melting black wax. "So, you furnish the place?"

"Nah, I wish I could take credit for all this great stuff." He shakes his head. "But I brought a company in."

"Right." Something jabs at my gut. I can't imagine hiring a company to do my furniture—just the thought intimidates me.

"You ready?" He hitches a thumb over his shoulder. "Your dinner awaits."

"But of course." I stand, covering my trepidation with a smile. "You're always a man with a plan."

"I am a planner, yes." He leads me into the dining table. "With my job, I pretty much have to be."

"That's for sure."

We sit across from each other at his stone and glass dining table that seats six. After swallowing a bite, I say, "This isn't bad." When my eyes close on their own, I'm forced to admit the truth. "Okay, this is the best BLT I've ever had."

"There you go."

We both go quiet as we eat, as I can't seem to focus on anything else. The crepe-like wrap, cheese, bacon, avocado, thin lettuce, and tomato melt together like a dream.

After Lucas finishes a few bites, he stops eating and leans back. I'm about to ask him what he's thinking about, but a growl coming from somewhere down the hall interrupts us. "What's that?"

"What's what?" he asks as another growl comes from the same direction.

"That. The noise you're pretending not to hear." I arch a brow. "Or was that a bodily function? Because I can give you your space."

"Come with me," he says sheepishly as he stands. He grabs a few extra slices of bacon and walks toward his bedroom. When I realize where he's going, I hesitate, my pulse surging.

"You coming?" He stops at the door to his room and looks back at me.

I approach and step into a rich bachelor's bedroom. High-end dressers, scant decor, a duvet but no duvet cover, and a huge king bed.

Lucas's bed.

I sit down on the mattress and shake off my nerves as Lucas walks to a crate in the corner of the room before opening it.

Gizzie comes strutting out.

"No!" I choke out. "Why do you have my mom's awful dog?"

"He's not awful." Lucas breaks the bacon into pieces. "Watch this." He throws bits in different directions, and Gizzie catches every single one, doing wild jump-work to reach them. "I'm fostering Gizzie for your mom. Just for a short time."

"Why?" I ask, staring at the dog. "Why?" I repeat. Gizzie and I exchange looks. His says, "Screw off." Mine says, "Watch your back."

Lucas interrupts our threats. "Let's just say Gizzie's having a little trouble adjusting to the puppies. I'm fostering him until he gets used to Dolly and Llama through supervised visits."

"Did he bite one?" I say, continuing to stare Gizzie down. He bares his snaggletooth at me.

"No," Lucas replies softly, looking away.

"Did he?" Now I'm staring at Lucas.

"It was only a technical foul." Lucas pauses, waiting for me to respond. When I hold my glare, he continues, "He tried, but he missed."

"Sweet mercy."

I act disapproving, but my heart is crashing like a cymbal in my chest.

Shut up, heart.

Lucas took in a dog. And not just any dog—an evil dog. I look away to hide my growing smile.

My eyes are drawn back when he says, "You reminded me of my mom today."

My breath flutters. "Really? How so?"

"How you handled yourself in the board room. Taking no crap, and not hesitating to stand up for what you believe in, at the cost of everything." He puts Gizzie back in the crate before he sits down beside me.

I'd be flattered by his words, and I'd love to hear more about his mom, but, man, his body's close to mine. And he smells amazing—a little different than usual, a mix of woodsy soap and fresh rain—which is wildly distracting. And with an up-close view of his striking features,

I have to fight the urge to study the sexy faded scar along his strong jawline. I hadn't noticed it until now.

"Also, thank you from keeping me from getting fired. Hugely." Lucas's gaze moves slowly from my eyes down to my lips. He's clearly no longer listening.

Our eyes lock, and I brush my hand against his thigh. "You're welcome. Hugely."

Lucas's Adam's apple bobbles as he swallows before he leans into me. His warm breath feathers over my jaw, then he brushes a finger over my lips.

He's going to kiss me. Again.

And I want him to. Again. I want the amazing-chef, dog-fostering Lucas to do a lot more than kiss me. But then there's the all-business, my-competition Lucas, and kissing *that* Lucas is the last thing I need.

"Sunsets," I blurt.

Lucas blinks. "Huh?"

"You wanted to know why I love sunsets."

"Oh, yeah." His face goes soft as he leans away. "I'd love it if you told me."

I nod, twiddling my thumbs in my lap. I take a deep breath before I finally say, "My dad." I think about the picture I found. I can no longer say I've never met him, so instead I say, "I never knew him. And he's gone now."

He reaches over and takes my hand. "I'm so sorry."

I shrug off the knot that always appears between my shoulder blades whenever my father comes up. "He was a one-night stand with my mom. His name was Henry Winter, and Mom met him at some protest. Apparently, he was a musician playing in a street band. Anyway, it was my fourth birthday, and Mom told me he finally wanted to meet me. So, I spent days getting ready, picking the perfect yellow dress, drawing a picture of him and me together, coloring it, then framing it. Mom bought a cake, strawberry, my favorite." I let out a jagged exhale. "We went to his house, which had a "For Sale" sign up. When Mom rang the buzzer, it was his probate lawyer who answered. The woman told us that there'd been an accident, and my dad was gone."

"Oh, no." Worry lines crease his face.

"Years later, Mom told me he'd OD'd." My voice cracks around the words.

"Oh, Sophie." He squeezes my hand. "That's horrible."

Lucas doesn't say anything more. He just wraps his strong arms around me and pulls me into a hug. Holding him tight, I let his smell, the warmth of his body, the way he makes me feel, take over and comfort me. I've never told any man this story before, not even my most recent ex, John, but I feel like I can tell Lucas. I don't know what that means, but it feels big.

I tuck a loose strand of hair behind my ear. "So, after that, Mom made me promise her I'd always keep looking forward. And when I watch the sun set, I feel like I'm looking at the edge of the world. A whole day, just being wiped clean. It means I can try for my dreams again tomorrow, and I don't need a dad, or anyone else, to make big things happen. And it works. Well, it mostly works. I'll get there."

"From the moment I met you, I never doubted that for a second," he says scratchily.

When I pull away, I meet his warm eyes, which have honey-gold rings around their black irises, and it feels like he's gazing into my very being. He's so handsome, and right now, there's something about the way his eyes dance and his voice drops an octave when he speaks to me. "You'll get there. I can see it in your eyes. Your beautiful, soulful eyes."

I lean in, and his mouth catches mine. The zingy notes of cherry and grapes from his rich red wine hit my lips, then my tongue, and it's an intoxicating blend.

Lucas's lips roam, and his breath skitters across my jaw. "You smell good." They move even lower, trailing his lips along my collarbone.

When his mouth reaches my ear, he nips at my lobes, and I shiver as sparks fly across my skin. He sweeps my hair over my shoulder, then peppers the nape of my neck with light kisses. His fingers trace circles up my back, leaving a trail of goosebumps in their wake. He's teasing me, and I'm not having it.

I turn my head, my mouth crashing into his. I pull him tight, threading my fingers through his silky hair, and when I do, it's as if all his restraint just... breaks.

He takes charge, all hesitation gone. His hands tangle in my hair as he pulls me closer, his tongue parting my lips before it sweeps over mine, rough, demanding. We fall into a haze, our mouths working in a desperate rhythm.

Taking a breath, I pull away and mutter, "What's this?"

"I stopped fighting," he rasps, breathless. He moves his kisses over my neck in a way that makes every part of me react.

I pull at the front of his shirt, and his silly cowboy top snaps completely open. I run my nails lightly across his molded bare chest and cut abs. My resolve has officially crumbled, every inch of my body aching for him. I want him. Maybe only for tonight, and maybe for all the wrong reasons. But every part of me wants every part of him.

I realize that this should all feel weird, but it doesn't.

It doesn't because it's Lucas.

His hands tighten on my waist. "You do things to me. I could—"

"Shut up and take this off." I tug at the belt of his cargo shorts.

"You got it, Sophie Fox."

.

23

Runaway Runway

Spotlights roam across the runway, camera lenses reflect from every corner, and each and every velour galley chair is occupied with a body dressed to the nines and adorned in something shiny from Tiffany. The flash of photography cuts through techno lounge music that echoes through the room.

Backstage, tension crackles in the air.

Everything is just *more* in the Big Apple. Speaking of, we're on the top floor, so there's a wall of windows that provides an evening view of the Hudson River and the Statue of Liberty far in the distance.

With Mom's help, I'm getting Wonton and Sushi ready to rock and roll RezQ's new sweaters, and I'm crossing my fingers the dogs will do just as they've been trained. We're not allowed to use leashes on the runway, so there's that.

I went back and forth, but in the end, I decided against using one of my walks to make a socially conscious statement. I, along with the other small designers, are only on stage twice, so there's no space. Hence, for tonight, that's been sidelined.

Nerves twine around my stomach like a knotted ball of Christmas lights.

Munch is modeling the all-important evening dress, and I don't care that she has dragon breath. She's the only dog I have who will do the twirl at the end of the runway the way I need. Plus, she looks stunning—her black fur the perfect contrast against the white silk dress. I opted against featuring my new, edgy RezQ gown. It isn't something that Pet IQ would likely carry in their stores—it's not mainstream enough—so I wanted to use this shot to show relevant petwear.

Missy is over at Fur Bebé's station prepping Mr. D, and his eyes meet mine from across the stage. I flash him the smile reserved just for him, and he returns the love with a bark and a blurred tail wag, but he knows to stay put.

"Calm down, Notorious D-O-G," Missy scolds. "Stay professional."

I turn away but continue side-eyeing Mr. D, who, by the way, looks dashing in his tuxedo. I hate to admit it, but his outfit is amazing—and the best thing I've seen Fur Bebé feature tonight.

It looks like Missy came through on at least one exceptional design.

Lucas materializes at my station and offers his muscles to bring in Munch inside her crate, which I appreciate beyond belief. I know he could get in trouble, but I *really* need the help. "Thank you," I whisper. It's the first time I've seen him since I was in his bed, and my body shivers from the memory.

A night that's forever imprinted on my brain sends dizzying rushes of adrenaline and heat through me, all over again. My body feels awake, alive. It was the best night I'd ever had, and not just because it was magical.

It was because it was with Lucas.

And he made himself vulnerable in a way no other guy ever has with me. It's because he made me vulnerable too, and for once, I didn't feel weaker for it.

"You didn't see me here," he whispers back with a wink.

A spark of electricity jumps the gap between us.

"Got it." I hold up a finger. "Mr. D looks phenomenal. By the way."

He fights off a smile. "Thank you."

A Bravo producer shows up backstage and calls Lucas and me over. The guy scrubs his goatee before he says, "So, we've decided to run a thirty-second feature of Puuccí's breakout fall design, and now, we're running short on programming time. I'm sorry, but since you two are the newbies, only one of you is going to make it on the air. We'll choose the crowd favorite. Good luck."

Oh, no.

I glance at Lucas, and his expression has gone stone hard. It's his all-business face, and I can tell that the Lucas from a minute ago is long gone. I'm certain the incredible evening we shared has been completely erased from his mind, at least for now.

When the music gets louder and the lights dim, my twine of nerves become ropes that chafe over each other in my stomach. But my dogs are ready and trained, so I take my place behind the curtain to walk out my models and give them treats.

As the other designers begin making their appearances on stage, the cheers of the crowd and the commentary of Madame Puuccí solidify that this is real. Until now, it's felt like a dream.

We stand at the edge of the stage, and I struggle to see as my eyes adjust to the bright lights. I bend down, give Wonton and Sushi a scratch behind the ears, then feed them a treat.

Madame Puuccí announces RezQ, and off we go to the end of the runway, my legs jittery as I walk.

Wonton and Sushi strut their stuff, which is RezQ drape-sleeved cashmere sweaters adorned with Swarovski crystals. When cheers erupt, I'm feeling more confident.

As the dogs perform their twirls, the applause swells, and I know I've made an impression.

I smile as we return backstage, proud that my sweet shelter dogs, both found abandoned and dirty at the side of the road, performed exceptionally.

The audience's reaction was good, but not good enough to solidify a spot on Bravo. I blow out a shaky breath before I dress Munch in her evening gown. Once it's on, everything feels just... wrong.

Sweat beads my brow as I think about the fact that Munch is my last chance to make it on the air, which means she's my last chance of getting interviewed by Madame Puuccí for RezQ to be in Pet IQ stores.

I'm second-guessing the dress I've chosen for Munch, and Mom must read my face, because she says, "Make the switch?"

After a nod from me, Mom holds her breath as she redresses Munch at lightning speed. In an instant, Munch is wearing my new bold, edgy sample because it'll get the biggest reaction from the crowd. Right now, that's all that matters.

It's a 1920s inspired dress, re-imagined with a see-through bodice of shimmering tulle. The silk hat's made of pearls and champagne peacock feathers, which matches the sleeves. The tutu has fringes, and there are champagne paw gloves to match.

I guide Munch out for my last walk. She does her thing, being the good dog that she is because she *loves* getting treats.

Her spin is flawless, and when the fringes of the tutu fly through the air, the crowd cheers louder than it has for any of the smaller brand's runway performances tonight.

"Well, what is this? A see-through gown." Madame Puuccí announces. "I'm most definitely interested. That's pushing the edge, RezQ—and I'm thirsty for more."

I'm floating when I return backstage, giving Mom a hefty high-five. She's got a glowing smile when she whispers, "That might just do it, Soph."

It might—that remains to be seen after Mr. D takes the stage.

Speaking of, Missy starts readying him, and I hear her say, "Okay, Fur Bebé is counting on you for the Bravo spot. So, do what you do best. Charm the crowd."

Missy's right, Mr. D is a crowd pleaser. Who can possibly look at that big overbite and tongue hanging out sideways and not smile?

And with that tux he's wearing, he's going to be unstoppable.

The thought makes me happy and sad at the same time.

Mom heads back to the dressing room to check the TV and see what's being shown on Bravo, which is airing on delay. As Missy prepares to take Mr. D on stage, he looks over at me. We exchange glances again, and I flash him another smile. His tail kicks up, and out of habit, I blurt, "You're such a good boy."

That does it. He wrestles free from Missy darts toward me so fast, she doesn't have a split-second to catch him.

He leaps into my arms, and I snuggle him close, whispering, "Just look at you, handsome." As I'm putting him down, I say, "Now go own it out there."

Missy shrieks, "Notorious D-O-G! Get over here *now*."

He curls tighter into my chest, clawing into me now instead of stepping onto the floor. I'm desperately trying to gently push him away. When it doesn't work, I look at Missy and say, "He's not going to come if you scare him. Offer him a treat."

She's digging in her bag when Madame Puuccí announces Whiffany & Co. Smithy Baldwin steps around Missy and prances onto the stage with a Pekingese wearing a corset with a black lace garter belt.

Lingerie? Really?

My stomach drops as Lucas rushes over. When Missy sees him, she turns to me and says, "How *dare* you speak to Notorious D-O-G right before his walk, Sophie. Talk about playing dirty."

My jaw wobbles. "I didn't mean to—"

"Sophie." Lucas's voice is steel as he approaches me. "Is that true?"

"I-I..." Swallowing hard, I'm desperately searching for words. "It just came out."

Glancing at Mr. D in my arms, Lucas's face turns a deep shade of red and *that* vein bulges on his forehead. Something shuts down in his eyes when he says, "I can't believe you did that." The ragged edge of his voice knocks the wind out of me. "I've never been so wrong about a person."

Before I can respond, Lucas turns and storms away. To where, I have no idea. Missy follows.

Through a blur of tears, I watch the other designers march their dogs on stage, but it's hard to process what's happening. I didn't mean to speak to Mr. D! I would never intentionally sabotage anyone else, even Missy.

Lucas knows that, right? The sights and sounds around me become tunneled and echoey, and suddenly, landing that Bravo spot seems insignificant.

Those ropes of anxiety are pulled so tight, they feel like they may tether and snap.

I've made a gigantic mess of everything.

I'm still holding and petting Mr. D, who's shivering. I'm aching to call Mom for help, but I don't want to move and send Mr. D running somewhere else, causing another problem.

Missy reappears near the curtain, as Fur Bebé's up next as the last walk of the evening. She's busy helping her team prep their dog, Kensington, but I can't see the animal because there are too many people in the way.

After Missy and Kensington strut onto the runway, I get a first look at the dog, and I draw in a breath so sharply I swear it would've echoed through the massive room if the techno lounge music wasn't drowning me out.

But I'm not the only one—a symphony of gasps fills the air, and everyone's face twists in shock and confusion.

Kensington—a giant gray poodle—is wearing an outfit of messy aluminum foil with a cardboard sign that says, "Not designed for baking," handwritten in marker.

Mom rushes beside me, studying the dog on stage before she says, "What is *that*?"

I look at her, desperate. "It can't be!" I cry.

The crowd erupts into nervous chatter, and Madame Puuccí announces, "Oh, wow. Color me stunned. Looks like Fur Bebé is protesting dogs being left in hot cars, which they should. This one's definitely tonight's crown jewel—and the perfect end to our show! No TV station pun intended here, but bravo, Fur Bebé!"

Missy pauses at the edge of the stage, and the confused crowd claps before they cheer. Then the cheers magnify into roars. This continues as the audience gives Missy and Kensington a standing ovation as the two exit the runway.

Turning backstage, I see Lucas in the darkest corner looking pale, agonized. My face contorts as I meet his hollowed eyes.

When I finally get the feeling back in my legs, I hand Mr. D to Mom and stumble over to Lucas, my stomach churning. "How could you?"

"I had to after what you did." His tone is cold, hard. Gone is the guy who'd held my hair while I puked and crafted me the perfect BLT. In his place is a stranger who doesn't even make eye contact.

My voice is weak, deflated. "I'm sorry I spoke to Notorious D-O-G, but it was an accident. I would never do something like that on purpose."

"Fine, Sophie. But this put things into perspective." Lucas's jaw is rigid, his lips twitching when he says, "It reminded me that I was brought to Fur Bebé with the sole purpose of landing a deal with Pet IQ. I have responsibility to my family foremost, then a fiduciary responsibility to the board and the shareholders, to do whatever it takes to make that happen. So, after Fur Bebé's best outfit—the one I designed myself—was taken out of contention, I had no choice."

In fairness, he warned me that night on his roof—he cleaves his work and personal life into very separate pieces, and his work persona is emotionless and cutthroat.

My voice is above a whisper when I say, "You *always* have a choice to do the right thing."

"How was what I did the wrong thing? No one owns the rights to raising awareness on social issues, not even you." His emotionless tone cuts deeper than his anger.

"That's a really good rationalization, but you know you got the idea from me and RezQ. And if it was an okay thing to do, how did your heart feel when you did it? Or don't you have one?"

His eyes narrow. "There's no heart in business."

"Really? What would your mother say about that?"

The sliver of light left in his eyes snuffs out as he glares at me, but I don't care as I say, "Come on, Lucas. You're here for the money, not the animals." I shake my head as I fight back the tears forming in my eyes. I *knew* that I couldn't trust him not to hurt me or let me down. That's what the men in my life do. "You pulled off this stunt but being socially conscious isn't Fur Bebé's brand. Your board *continually* refuses to do anything to help the animals in need." My tone turns to acid. "But who cares about the truth? After all, it's just business."

"It *is* just business, Sophie."

"You know what? You're right." I nod slowly. "Which is why I'm not backing down, even if you land the Pet IQ opportunity. I'm going to work myself to the bone proving to you, Missy, and every person like you two that in the long run, even in business—*especially* in business—doing the right thing wins out."

And mostly, proving that to myself.

Lucas stands silent, red-faced and vibrating with anger.

I take a step toward Mom, who's begrudgingly returning Mr. D to Missy. Keeping my eyes trained on Lucas, I grit, "You're going to fail because you're a fraud."

When I storm away, my knees almost give out.

24

Sentimental Slippers

I shimmy through the strip of space between the Winnebago's kitchenette island and its swivel chair before slumping into it. Lucas's box of Trolls Band-Aids sits on the counter, and images of the day he gave them to me rush into my mind.

Mom grabs that bottle of Vigne d'or Reserve Malbec that Lucas gave me and comes to the kitchenette island.

When she pops the cork and takes a swig, I say, "Mother, it's 9:30 in the morning." I rip the bottle from her fingers. "So, what's the plan now?"

In life's game of Chutes and Ladders, I just slid back to square one—no job, no prospects, and stuck living with my mother in a Winnebago.

She grabs the wine back, guzzling it before breaking into a coughing fit. Barely able to speak, she croaks, "No plans. Screw plans."

"Screw plans," I parrot, grabbing the Band-Aid box and chucking it on the floor. "Lucas and his grand planning."

Mom picks up the Band-Aids and hands them to me, wrapping her hands around mine.

Tears spill onto my cheeks, and she takes me into a hug. A *real* hug, holding me tight.

Why is it that when it's just Lucas and me, everything seems so perfect? And then reality hits with work, everything crumbles like a taco shell? My lips tremble, and I hold on to the edge of the counter as my world falls apart beneath me. "I let myself care about him because I thought he cared about me too."

Everyone wants to know why I don't let people into my heart. Well, this is why.

Work always creates an infinite crevasse between me and relationships, and this is no exception.

"I know, hon." Mom rubs my back. "Let me get you some chips."

As I consider her offer, my lips pucker into a pout. "Do you have Cheetos?"

"I always have Cheetos." Mom gets up, and I space out while she buzzes around. I can't pull my brain out of the fog enough to pay attention.

When she returns and puts the open bag of Cheetos in my hands, my mind returns to the room. After a few fistfuls of neon orange crunchy bliss, I stare at the wine bottle for a beat, then take a swig. It tastes like spoiled dessert wine. Spewing it from my mouth like the fountains of Bellagio, I say, "What happened to this?"

"I added Splenda to it," Mom says. "It was bitter as quinine."

I gasp. "That was a seventy-five-dollar bottle. Wasted."

"How's it wasted if I'm drinking it?" Mom sits next to me.

I'm not sure if she has a decent point, or if I'm too heartbroken to care. I blink back the pinpricks needling the back of my eyes. "We were about to get that Bravo spot. And we'd worked our butts off. People like Lucas, they don't get how hard it is for us, starting from nothing." I lay my head on the counter and into a powdery puddle of Splenda. "I thought he and I had something special—bigger than where we both came from. He seemed to really appreciate that I moved out on my own without a dime and made it as far as I did. But in the end, it didn't matter to him. It meant nothing. He stole my concept and used it for his own benefit."

Mom runs a hand over my hair. "What you've accomplished does mean something, honey. It means everything—to those who care more about character than money. It matters to those who care about things that matter. And it will be *everything* to the man good enough to deserve you." She stares into space, the gears of her mind revolving. "Lucas does appreciate what you had to overcome to get where you are, but he's also been fed with a silver spoon." She winces. "And, come on, Soph. His balls were in a vise."

"Still. I can't believe I was so naïve." I lift my head and lick the Splenda off my lips. "It felt different with him. This is silly, but I thought I might've found The One."

"Finding your 'one' is useless if he hasn't found his."

"Well, that's painfully true, isn't it?" I bite the inside of my cheek, the sting of tears still fresh. I've fallen for someone who, apparently, cuts off his feelings like split ends.

"I wouldn't give up on Lucas just yet. He's a little lost, and I think he's struggling between the world he came from and the world that suits him. If he finds his true self, he'll be a perfect match for you. But if he goes back to his old life, well, living *that* life would smother the beautiful thing that makes you who you are."

"Thanks, Mom." Her warmth and wisdom dull a little of my pain.

She stares off into space. "I didn't get around to opening his third eye, dammit. I knew I should've made that more of a priority."

I close my eyes. "Right."

Mom wanders over and stands at the counter, quiet, for just a bit too long. So, I ask, "What's going on in that head of yours now?"

She hesitates, her eyes clouding over. Finally, she says, "I've been talking to your dad, Soph."

Here we go. "Did you channel him again? Or was it the Ouija board? Because I asked you to stop doing that."

"I know, but it's different now." Her face turns desperate. "I talked to his subconscious, not his ghost, like I thought. Something's changed. Maybe he's been reborn."

I shoot her a glare. Why does she do this crap? Dig up painful history at the worst possible moment? "Really? And what did his new self say?"

"He misses you."

I squeeze my lips tight, fighting not to lose patience. "How could he miss me when he never even knew about me?"

"Because he's your father, that's how."

"*Was*. And he *was* a sperm donor." I inhale a large breath and count to ten in my head. We haven't discussed him in a long time—years. I guess she's due. "Why are you bringing him up now?"

"Soph, did you get the results from the OriginLinx kit?"

I groan. "How did you know about that?"

She won't meet my eyes. "I found the test wrapper in the garbage."

"Really? So, you're garbage digging now?"

"I prefer the term, 'immersive sleuthing.' Anyway, did you get the results?"

Not yet." That's not a lie, I haven't, and now that I've had time to think about it all, I've gotten increasingly nervous. Now, part of me hopes the package got lost in the mail.

"Let me know when they come in, Soph. I'm so excited for you to know your dad's side of the family. I just want you to find your peace with him, honey."

"Oh." My anger dissipates a bit.

"When I finally let go of the anger with my parents, I was free." She heaves out a sigh. "Your dad hurt you. Deeply. In places you don't even realize. I just don't want him to keep hurting you."

I think about the picture I found of him and me. He *did* meet me, and he didn't want me—and that is a fresh, gaping cut into the wound I've spent almost a lifetime building a thick scar around.

And that's Mom's fault. Why hasn't she told me that I'd met my father? I found out anyway, and now it hurts all over again. I go to scold her over what I found, but the words die in my throat.

I can't bring myself to confront her with it. Not right now, not after everything I've been through.

Her voice is gentle. "You're so afraid of people leaving, you push them away before they can."

I sit quietly, my jaw clenched as I fight off the urge to defend myself. I'm angry at her, and I want to argue, but I know she didn't tell me about me meeting my father to protect me. That's what she's always done. And, clearly, I'm damaged enough from what he did—why exacerbate it? Finally, I say, "You're probably right about that."

I put my robe on, giving up on getting dressed for the day. My feet are cold, so I put on my slippers. As soon as I do, Mom points at my feet. "Those look snazzy. Are they comfy?"

"Oh, yeah. Dreamy." I slide one off so she can feel the chenille.

As she runs her finger over it, a wistful smile spreads across her face. "Remember those ridiculous slippers I bought you when you were little?"

"The hedgehog ones," we say in unison.

"Of course." I put a hand over my chest. "I loved those things *so* much. I wore them every night." I look up in thought. "I wonder what happened to them?"

"I had to sneak them out of your closet and throw them away." Mom sticks out her tongue. "They were in shreds, and you *refused* to stop wearing them."

My mouth curves. "Remember when you gave them to me? You had them sitting in the back seat of the car. You were picking me up from school that day because I had a dentist appointment." I tap a finger on my chin. "Now that I think about it, that was a smart move. You distracted me with the best gift ever so I didn't whine about having to get my teeth cleaned."

"That's not why I had the slippers that day."

"It isn't?"

"No." Mom's smile fades. She stares at nothing before looking back at me. "It's the day I'd finally earned enough in tips to afford them. I got off work and ran straight to the store, crossing every finger and toe they still had a pair left in your size."

"Oh." A spike of guilt jabs my rib cage. Memories rush back of all the times I'd badgered Mom to buy me things. I'd given her such a hard time when I didn't get them. I never could've imagined what she'd gone through for a silly pair of slippers. "I didn't know."

"Of course you didn't, honey." Mom approaches and strokes my shoulder. "That's just what moms do."

"Well, thank you." I put my hand over hers, swallowing the scratchy lump in my throat. I think back to all the things she did—and sacrificed—for me, without a second thought. The days she literally gave me the sweatshirts off her back when I was cold, or the nights she stayed up taking care of me when I was sick. And now, she moved to

Atlanta to live in a Winnebago with me to help me get my life back on track. "Thank you, Mom. For everything."

"You're welcome."

# # #

It's been two days since the runway show, and I've spent both in bed. I said I was going to keep on fighting, but so far, I haven't been able to muster the energy.

Lucas landed the Bravo spot for Fur Bebé, and I'm sure he's meeting with Madame Puuccí any day now.

So, I'm not exactly sure what I'm fighting for, except the principle of it all. Which I want to do—I *should* do—but man, I'm tired. And what's the point?

It's early Tuesday morning when there's a knock at the Winnebago door, and I crawl out of bed to check the peephole. I'm shocked to see Eva standing there—she never comes by at this time. She's usually in a meeting or on her way to court.

I open the door. "Shouldn't you be working?"

"Can I come in?" she asks, desperate. She's dressed in her jogging clothes, which are designer, pristine. Even her dark locks—pulled back for her morning run—look stylish and ready to hit the town.

"Sure, of course." I smooth my plaid pajamas, which are pilled. I should really consider upgrading my nightwear.

After she blazes through the door, she says, "Okay, I know you've needed time to regroup after everything that went down at the runway show, and I've tried to give you that."

"Thank you."

She flips up a palm. "But it's been sixty-one hours, and I'm sick of waiting. It's time for your dog weddings."

"Huh?" I run a hand through my bed head. "My dog weddings," I mumble, thinking about that dumpster fire of a presentation I gave to Fur Bebé, which feels like a lifetime ago. "Wait. How do you know about that?"

"Riley told me. You should do it."

"The idea that Fur Bebé shot down? Well, they didn't shoot it down. They were too shocked to even do that."

"What are you talking about?" Mom descends her cab bedroom stairs, her eyes perked.

I hesitate, shivering from the memory. "My disastrous dog wedding presentation. Since there aren't pet bridal shops, I thought it'd be great to offer pet engagement collars, tuxes, and veils."

Eva tucks a loose strand of hair behind her ear. "Sounds like a line for the wealthy. Which means mega high profit margins."

Mom buzzes over, tightening her robe. "Ohhh, we could even offer the richy rich one-on-one consults. It's critical to match dresses and veils to each dog's color tones and personality." She turns the coffeemaker on.

My face pinches. "Can't you just say you have a pug and match that?"

"No! There are apricot pugs, black pugs, fawn pugs and silver fawn pugs. And they all have different bone structures. Jeez, Sophie. I thought you were the expert."

"Oh, yes. Sorry. Different bone structures." I cock my head. "You're not serious."

"I'm as serious as a bad perm." Mom stops what she's doing to stare me down. "Eva and I are right about this. Wealthy people will love it."

"I don't know." I sigh. "Fur Bebé executives thought I was off my rocker."

"And that's the reason why you should do it." Eva grabs my hand and squeezes. "They're schmucks."

"True," I murmur.

"It's a great idea," Mom says. "And it's definitely different. Promise me you'll consider it."

"I promise," I say, not meaning it.

"Sophie, don't lie to me." Mom folds her arms. "*Really* promise."

"Yeah, promise, Sophie." Eva releases my hand and folds her arms too.

I groan. "Fine. I promise."

"Whatever." Mom flicks a hand, annoyance flashing in her eyes. "You won't. You never listen to me."

There might be some truth to that. "Okay, so dog weddings. How about I design a sample?"

Eva jumps into the air, clapping. "How *about* that."

25

Crowded Space

I get back to the grind in my closet office on Wednesday to start on RezQ's new bridal collection—Vera Wag. Today, I'm designing my flagship doggie wedding dress.

Unable to follow through with the mouse-trapping device, I nod at the hole in the baseboard to acknowledge the truce my rodent companion and I've reached. I named him Woody, as he clearly has a passion for shredding wood, and I respect that.

Now. What can I do to bring a gaggle of press to this new collection? What would Mom do? When an idea pops into my head, I don't overanalyze it, I just do it.

I dial up Raven Monroe, the famous fitness guru, and leave her a voicemail, offering up what I hope to be a tempting proposition. What do I have to lose?

When I hang up, I see an email from OriginLinx in my inbox.

Crap. There it is. I take a deep breath before I open it and start reading. It says that my kit's been processed, and I need to finish setting up my account to start finding relatives.

I go to click on it, and something stops me.

It's my trembling fingers.

I know Mom wants me to find family on my dad's side, but I'm not so sure. Do I really want to open that Pandora's box? Do I really have the emotional bandwidth to handle this right now?

I sit in silence, staring at my computer screen for an inordinate amount of time, frozen in indecision.

There's a knock at the door followed by Riley's voice. "It's me."

I exhale the breath trapped in my lungs. "Come in, Riles."

She floats in, a huge smile on her face.

"I picked up your pistachio latte," I say, sliding hers over to the edge of my folding table.

She lets out a happy sigh but doesn't come get it. "You're the best, thank you. So, guess what?"

"What?"

Riley opens the door wider, and Eva and Mom step in beside her.

"Surprise!" Eva throws up her arms and knocks a box of paper clips off, which hit the floor with a symphony of pings. "Oy vey! It's bright in here."

Eva tries to bend over to pick them up, but then hits Mom with her bum.

"Here, Eva, get those with my magnet." Mom pulls something out of her beach-bag sized purse and hands it to Eva, who goes into a vertical plié before coming up with a mass of paper clips stuck to a black strip. "Thanks, Skye. You think of everything."

"What are you all doing here?" I skim my eyes over the three of them, a triplet of guilty faces. "Oh, no. *What* are you all doing here?"

Now I really feel like a police officer, interrogating my perps. I was thinking about investing in a light-dimming panel, but maybe not.

Riley's practically bubbling over. "Skye told us to meet you here. She has a plan."

Eva wrings her hands. "I'm a little scared."

"You should be." I arch a brow.

"Don't be scared—be pumped!" Riley whirls her fist. "The RezQ team to the rescue, reunited for another mission."

"That's right." Mom gives Riley an approving back slap.

Riley shrugs. "And it's getting me out of some silly soirée at my parent's neighborhood's club tonight."

Mom reaches into her magical purse and pulls out a flask. "Cheers," she says, holding it up. Then she grabs the stack of mini cups by the broken water cooler and pours us each a shot. After handing them to us, no one says a word as the three of them scoot over to my desk and we tap our cups together.

After slamming her shot, Mom glows. "To the wedding of the year."

I drink from my cup before barking out a nasty cough from the whiskey burning its way down my throat. I rasp, "What have you done, Mother?"

"It's not what I've done." She lifts her chin. "It's what I've discovered." She peers around the space, building suspense. "Next Saturday, Missy and Eben are getting married at Chateau LeBlanc in the Blue Vine Mountains... and it's being broadcast live on a special episode of *Bridesmaid to Bride*!"

"*What?* Missy went back to Eben?" Eva yaps, her face still contorted from her whiskey shot.

"I *did* put him in the freezer to call in his cosmic boomerang," Mom says. "And apparently, *she's* it."

"They do deserve each other." I shrug.

"Exactly," Eva says.

Riley snatches her coffee and sips away, uncharacteristically quiet about the topic, especially considering how much she loathes Missy.

"Saturday night, the wedding's being aired live at seven p.m." Mom shimmies her way into my guest chair. Then she reaches into her massive purse before she says, "They are doing a call for extras. We're going to land a spot and bring in dogs wearing RezQ's wedding collection. My plan is airtight." She flops a packet of papers on the table, the top one a map. "We start preparations tonight—0500."

"Holy blazes of a fiery inferno." I close my eyes. "Absolutely not."

Riley's mouth curves conspiratorially. "This is the big one. People will see your designs and orders will come rushing in. Madame Puuccí will have no choice but to consider you for the Pet IQ deal."

"Soph, we need a bride and groom." Mom's lip curls. "Not Munch."

"No, we don't because we're not crashing Missy's wedding." I sit up in my chair like I'm a boss. Which I am. Of this tiny supply closet, but still. And I know Eva and Mom have a point about Missy's televised wedding getting us huge PR but breaking into it isn't right. It's also not feasible. "There's going to be camera crews, security teams, decorators, planners... I mean, this is way too dangerous. Nope."

"I'm with Sophie." Eva sucks air through her teeth. "My dad will kill me. Dead."

"We get to stay at Chateau LeBlanc for the weekend with a gorgeous view of the mountains and a bunch of horny groomsmen." Mom's voice goes up an octave. "I mean, if you want to pass that up."

"Ohhh... come on, Eva," Riley prods. "Where's your sense of adventure? *Smoking* hot men."

"Maybe..." Eva bites her lip.

Riley's sparkling eyes meet mine. "Okay, I know something else about the wedding that could be huge for us."

I lean over my desk to slap Riley on the shoulder. "So, you *knew* about this? That's why you were so quiet?"

She shoots me a scowl. "I work with the bride, and it's all she's been talking about, so yeah." She exhales dramatically. "The Pet IQ executive team is going to be there."

"What?" Okay, now I'm interested. "Why?"

Riley says, "Madame Puuccí announced that the final contenders for the Pet IQ opportunity are Fur Bebé and Whiffany & Co. We need this huge PR event to seal the deal for Fur Bebé."

My face crumples. So, it's done, and I'm not on the list. I'm not surprised, but it's still hard to hear. "Oh."

"So, that's why you need to do this." Riley stares me down. "It's your last shot."

My nose scrunches. "I think it's more like one of those chuck-the-ball-from-half-court kinda shots."

Mom says, "So, Soph. Missy has selected over a thousand bouquets of pink roses for the decor. You're the official flower mister. That's how I got us a room."

"Why am I getting the crap job?" I scowl. "Nope."

"I know something else, Soph," Riley says softly, the sparkle in her eyes dim with pity. "There's a whole special set up for Notorious D-O-G. He's the ring bearer."

"Mr. D!" My heart pinches, and my eyes mist. "*Missy* gets him as the ring-bearer, and I don't?"

Riley touches my shoulder. "Well, you're not getting married, Soph. I'm sure he could be yours too when that happens."

"*If* that happens," Mom cuts in.

"Mr. D," I blubber on, ignoring Mom.

That's my final straw. I groan before I say, "Okay, let's do it, but only to pitch Madame Puuccí. No dogs in wedding wear."

"Eva's gotten requests for engagement bracelets. From Novu Villa country club members." Mom plunges on. "Can you make one for the bride and one for the groom, Soph?"

"Nooo," I drag out. "No dogs. I mean it. That's a hard line." I can't ruin anyone's wedding.

Riley fiddles with one of the paper clips. "Let's just prepare the wedding collection and get it up on your FaceSnap account. Then, as extras, we can have the RezQ name somewhere on us."

"They'll be checking for that. I'm sure they don't allow promo of any kind." Eva squeezes by Mom and sits on my desk, making it sag dangerously low.

Which really says something, since Eva's a waif of a thing.

"No to that too," I say, my tone firm. "I can't stand Missy, but we're not using her wedding as an advertisement."

"Okay, Soph." Riley bends the clip into a bobby pin shape. "Chill."

"But we are still going to take on false personas, break into a wedding, then hit up Madame Puuccí, the biggest pet fashion icon in America?" Eva flutters out a breath, her golden-tanned skin paling.

The door flies open and West pops his head in. "Hey, I thought I heard a party in here. I brought sustenance—from Deborah." He holds up a brown bag.

"Bring it in, Westie, I'm starving." Riley throws her arms out.

He says nothing as he stares at Eva. "We haven't met." His voice cracks, like he's suddenly thirteen.

"I'm Skye, Sophie's mom." Of course, Mom thinks he's talking to her.

"Hi, Skye." He smiles. "I'm West…"

There's a pause as we wait for him to finish what he's saying, but once again, he's staring at Eva.

"Eva, my cousin, West, West, my friend, Eva," Riley cuts in, wagging a finger back and forth.

West side-steps past Mom and hands Eva a cinnamon roll first, radiating his best smile. "Beautiful name."

Wow, I didn't get that kind of treatment when he met me.

"Thanks, West, you're the best." Eva lifts the roll. "And I'm a poet and didn't know it."

West lets out a laugh, his eyes shimmering. "I *am* the best," he says before doling out cinnamon rolls to the rest of us.

Man, talk about sparks flying. At least on West's part.

"Thanks, Westie, you rock," Riley mumbles after taking a bite. "Now we're in the middle of a top-secret meeting, so scram."

"Ten-four." He salutes. "I'm right across the hall fixing computers, so I'm sure you will be seeing me again soon," he says before backing out the door.

"I'm sure," Riley says, her voice tinged with sarcasm.

Mom smiles conspiratorially. "Wow, what a cutie patootie. Eva, keep an eye on that one."

Eva's big brown eyes go even bigger. "Huh?"

Mom licks off her fingers and whispers, "Soul connection," to me and Riley. "Anyway, Soph, so that was a yes on crashing the wedding?"

I slink in my chair. I can't believe I'm about to agree to this—it's never okay to crash someone's wedding, even the enemy's. But it could work if we slip in, talk to Madame Puuccí, and slip out, sight unseen? I know I'm rationalizing this, but at the same time, I have to do everything to create my own success. No one is going to do it for me. "I guess. So, when do I try to pitch her?"

"In the lobby or something?" Riley twists her flowing red hair, then places her homemade bobby clip in it. It actually looks cute. Of course it does.

"But Missy and Eben *can't* know we're crashing their wedding." I bite my lip.

"It's all taken care of." Mom smacks the paperwork.

Unfortunately, I'm sure it is.

26

The Ride

2^6

Late Saturday afternoon, my ringing cell phone stirs me from a deep slumber. I was working on Vera Wag, but I must've nodded off. Clearly, I'm exhausted. I reach to the nightstand, grab my phone and fumble to answer it.

"Mom?" I croak.

"Soph! I need your help. I'm stuck in the middle of nowhere."

"Huh?" I rub my eyes.

"I borrowed your car and came out to do an astral traveling session with Vorian-5, but when I stopped for gas, I locked the keys in your car. Can you come on the Harley and bring your spare?"

I groan. "Why did you take my car?"

"Soph, stuck in the heat. Focus."

I don't have time for this. "You do all sorts of questionable stuff. Don't you know how to do something normally questionable, like jimmy an old car lock?"

"I tried. I'm only human. And I'm at a gas station in the middle of nowhere in Georgia. I could die of heatstroke."

I sigh. "Okay, I'm coming. Tell me where you are."

"Just put in the Ride 'n Roll gas station along highway 140, about forty-five minutes north." She clears her throat. "Call me the second you get here, okay?"

"Okay, bye."

"Bye—don't forget to call when you get here."

"Okay, okay."

I drag myself into jeans and a T-shirt, then pull my hair into a ponytail so I can put on a helmet. Then, I put on Mom's leather jacket and black boots.

With the wind in my face and my foot on the gas, riding the motorcycle gives me a rush of adrenaline I've missed.

I've done pretty well so far at not giving up the fight for the Pet IQ opportunity, but it's getting harder and harder. Raven Monroe hasn't returned my call—yet. This is just the mood lift I needed. My lungs fill with fresh air, and my problems seem further away. I need to do this more often.

About forty minutes outside of Atlanta, I see my car parked at the Ride 'n Roll gas station, which clearly got its name because it's a biker's hangout. I blend right in as I roll up, getting waves and peace signs from those mulling about. I put my helmet in the back storage compartment with the spare before I strike up a conversation with the gang of graying, long-bearded bikers in the parking lot, making their day when I compliment their "V-Rod muscle machines."

But I don't see Mom anywhere.

I think about calling her like I promised but stop myself. She was just a little too insistent about it, and I need to find out why. I go inside the gas station, combing the aisles, but Mom isn't here either. Getting more suspicious by the second, I head to the back to find a patio door.

Outside are tables and chairs filled with bikers eating the food from the tiny deli inside the place.

Peering out the patio door is when I see Mom, sitting at a table and chatting... with Lucas.

Lucas? She's hanging out with *Lucas*?

Before they see me, I duck and rush back through the store and go out front before making my way along the side of the building into the bushes so I can eavesdrop on them. I can't believe I'm doing this, but apparently, Mom has worn off on me. I *have* to find out why these two are chilling together after what went down between him and me.

"I wish I still had Jerry's alpha-beta counter," Mom says. "I want to test my waves here because I know they'd be off the charts—I already blew that machine up once."

This is the crap I have to listen to while I'm getting scratched by branches?

"What happened to it?" Lucas asks.

"The last time I hooked myself up to it, it made a popping sound and started smoking. I think my energy was too much for it."

"So what exactly are alpha-beta waves?" By Lucas's tone, he sounds like he legitimately wants to know the answer.

"It's the level of brain activity in your sixth sense."

"Got it," he says.

And I have my answer. Mom is trying to open Lucas's third eye, which means she's trying to make him grow into my suitable mate. Or something like that. But why is Lucas still hanging out with Mom?

It doesn't matter. I've heard enough, and I walk around the corner and approach them. "You two are *sneaking* to hang out?"

"Oh, hi, Soph," Mom squeaks out. "You were supposed to call me when you got here. We were discussing Gizzie. Lucas wants to adopt him, and I've decided to grant Lucas permanent custody."

I open my mouth to argue, and then I realize that it's just my pride getting the best of me. I can't stand that dog, and Lucas taking him is the best thing that could happen to me. Lifting my chin, I say, "As long as Lucas commits to providing Gizzie a loving home, then I'll agree to relinquish custody." I realize I never had custody of Gizzie, but whatever.

Lucas's contrite eyes lock with mine, and it's almost as though we exchange silent apologies.

"Anyway," Mom plunges on, "Lucas and I went to Vorian-5's astral traveling session today. Vorian-5 owns a spaceship. Super nice kid."

"The Vorian-5 who gave you my car?" I say, realizing she's creating a diversion.

"Yup. We all went with him to Kepler-186f." She hands me a home-printed brochure with a picture of him standing in front of his spaceship on the cover. It's a round wooden structure with Christmas lights hung over it. "On his home planet, his name represents his outward fierceness and inner softness."

"He looks about as fierce as a tabby cat."

"Well, this is just my personal opinion, but I believe he's actually only half Kepling. I get the feeling his father was an Earthling, but don't tell Vorian-5 I told you that. On our planet, he goes by Jared, and he's a tax auditor during the week. On weekends, he hosts astral travel sessions in his backyard. Anyway, he identifies more with his Kepling lineage, so he prefers that his fellow astral travelers call him Vorian-5."

"Does he open third eyes?" I ask seriously. I want verbal confirmation that Mom brought Lucas here to open his third eye.

"You know what, Soph? Vorian-5 worked very hard to get his spiritual-awakening certification," Mom snaps, assuming I'm being sarcastic. I guess I deserve that.

"He's a trained professional, Sophie." Lucas's tone is even. "And he did get mud off my third eye."

"Really?" I shoot Lucas a puzzled look. He can't be serious.

"Oh, Soph, that reminds me. We should be collecting stones." Mom peers around. "Vorian-5 told me that some ones here have powerful healing properties."

"How will I know which ones to choose?" I say, too tired to fight.

"Just select ones you're drawn to. Ones that speak to you." She wanders off the patio to pick up a smooth red stone and put it in her purse. When she gets back, she says, "I'm starving," as she heads for the door. "I'm going in to get some food."

"Me too." Lucas stands, and I follow them both inside.

Heading down the aisle, I see a sign hanging over the hot dog warmer that advertises, "Easy Sliders."

"Now those look good," Lucas says before he fixes himself one. Giving in, I make one too. I think back to Lucas's amazing BLT and wonder how we've fallen this far since then. "I think you're just starving." I look over to see Mom talking to the cashier, and she gasps in surprise. Then the cashier zips around the counter with a glowing smile to shake Mom's hand. Exclaiming how honored he is to meet her, he hands Mom a magazine, and she writes something on it.

Crickey. What has Mom done now? When she finishes, the cashier puts his arm around her and takes a selfie. Then he runs to the door and opens it before yelling that a magazine cover girl is in the store. He orders the motorcycle gang to "get their butts inside The Ride *now*!" as he waves the magazine in the air.

I grab Lucas and shoot up to the counter. The bikers bust through the door and ask Mom for autographs. She stands in the middle of the gang, signing magazines and getting her picture taken.

Mom has groupies.

"That's so awesome. Congratulations," Lucas says after he snatches a copy of the magazine.

"Holy smokes!" Mom has a dazzling smile. "I never imagined I'd be famous."

I peer over Lucas' shoulder. He's holding a copy of *Hog Honeys* magazine with my mother on the cover. She sits on the Harley wearing a fringed leather corset and black leather biking short shorts. An elaborate temporary tattoo crawls out of her cleavage and onto her arms.

I shake my head. The fact that I'm not shocked that my mother is on the cover of a biker magazine is more shocking than my mother actually being on the cover of a biker magazine. "So, when were you in a biker gang?" I try unsuccessfully to hide a smile.

"When we rescued Jimmy Chew."

"Oh, duh," I mumble, but I'm proud of her. I never saw that outfit, so she must've changed by the time I got home from work that day.

"Ah, that was the best bust ever." She smiles wistfully. "Making the cover of *Hog Honeys* is just an added honor."

"Congrats, Mom." I turn to the cashier. "Can you get us five more copies, please?"

"You look great, Skye." Lucas studies the page. "I didn't get a chance to really see your tattoo before. "Is that reincarnation represented in your ink?"

"Yeah, you got that. And see the aura around the new soul? That's our destiny. We take it into the next life with us."

Lucas tilts his head and inspects the cover closely.

Lucas is examining Mom's cleavage. Suddenly, the easy slider dog becomes lead in my stomach.

Mom's glances at her phone, then stuffs her hot dog in a paper bag and begins texting.

"Everything okay?" I say, knowing good and well it isn't.

"Vorian-5 says he wants to go back to Kepler for good."

"And that's bad?" My face pinches.

"Very bad. He thinks jumping off a cliff will force his Kepling wings to emerge and fly him home. I need to go. I'm gonna have to talk him down from the ledge again. Dammit. Soph, can you take Lucas home on the bike? Vorian-5 is deathly afraid of motorcycles."

"Sure." I don't want to be anywhere near Lucas, but right now, we have to put aside our squabble. Someone's life is on the line. Without hesitation, I hand Mom the spare key. "Just make sure Vorian-5 is safe."

Mom hugs her adoring fans before rushing out the front door.

Leaving Lucas, me, and a motorcycle.

# # #

"So, you know how to ride on the back, right?" I barely meet Lucas's gaze. "Since you rode with my mom that one time."

"Yes."

"You're going to get cold." I look around the store. "Maybe you should buy one of the sweatshirts they have here?"

After Lucas has one on that says, "Just a man and his hog," we make our way outside to the bike. I pull out the helmets, handing Lucas the spare. After putting mine on, I catch him staring at me. "What?" I say.

"Nothing." He kicks his shoe into the ground. "You look good as a biker."

"Thanks." Unwelcome butterflies return to my stomach, but I refuse to be charmed by him. I remember his words, loud and clear—*I've never been so wrong about a person*. I climb on the bike waiting for Lucas to sit behind me when he says, "Can we make a pit stop on the way home?"

"A pit stop? Where?"

"On the drive here, your mom and I passed this great lookout point." He clears his throat, jamming his hands in his jeans pocket. "And sunset is approaching. I'd hate to miss a view like that."

I want to see the view too, but I'm scared of the feelings I tend to get when Lucas and I are taking in the sunset. But if I say no, he'll think I care too much, and I don't want that either, even though it's true. "Fair enough request."

As we ride, the warm day transitions into the perfectly cool evening. Lucas wraps his strong arms around me, and it feels impossible to believe I can't get used to being held by him like this. It's the most perfect place in the world for me to be.

But I make the decision to try to enjoy it for what it is—something that feels really good, just for today. I lean back so I can feel him against me.

I'm free, taking in each moment when he squeezes me a little tighter. When we get to the lookout spot, I'm floating as I park the Harley and take off my helmet. When I turn around, it's the old Lucas gazing back at me. His face is flushed, and he's wearing *that* smile, the one that lights up his face and turns his eyes to shimmering chips of amber. "That was amazing." He sighs.

"It was," I say, but I'm probably referring to something different than he is. And that's okay—or at least, it has to be.

We walk to the rail to see Atlanta in the distance, set against the dusky backdrop. I can't believe a random spot along the highway has such a spectacular vista, possibly the best I'd found since living here. I even have the urge to log onto Yelp and share my random find, but don't. Instead, I take a seat on a wooden bench and soak in the scenery.

While I sit, I think about Mom's request to collect stones that "speak" to me. I see one; jagged, light gray, ugly... except for its dusting of light blue. The fact that it got my attention makes me wonder if it is, indeed, "speaking" to me, so I pick it up and put it in my pocket. I can't believe the crap Mom convinces me to do.

Lucas joins me, handing me some bottled water he bought at the gas station. "Thank you," I say as I take it. I don't plan on talking to Lucas—I've shared more than enough with him. So I sit quietly, letting the cool breeze brush my face.

"You deserve it all, Sophie," he says, whisper-soft.

"What?" I turn and meet his gaze, which is sad, broken. Despite everything, I can't bear to see that expression on him, so my eyes dart to the ground.

Lucas put a finger on my chin and tips it up so I meet his eyes when he says, "You deserve it *all*. Recognition for your work, someone who's got your back. Killer sunsets."

I swallow back my pride, the thing that's telling me to stonewall him and simply nod. Instead, I let the corners of my mouth tilt upward. "So do you."

"I didn't mean what I said—about being wrong about you. I knew what happened with Mr. D was an accident, but I was hurt and angry. You're the most straightforward, honest, and fair person I've ever met—to a fault. I'm sorry for what I said."

"Thank you." His words warm me and scare me at the same time, so I say, "Hey, I've done questionable things—crashing your meeting with Frank Franklin." A weak laugh whisks out of me, an attempt to keep Lucas from knowing my most innermost thoughts. The laugh dies when I realize its futility. "I do have this doggedly stubborn need for life to be fair. I'm working on it."

"I wouldn't. The world needs more people like you in it." He fidgets on the bench seat. "If I ever got serious with someone, that's what I'd want."

Besides being deeply flattering, his words and nervousness make a bulb flicker on in my head. "You've never had a serious relationship?"

"No." He evens his lips. "And although I'm sure you think it's because I'm closed off, it's actually because work always gets in the way."

"Fair enough. I haven't had a serious one either. For the same reason. Or that's the reason I give, anyway."

Lucas's whiskey eyes linger on me before drifting upward. "Check out the sky now."

I follow his gaze to find my sunset thirst delightfully quenched. The twinkling city lights glow against the shadow of clouds in the red sky. It looks like something out of a sci-fi movie. "More than I'd hoped for." When I look back at Lucas, he seems to be studying my face. "What?"

His gaze intensifies as he sits silently. Then his usual glow dims as a heaviness makes his strong, broad shoulders sag, just a touch. His mouth twitches before he says, "I was thirteen. Mom was forcing me to go with her to one of her meditation classes. She wanted to teach me how to become more in tune with myself, and I was giving her grief about it—being a mouthy teenager. We were arguing when Mom drove the car into a power line pole..." he trails off, his voice turning into a croak. He takes a moment to compose himself, his jaw tensing as the effort. His voice is hollow when he says, "Everyone always tells me it wasn't my fault, and I know it wasn't, logically. But I was being rude and distracting her. And all I got was a broken finger? That was it. A silly broken finger."

My breath is frozen solid in my chest, and my heart feels like it's in a vise. "Lucas, I'm so sorry."

"So..." He stares into the distance. "I know I can never really make up for what happened, but I owe it to Mom to spend my life doing what she wanted most—me finding peace and balance."

And *that's* why he does these kinds of things with Mom. In this moment, I regret everything. Regret being ashamed of Mom and her Winnebago. Regret not being more grateful. Regret giving her a hard time about her beliefs, which have only helped people—including me.

As though Lucas's thoughts echo mine, he says, "And you know, my mom wasn't wrong. I'm not sure it matters exactly what I believe, but rather, what my beliefs give me. I do the best I possibly can, but at some point, I have to relinquish the power to something bigger than myself. There's peace in that."

"That's very wise, Lucas Nevarez."

"Thank you." He hesitates, the peaceful look fading from his face as his backbone goes ramrod straight, as though he's run out of energy for third gear and has to downshift into first. A ragged edge creeps into his voice when he says, "I'm sure a psychologist would say I became a cutthroat executive because of what happened. I needed to conquer the world. But I dunno—I'm just trying to figure my way, like everyone else."

The corners of my mouth curve. "A superhero. Maybe the socks weren't such a bad choice after all."

His lips split into a pained grin as he shakes his head.

I feel the invisible shield I put up between him and me fading as my anger dissipates into the crisp, cool air. Without my permission, my body moves closer to him, and my voice emulates the soft hues of the horizon when I say, "I know your mom's not here to tell you this. But I promise you, wherever she is, she thinks the world of you now. She's very proud. You know that, right?"

He glances down, and when he looks back up, his eyes are like pools of melted gold. "I don't know if I know that. Or if I ever will. But it feels really good to hear you tell me that." His gaze intensifies on me. "Anyway. Here I am, going on and on about my problems."

"I understand. Dad issues here." My eyes flick away, and I turn, closing the book on the subject.

Lucas bends down to the ground before picking up a rock and throwing it over the cliff's edge. "Just another thing we have in common."

"Yeah. That one isn't so good." I don't want to dwell on that, so the corner of my mouth perks when I say, "You don't drink coffee through the stirrer straw like I do."

"I remember the first time I saw you do that. I realized that you have it right and the rest of us have it wrong. The stirrer stick *is* a straw. Why not just make it a stick if it's not intended to be used as a straw?"

"Exactly." I slap my hand down on the bench.

"And," he says, the lightness returning to his tone, "drinking through straws is more fun."

"How do you understand me so well?"

"I don't know. Maybe it's because my mom was a lot like your mom," he says. "Well, Skye's one of a kind, but my mom had a lot of similar qualities and the same wackiness and unique spiritual beliefs."

"Tell me more."

He speaks about his mom with fondness, chuckling at her unorthodox ways. It isn't long until we get into a competition of whose mom humiliated whom the worst in high school.

"Get this." I smile, sure I've already won. "My mom once hosted a firewalk and invited my Algebra II teacher as a date."

"Oh, yeah, my mom once marched in front of my school wearing an outfit made only from recycled toilet paper to protest the fact that the school didn't recycle. And no, it didn't get them to start."

"You win," I say, laughing. Right now, it feels like I've known Lucas my whole life.

There's a beat of silence, and I sense another mood shift in the air.

Sure enough, Lucas touches my back, and my eyes roam up to his face that right now, radiates emotion. Our eyes stay connected like industrial velcro, and his adoring gaze turns fiery.

This is how he looked in bed. Which I want. I *need*. I need him to wrap himself around me and never let go. He'd given me an experience that will live in every cell of my body for as long as I breathe. The way he moved. The way he touched me, ever so gently. The way he instinctively just *got* me.

Every fiber in my being wants that again.

Except when it's over, Lucas would shut me out again, and all I'd be left with was more emptiness and regret.

This is just adrenaline-fueled lust, and I have to rise above it. I scoot away and smooth out my jacket, breaking the spell.

"Hey," he says, his voice husky. With one word, he lures me back. Not able to fight it, I met his eyes again. At this moment, I could fall into him and never come back. I want to, but I can't. I simply can't allow it. Lucas brushes his finger across my cheek as his eyes crawl down my shirt, a glazed look in them. He wants me too.

But he must be having all the same thoughts because he draws in a breath and drops his hand. My heart sinks when he scoots away.

"We should get back." His eyes go inky, his exhale forced.

"Yes. We should."

27

The Big Fish

I'm thrilled and proud of Mom—she convinced Vorian-5 to be happy staying on earth.

Besides that, it's been quite a week preparing to crash a televised wedding. Well, and design, pattern, and sew my Vera Wag collection. Plus, devise a plan to rescue RezQ.

A sad pun that is.

Tomorrow's the wedding, but our sting op starts tonight.

Walking into the Chateau LeBlanc's signature restaurant, I take in Scaldi's Vegas-like Renaissance decor with Michelangelo prints, faux cracked walls and flickering battery-operated candles. Mom, Eva, Riley, and I make our way to a stone-paved veranda where a fountain rains on a European statue and sit at a table shaded by a large umbrella.

It's the perfect mid-October day in Georgia, seventy-eight degrees with a gentle breeze, the sweet citrus smell of shedding magnolias drifting in the air.

The *Bridesmaid to Bride* producer and film crew are meeting here later to make a plan for Missy and Eben's wedding. Mom found out about the meeting from "the weakest link" in the bridal party, whomever that is. Mom won't reveal her source, and that's terrifying.

Right now, our plan is to plant bugs and listen in. West got us all set up with everything we needed. Bugs, bluetooth earbuds, and a signal dish on the roof of the Winnebago. After we hear the *Bridesmaid to Bride* team meeting, we're going to make our own plan for tomorrow's wedding.

Wearing our wedding crasher gear—sunglasses and hoodies—Riley, Eva, and I chow down Scaldi's award-winning spaghetti and meatballs. Mom plants her bugs on the patio while "soaking in the atmosphere" and "studying the statue." She finishes up by the time we pay the bill.

This week, *all* of us created, designed, and sewed day and night. We had an assembly line going with hip-hop music and three pizzas.

My family and friends are the best.

After we leave the restaurant, Mom parks the Winnebago behind three large trees in the back of Scaldi's patio. Then she removes a floorboard from under the dining table, revealing a junk food heaven: Twinkies, Ding Dongs, Ho-Hos, the works. "This is my management system for stake outs. These things are a snore."

"Ugh, no thanks. I'm never eating again." I pat my overly full tummy.

"Does somebody smell mold?" Eva scrunches her nose.

I look at Mom. "Told you."

Two hours later there we sit, bored out of our minds and hogging down cakes full of hydrogenated oils. I was going to use the time to buy Billy Road tickets, but there aren't any left. I pull my headphones partially off and signal Riley to do the same. When she does, I say, "I can't believe Billy Road is already sold out. Tickets went on sale a few hours ago."

For some reason, Riley's face twists in guilt.

"What?" Dread pinpricks its way up my spine.

"You'll get to hear Billy Road tomorrow night—if we hide. He's playing at Missy and Eben's reception."

"No way!" I squawk. First my job, then Mr. D, and now Billy Road? "How does Missy have *everything* I want in life—"

"Shh, stop whining," Mom snarls. "Listen."

I sniff. "Fine."

We planted several bugs, which means we have the arduous task of listening to numerous conversations at once through our headphones that are connected through bluetooth. But something weird is happening—we're about an hour and a half away from their scheduled meeting, and except for the sounds of the wait staff setting up, Scaldi's has gone silent. The only conversations we're picking up are things like, "the wine table goes there," or, "the centerpieces are stacked in the corner."

The staff chatter goes on for almost an hour until I hear *that* hair-raising shrill voice.

"This is not the color of roses I ordered! These are pink *lace*, and they're supposed to be pink *paradise*."

Missy.

She can't be here, can she? Just the producers and film crew are supposed to be meeting tonight. I have to be hearing things—like some sort of post-traumatic stress symptom where I imagine her shrill voice at random times.

"Are you the bride, ma'am?" a male voice asks.

"Yes, and I want to speak to the decorating crew. Right now."

It's not post-traumatic stress. It's really Missy. "*What?*" I look at Mom and Riley, and they're both scowling. "Why is *she* here now?"

"What's wrong, babe?" It's Eben.

"Your tacky fiancée wants her roses fuchsia, not baby pink," I sneer.

Riley lets out a snort that makes me smile—for a second—until, in my headphones, I hear a mention of the bridal party arriving, and I realize the implications of what's happening. One look at Mom, and I know she's thinking the same thing.

I rip off my headphones. "This is the rehearsal dinner, not a planning meeting!" I look at Mom. "Who's your source?"

Eva and Riley join me in scolding Mom with our eyes, and Mom finally caves. "The information I got was good, don't worry. It's from a bridesmaid, Eben's sister. She hates Missy's guts and can't believe her brother's marrying her." Mom rolls her neck. "Just trust the process."

Trust the process?

"How did you even talk to Eben's sister?" I shake my head.

"I called her." Mom shoots me a "duh" look.

Fuming, we continue to sit and wait, and sure enough, the rehearsal dinner kicks off. The groomsmen arrive, and Riley says, "This is *killing* me. I want to see all the hot men! I'll pick the best and... bow chika bow wow."

"Do it," I reply. "Dare you." I'd love to see Riley actually follow through with one of the imaginary conquests she brags about.

"I will. The best man, Hudson, is hot." She lifts her chin. "And tonight, he's mine."

"Wasn't he written about in *Love Buzz* for hooking up with, like... everyone?" Eva's face puckers.

"That's the point." Riley curls her lip. "I'm not marrying him, I'm enrapturing him. He'll have skills."

"Amen," Mom says.

Eva laughs. "Soph, are you hearing this?"

"Unfortunately."

The four of us suffer through Missy's ear-piercing laugh as she welcomes everyone. After, Hudson gives his best man toast, which includes a "funny" story about how Eben and Missy broke up before they broke up for good. Well, until now. Apparently, Hudson had been a cheerleader during Eben's transgressions. But of course. The best, though, is having to hear Missy's snarls to the staff.

Talk about torture. I'm lying on Mom's couch as we wait to see if anything is said of the wedding plans for tomorrow. Two more infinitely long hours pass, and we've managed to eat another round of Twinkies.

Then when it's all over, we finally get our *Bridesmaid to Bride* team meeting.

"Told ya!" Mom hollers, doing a fist pump.

"Good job, Skye!" Eva flashes her brilliant smile as she high-fives Mom. "We shouldn't have doubted you."

The wedding decorations are to be finished first thing, but the flowers aren't arriving until three o'clock. The film crew is arriving "on set" at five, two hours before the wedding.

But the key information is this: Madame Puuccí will be in the wedding gazebo at four o'clock, sharp, doing pre-interview pictures for a *Vogue* spread on how she designed the outfits for Mr. D, the ring bearer, and the flower girl—a poodle named Lady Godiva.

This is my chance.

# # #

Unfortunately, the four of us have to pile into the hotel room for the night because Mom and I were only able to afford just the one. But that doesn't stop us from enjoying the place. For me, it's a massive upgrade from the Winnebago.

Our room has a monstrous walk-in shower with a bench seat, so Eva, Riley, and I are running scalding water against the wall to make our own sauna. In our bathing suits, we're hanging out, sitting on the bench seat with wine. Mom is with Dolly and Llama watching some detective movie.

Riley's a bit tipsy when she says, "I'm going to take you both guy shopping. There are hotties all over Atlanta waiting to do lots of things to you. I mean with you. Or both. Believe me, I've looked."

"Riley, you do remember that you were supposed to 'bow chika bow wow' with the best man tonight? And now you're sitting with us in a shower?" I gulp my wine.

"His face was hot." She curls a lip. "Until it started talking."

"Yeah, Soph, he *was* gross," Eva says. "And you're one to talk. What happened with Lucas?"

"Nothing happened with Lucas," I blurt, a little too quickly, avoiding her probing gaze.

"Define 'nothing.'" Riley's head bob is out.

I furrow my brows. "Okay. Stuff.'"

"I knew you were hiding something!" Riley smacks her hand on the bench seat. "Define 'stuff.'"

"Some light exploration," I mumble.

"Exploration?" Eva scrunches her nose. "What are you, an astronaut?"

"Did you get your hands on the goods or not?" Riley tilts her head.

"Fine, everything happened!" I cry. "All of it. And it was the best of my whole life." And it can never happen again, which makes my heart nearly implode with longing.

Riley waggles her finger. "I knew it!"

"It's over," I mumble. "So it doesn't matter."

"Over, smoover." Eva high-fives Riley, splashing some of her wine on me in the process.

Mom comes busting through the bathroom door. "We got it," she says, her voice ringing with excitement.

"Got what?" I say, more than grateful for the interruption.

"Proof that Yum Breath Company hid the fact their chews have been linked to over two thousand pet deaths. Two thousand! They're covering it up, and we got 'em."

My stomach churns. "That's a hefty accusation. You're sure? And who's your source?"

"I never reveal my sources—"

"Ugh, please stop." I flop my head back. "This is big, and we need to know how you got this information."

Mom sniffs. "Fine. West is here in the hotel room with me. That's all you need to know."

West? Mom's now roped into him into doing something questionable? "Oh, jeez."

Riley squeezes her eyes closed. "I'm gonna kill him."

"So, nobody come out of here naked or anything." Mom points out the door. "West found investigation documentation on the chews that showed deadly results."

"They're *really* covering up the fact that they're injuring and killing animals?" Any relaxation I'd gained from our faux spa experience has evaporated.

"Scumbags!" Riley takes a big swig of her wine.

"Think of the injury lawsuits. The insurance claims. The indictments. They're finished." Eva's tone is all business.

I go silent as my cheeks get hot as rage courses through my veins. I grit my teeth when I finally say, "They have to be stopped. Now."

"They're about to be," Mom says as she walks out the door.

28

Wedding Crashers

The next morning, we're up at the crack of dawn to snatch the surveillance bugs from the back veranda of Scaldi's before it opens. Then we head to Chateau LeBlanc to scout it out. After finding the grounds where the wedding's going to be, we map out the nearest parking, escape routes, and hiding areas.

It's clear that the bride and groom are going to stand in the large and elegant castle tower gazebo with a spectacular view of the Blue Vine Mountains as their backdrop.

That's also where Madame Puuccí's going to be for her interview.

With that in mind, we devise our plan.

Good news: the gazebo tower has a stone ladder along its backside so that I can climb to its roof and watch for Madame Puuccí from behind the ledge. I can also retreat up there if I'm on the verge of getting caught.

If I *do* manage to corner Madame Puuccí to pitch her, Mom and Eva are going to hit up the scene as workers to distract anyone from coming near us.

Riley's dressed to the nines—and looking like a model—ready to sit at a decorated cardboard table with sparkling waters on ice to hand out to guests. We made her a fake hotel badge.

Her job is to keep a watchful eye on everyone entering the premises, then notify the sting op team if security approaches before my renegade pitch with Madame Puuccí.

We search for a place to park the Winnebago so that it's hidden, but within reach, so our equipment works. The instructions said the bugs can't be over three-hundred yards from the dish on the Winnebago to get a signal. Not an easy task. But Mom finds a semi-truck in an adjacent lot and parks behind it.

As Missy's fake flower waterer, I can position myself to jump in and give my pitch. Mom gives me her mask, apron, rubber gloves, spray bottle, and sunglasses, then digs through a plastic sack and pulls out a hot-pink lace bra. "You need to wear this. It's already pre-wired with a microphone, so you don't have to worry about it popping out anywhere. It should be your size, I checked."

I take the bra and inspect it, finding a diamond heart dangling from the middle. "Thanks. It does look like my size. But definitely not my style."

Mom touches the diamond heart. "Maybe this'll be a good luck charm." Then she hands me the earbuds so I can hear her, Riley, and Eva. Eva and West are going to use the downtime in the Winnebago to find out any more information on the ingredients and studies of Yum Breaths. They're to go through the internet with a "lice comb," as Mom put it.

I can't believe today is another sting operation, hopefully my last.

At around three fifteen, I walk—with my samples in a backpack—to the wedding grounds where legions of satin hot-pink covered chairs face the gazebo, crawling with vines of baby and hot-pink roses. Matching floral arrangements decorate the aisle chairs. Missy is *not* going to be pleased with the baby pink flowers.

I spray the floral arrangements, walking up the aisle with the intensity of a woman on a mission. I pass a hotel employee who's tying bows around the satin guest chairs.

"Excuse me, who are you?" The employee approaches me warily.

Without so much as a glance in his direction, I say, "I was hired by the bride, Missy Mulligan, to make sure the flower arrangements are properly watered."

"Why wasn't I informed of this?"

I sigh. "Look, I'll just call Missy and tell her you aren't letting me work." I grab my phone. "What's your name?"

"No, no, don't do that," he says, panic in his voice. "Just hurry."

"You're going to want to vacate yourself and the other workers for about twenty minutes. The stuff I'm spraying is great for the plants, but isn't good if you breathe it in." I make a serious face. "Toxic." I point to my mask.

He groans but ushers out the bustling workers.

As soon as they're gone, I bark, "Get moving, now's the time," into my microphone.

"Hold on," Mom says. "We have a problem. There's the van here with some of the film crew. They can't see us—I gotta move the Winnebago."

Great. That's going to waste precious minutes. I continue down the aisle, misting the floral arrangements on the chairs as I make my way inside the gazebo. Once there, I shake my head at what I see hanging—cages of doves, apparently waiting to be released.

I mist the dozens upon dozens of roses—hot pink and baby pink—that surround the arched entry. I'm supposed to look for hiding places in case I need to duck. Looking to see an attic door in the ceiling, I whisper into my microphone. "There's an attic space in the gazebo."

"See if it's easy to access," Mom says.

I tug at the rope attic door handle, and it comes down, revealing a collapsible ladder. When I expand it and step up to peek into the space, I see speakers, decorations and a box of wedding supplies. I lean into my microphone. "I could hide up here if I can't make it to the gazebo's roof."

There's silence on Mom's end for another minute before she yells, "Hang on!"

Then I hear West and Eva squealing like baby pigs.

"What happened?" I ask in a frantic whisper.

"Yeah, what was that?" Riley cuts in.

"We're fine, Soph," Mom says in a tone that indicates they're anything but fine.

"No biggie." Eva heaves out a breath. "Your mom just drove us into the Grand Canyon. I think I have a concussion."

"You're fine, Eva," Mom says. "You had your seatbelt on and it's just a tiny ditch."

"Yeah, you can really hide a Winnebago in a tiny ditch," Eva says. "And let me tell ya, Soph. We're hidden. Like buried treasure."

"Wow that was a doozie!" I hear West in Eva's microphone. "Skye, you drive like Riley does."

"I can hear you guys, remember?" Riley says. "And if anyone cares, I'm in place and handing out waters."

"Thanks, Riles," I say.

"Eva, go back and look in that van," Mom says, out of breath. "The crew left, and I saw dogs in there. It's getting really hot."

"I need you guys here," I yap. "I got the area cleared."

"We gotta get those dogs out of the van first!" Mom cries. "There's a whole bunch of them. I *cannot* believe someone left animals in there."

My heart squeezes at the thought of any dogs overheating. "Okay, but hurry."

I'm ready to head to the gazebo's roof when I hear a voice. Not just any voice, but Lucas's voice.

Just the rich baritone sound of it makes my heart flutter and sting at the same time.

But it can't be. "Lucas isn't invited to the wedding, is he?" I ask Riley.

"Yeah, Missy invited all the board," Riley says.

Eva's out of breath, clearly too preoccupied to pay attention to me or Riley. "The van is locked, Skye. We need to bust open a window."

"I think Lucas is here now." I take a step down the ladder and peek out. There's the film crew with Lucas and others who appear to be groomsmen. And they're all heading toward me.

Crap! "I'm hiding," I whisper into my ear bud. "I thought they said five o'clock!"

"Son of a biscuit!" Riley yells.

Eva, West, and Mom are a murmur, clearly focused on their new dog rescue mission.

I climb the ladder and crawl into the attic on all fours, balancing my backpack while placing my hands and knees on a beam that makes a cracking sound. It's got to be stable, right? This is a storage space. I reach through the entry to fold up the ladder and pull the attic door closed. Safely out of view, I murmur, "I'm in the attic."

The *Bridesmaid to Bride* director says, "Okay, everyone, crowd into the gazebo with your whiskeys. Look like you're chatting and having a wonderful time."

Ah, crap.

Before I know it, a bunch of dudes are below me, talking sports, scotches, stocks, with forced laughter. I hear a voice boom, "Hello, all you *Bridesmaid to Bride* fans. We're here at Chateau LeBlanc waiting for our very special wedding between Eben and Melissa. But while we wait, we want to introduce you to some of the single groomsmen that just might become the next *Groomsman to Groom*!"

Seriously?

"Abort mission," I whisper into my microphone.

"No kidding, Soph," Mom says, struggling for a breath. I hear a loud bang, and I assume she's trying to bust a window.

Good gravy, there's a torrent of shenanigans happening right now.

The host continues to ask all the guys a bunch of silly questions, like what they do for work and fun. When Lucas is called up, the announcer says, "And this is Lucas Nevarez, CEO of a pet retail company at just thirty-two years old. Now, we've heard you have quite the reputation for being a cutthroat executive. Is this true?"

Lucas chuckles. "Yup, so if I'm the next *Groomsman to Groom*, watch out, ladies. You *all* might be going home the first night."

I hold back a snort. Lucas obviously doesn't want to be on the show, and he's blowing the interview on purpose. That's so him.

"All righty, then," the announcer continues, "Hearing it straight from the brutal CEO from Wall Street. Let's move onto another potential contestant."

The announcer continues his interviews until I'm sweating. No, that's an understatement. I'm dripping, from every pore. It might be a pleasant eighty degrees outside, but in this attic, it had to be a sweltering three-hundred and eighty. I lay, stomach down, on top of a beam, Mom's ridiculous pink lace bra boring a hole through my skin.

The announcer discusses Eben and Missy's honeymoon plans (the Virgin Islands), what a beautiful bride Melissa is (yay) and how there's a surprise at the end of tonight's wedding (also, yay). Listening to this crap is bad enough. Listening to it while sitting in a sauna struggling to breathe is torture.

Besides getting heatstroke, my body aches and my legs tingle because I can't move in the cramped space.

"Excuse me, I'm sorry to interrupt," an unfamiliar female voice says. "But I'm here to finish decorating."

"Oh, yes, have at it," the announcer replies. "We're just finishing up."

I think of an escape plan as I listen to the sound of rustling flowers, stapling, and off-key humming. I'll just tell the decorator I'm hotel staff and needed the gardening mister out of the attic. I move to open the door when Riley cuts in with, "Abort, abort!"

"What's going on?" I squeak.

Riley says something, but I don't hear it because just below me is Missy's voice.

No, no, no.

"Hello, Krista, this is my mom, Kitty," Missy says. "Don't mind us. We're just here to take a look at everything."

"There's pink lace everywhere." It's another voice, similar to Missy's, but older.

"Is there a problem, Kitty?" the decorator asks.

Kitty busts out a dramatic sigh. "Yeah, this isn't gonna work. Missy doesn't want pink lace."

My stomach drops.

"I don't understand. This is what was ordered." The decorator now has panic in her voice.

"I told them last night," Missy screeches. "I *cannot* believe they still put all the pink lace roses out."

"It's fine, dear," Kitty says. "Let's just remove all of them ourselves. I don't want to trust anyone else to do it, they might leave gaps. It'll only take a little while if we work on it together, Missy."

"Okay, I'll just have them move Madame Puuccí's interview to the gardens," Missy says.

Nooo.

"Hell's bells!" Mom says. "I don't see Mr. D inside the van. That's good."

"That *is* good," I whisper, relieved.

When Missy and Kitty finish an hour later, I'm delirious. And royally screwed.

The place is now abuzz with caterers, photographers, florists, videographers, the film crew, and one very pushy wedding planner with a squeaky voice.

The only thing keeping me from losing my mind is that I'd dumped out the box of wedding paraphernalia, using a tiara I found to pull my hair up off my neck. I also put huge cubic zirconia wedding rings around each of my fingers, wishing I could snap a photo for Mom, Riley, and Eva. Oh, and West too.

By the time the wedding ceremony begins, I'm so hot I struggle to breathe. I have to do anything to cool down. I need to take off my shirt.

It's Missy's turn to recite her vows. "Eben, our love is like this wedding ring I custom designed..."

I squirm, trying to lift my sopping wet shirt above my head.

"...virtually flawless, brilliant, transparent—" Missy pauses.

My top has suctioned to my left arm and neck.

"...enormous, rare and unbreakable," she ends, sniffling.

I roll my shoulder to loosen the shirt's hold.

Below me, the preacher says, "If there's anyone who objects to this marriage, please speak now or forever hold your peace."

My top finally gives way, relieving my neck of the pressure, but causing me to topple over. A loud cracking sound blasts my ears before a refreshing cool breeze hits my body.

I hear someone say, "Holy hell," just before I fling through the air. I grab a hold of the ceiling beam, and my sunglasses fall off as my legs dangle before the beam breaks for good. I fall onto the wedding arch, and it crumbles beneath me. Logically, I know all the branches jabbing into my skin should hurt, but I must be in shock because I feel no pain.

The backpack hits the floor with a thud, just missing Eben.

Then the flutter of wings fills the air as the doves, whose cages I knocked over, fly to freedom.

Lucky them.

# # #

Gasps echo through the crowd before Missy's high-pitched squeal tears through my ears.

"Shall I take that as an objection?" the preacher deadpans.

In my ear bud, Mom yells, "Dammit!"

Behind me, Eben screams, "What the—?"

I stand, drenched in sweat, covered in cobwebs and wearing a tiara, fake wedding rings on all fingers, cutoff shorts and Mom's hot-pink lace bra. A bra that matches the army of bridesmaids standing to the side of me. I look down to make sure my microphone is still hidden. It stayed put, so at least there's that.

I turn to a sea of faces staring at me. I meet Lucas's gaze, and his eyes are huge as he shoots me an utterly shocked look. A pillow of white lace and taffeta charges toward me, and I realize it's Missy who's jumping on top of me.

And I know whatever I'm about to get, I deserve it.

"You psychotic witch!" she howls. A left-handed hook lands on my jaw, knocking me further into the sharp branches. An intense pain radiates from the blow. Apparently, the shock has worn off.

Mr. D barks his head off, and I feel his tongue on my hand. "I'm okay, buddy," I say, not sure if that's true.

I was so happy that Urban Productions lawyer disappeared, and I hoped that was the end of Missy suing me. But now, I'm going to bet he'll be back.

A group of people surround Missy, lifting her off before she can re-attack me. For a split second I feel sorry for her, as her poofy princess wedding gown is now covered with grass-like stains from all the flower stems.

Lucas is rushing toward me, but he's stopped by the best man. Another buff guy in a security outfit takes me from Eben's hold.

"Sophie!" Mom's voice hushes the crowd as she hustles down the aisle, along with a crew of dogs dressed in hats and ties. I *cannot* believe Mom managed to show up with dogs. "Sorry, everyone, but we've got a problem. These dogs were left in crates in a hot van, and my daughter was up there helping us on a lookout rescue mission." Mom stares at me. "Clearly, she got overheated."

Riley, Eva, and West join Mom, all looking at me with bulging eyes.

Mom faces the audience as they let out a symphony of gasps and nervous chatter. "I'm very sorry, everyone. Now that all the animals are safe, you can continue with your wedding."

Mom grabs the backpack, and I hang my head as the security guard wraps a cloth around me before escorting the four of us away. I should be boiling with embarrassment, but I'm too terrified. What if I've ruined RezQ's reputation for good? I hope with everything in me that Mom's story has thrown everyone off.

The security guard leads us off the grounds and back to the hotel. As we walk, I'm too shocked to feel much of anything.

But what I do feel in this very moment is relief and gratitude. No, I'm not going to pitch to Madame Puuccí. And there's a chance I just made the world think I'm missing a few screws.

But I've never been more glad to have Skye as my mother.

No one else on this planet (or universe?) would have the instantaneous street smarts and wicked creativity to figure a way out of this mess. Mom loves me more than she loves anything, including herself, which she shows every day by doing things like this—saving my butt.

I turn to see Lucas behind us, but the security guard keeps hold of us until we reach the hotel lobby. Once the guard releases my arms, he says, "You *really* need therapy. Please get it."

"Thank you," I say before looking back at Lucas.

"Sophie, wait up," he says. "I have to talk to you. It's really important."

Mom rips the shirt off her back, showing off her oversized sports bra, and hands it to me, along with the backpack. Then she gives me a shove. "Go get him."

I flash Mom a weak smile, saying "Thank you," before I slip the shirt on as Mom scurries out the rotating door and hopefully, straight to the Winnebago.

29

In the Toilet

"Come with me." Lucas rushes through the lobby.

"I'm pretty sure I'm supposed to leave," I whisper.

"Whatever." He whisks me along, and when we get to the women's bathroom, he says, "Go inside."

"Huh?"

"Madame Puuccí's *Vogue* interview got canceled because of Missy. They didn't have another place ready to do the photoshoot, so they nixed the article. I told Madame Puuccí that Trish, one of *Vogue's* senior editors, drank four cocktails at the pre-wedding mixer, which wasn't a lie. So, Madame Puuccí's waiting in there for Trish to get her interview back. Madame Puuccí didn't see what happened at the wedding ceremony, which is good for you. Here's your shot."

"Wow, Lucas. Thank you." I blink, regarding him with shock and amazement. "*Why* are you helping me? Again?"

He shakes his head slowly, defeated. "I can't *not* help you. But get in there before I change my mind."

"Got it." I rush into the bathroom and when I step to the sink, I see Madame Puuccí's signature stilettos under one of the stall's gaps.

Bingo.

Sure enough, when the stall door swings open, it's her. The instant she sees me, she skips the sink and b-lines it for the bathroom door.

"Wait, Madame Puuccí."

She turns slowly before looking me up and down. "You look like hell."

"Thank you."

I hear a click outside the bathroom door, and wonder what just happened, but I plunge on. "I have some amazing news about RezQ."

"I don't care, Ms. Fox. Truly." She pulls at the door's handle, but it won't open. She gasps. "I'm *locked* in here?"

"Hello, Madame Puuccí." Lucas's voice echoes from the outside. "Just hear Sophie out. Then I'll open the door."

"Two minutes," I blurt, holding up two fingers.

"You people have lost your minds." She pats her tall bun, slowly turning toward me.

"There might be something to that." I reach into the backpack and pull out my best Vera Wag wedding dress—a sequined Victorian gown with gold embroidery and a matching crown. "I'm working with Raven Monroe to host a dog wedding for charity. Two thousand dollars a head to attend, and we've already had several VIP guests RSVP." Okay, *several* is a bit of an overstatement. We have three, Raven and her two besties, but still. "It's getting written up in *Atlanta Wedding Magazine* on how the wealthy are doing something big to help the overflowing rescue shelters here in Georgia." That part is one-hundred percent true. I raise my chin, pausing for effect. "Dog weddings—it's the next big thing, Madame Puuccí. Ride the wave with me."

She studies my face, clearly trying to figure out if I'm brilliant or bananas. Finally, she says, "Pet IQ's board has already chosen our finalists—Fur Bebé and Whiffany & Co."

"You may want to rethink Fur Bebé. During the wedding, they just got called out on keeping the animals in a hot van—on live TV."

"Did they, now?"

"Yes. By my mom," I say proudly.

"That's right. Your investigative mother." Her eyes brighten, but then they narrow before she groans. "Dammit. That was actually a persuasive little speech."

"Thank you."

A long, pregnant pause fills the air, and this is where my negotiation training kicks in—I know that the first person to speak loses, so I super-glue my lips together as I wait it out.

"Okay." She waves her canary yellow fingernail in the air. "The board has approved and finalized the two others, but I will enter you as a one-time CEO pick. You can join Fur Bebé and Whiffany in the final presentation to the Pet IQ board next Thursday."

I pump my fists. "Thank you—you won't regret it." I'm beyond glowing. I didn't just land the final presentation, I did it with my friends, my mother, and Lucas.

And that's so much better than landing it on my own, which I could never have done.

Maybe Lucas and I could find a way to fit the pieces of our lives together—personal *and* business? We have to because... I stop myself from thinking what I'm about to think.

But the voice in my head says it, loud and clear—like a car stereo on full blast.

I love him.

I'm in love with Lucas Nevarez.

The thought makes euphoria wash over me, a spell that's transforming my being. I thought I'd felt love before, but it was nothing like this. Now, whatever happens, I'll know what it's like to love someone. *Really* love someone, from the amber flecks in his eyes and odd obsession with superheroes, to the way his lips twitch when he's cherry-picking his words. I love his kind and generous heart, witty and brilliant mind, and fiercely protective nature over me, even when it's detrimental to him. But it's more than that. Mostly, I love the person I am when I'm with him.

And I can never unknow all these things.

I'm yanked back into the moment when Madame Puuccí bangs on the door. "Let me out, Lucas—or Fur Bebé's out of contention to be in Pet IQ stores."

The door swings wide open, and Madame Puuccí rushes away, her heels tapping on the marble floor.

# # #

"Thank you, Lucas," I squeal in a whisper.

"You're welcome." In one hand is a first aid kit, the other, an ice bag. He must've gotten those from the front desk. He steps toward me, his fresh-soap smell filling the air around me, which makes my brain go full static. How can he smell *that* good? "Are you okay?" he asks, his voice soft.

"More than okay."

"That sock to the eye looked like it hurt." His eyes flash. "Eben's jerk of a best man took me out when I tried to get to you."

"It did hurt but thank you for trying."

He hands me the ice pack. "Here."

"Thanks." I put it on and force myself to keep it there while it stings.

He holds up the kit. "You've got more cuts than I can attend to here, so this is for when we get back to the Winnebago."

"You're the best." I look down to see scrapes, dried up blood, and freshly forming bruises all over my arms and legs, I'm sure from all the branches. And now that he's mentioned it, my bum *really* hurts.

I look up to see that, in contrast, he's wearing a suit and looking razor sharp. Self-conscious, I run a hand over the fresh cuts and bruises that cover my face. "I can't believe you trapped Madame Puuccí in a bathroom for me. I don't know how to thank you enough."

"You don't have to."

I pull him into a hug, excitement pouring from every cell as I press my body against his. Without my permission, my mouth blurts, "I'm falling for you, Lucas."

His body goes stiff before he pulls away.

Oh, no.

My heart constricts, and all the tingling and excitement vanish in a split-second, like someone cut the power. "What was that?"

He meets my gaze, his eyes splintering. "Let me walk you back to the Winnebago." His tone is cold, clipped.

"Okay." My stomach drops to my toes. "So, what's up?" I say, dreading his answer.

He walks in silence before he says, "What happened between us was a mistake."

His words knock the wind out of me—what's left of it—and I blink for a moment as the impact settles in. My tone has an edge when I say, "It sure didn't feel like a mistake when you bandaged my wounds, cooked me dinner, and invited me into your bed."

He stops walking and closes his eyes, clearly needing to collect himself. "I wasn't thinking. I let my attraction to you get in the way of reality."

I swallow hard, fighting the mist out of my eyes. "It was just an attraction, nothing more?"

"As you know, I came to Fur Bebé to land this Pet IQ opportunity. Things between you and me are making this too complicated." His jaw clenches, pain flashing through his eyes. After a sharp inhale, his lips twitch as he says, "In fact, I think it's best if I return to Boston and work remotely. I need to focus on work and do what I've been hired to do."

He didn't answer the question, but regardless, his words are like a razor slicing into my deepest insecurities. Yes, he just helped me secure a pitch spot against Fur Bebé, something his board would surely fire him for if they found out. And yes, I know he's from Boston, but the idealistic part of me hoped Atlanta would become his home.

So, what he's saying makes sense. Logically.

Illogically, my heart is splintering into a million pieces. An ache so sharp and deep, it feels like it'll never quite be the same.

It probably won't.

I've become numb to the aches of my cuts and bruises, and I realize I preferred that to the pain I'm feeling now.

I shouldn't have let myself fall for him because I was right all along—a big city Harvard boy like Lucas would never love a community college, small-town girl like me.

The thought breaks me. I nod, feeling like a hollowed shell, but I thrust all my willpower into keeping my face even. "Right."

My brain reels through everything he just said. He's heading back to Boston, where he can work remotely for Fur Bebé. He said what happened between us was a mistake.

The words pain me all over again, but worse this time around. My walk speeds up, and the hurt and anger are bubbling up inside me like an instant pot. I remind myself why this is happening.

I'm screwing with his job and his family's business.

But that's logic, and the way I feel about him defies logic. How can he not feel equally illogical about me?

Doesn't he love me too?

Of course he doesn't.

I turn toward Lucas, unable to meet his gaze. "Good luck with your life in Boston."

He hands me the first aid kit. "And good luck with RezQ, Sophie. I know it will be a success, regardless of what happens with Pet IQ."

It will be a success *with* Pet IQ. That I will make sure of.

# # #

We spend the night in the hotel room, chowing down popcorn and watching old Audrey Hepburn movies. As much as we would've loved to see Billy Road perform at the reception, we weren't particularly in the mood for getting arrested.

This morning, Mom's in the Winnebago, which is running and waiting for us in the loading area.

When I step out of the rotating doors with my suitcase, I can't believe my eyes.

That's Billy Road standing at the driver's seat window, smiling and talking to Mom. And was that a laugh?

Is my idol, Billy Road... *flirting* with my mother?

I approach slowly, as though I'm entering an alternate universe where we're all cartoons and any minute, the whole scene is going to have the word "boom" written into a jagged cloud over it before it all disappears.

And oh, no. Mom's still in her pjs!

"Hey, there," I say, my voice hesitant.

Billy Road looks at me and flashes a genuine smile, which shows the creases around his eyes and forehead. Up close, he looks older than he does on TV, but he's got a charisma about him that you miss on the screen. His eyes are almost otherworldly, and there's a sparkling energy around him. I guess that's what Mom would call his aura. "You must be Skye's daughter, Sophie." He extends his hand. "It is wonderful to meet you."

I shake it, my hand numbing from nerves. "Mr. Road. I'm such a huge fan."

Really cute, Sophie. That's what *everyone* says.

Eva and West come through the doors. "I'm a huge fan too," Eva chirps.

"Me three!" West is so happy, he looks almost buzzed.

Billy Road chuckles, clearly used to this kind of situation. "It was really nice meeting you all."

"Yes, you too," I say, before thinking "duh" again. When I look at Mom, she's gone googly eyed. It's not like her to get starstruck, but I'm sure it's next level when one actually flirts with you.

And hello, it's *Billy Road*.

Billy Road walks away with an actual swagger.

"What was that?" I say to Mom, shocked.

"He dug me, like everyone does," Mom deadpans, but her glazed eyes tell a different story.

"That was *awesome*!" Eva squeals.

"It was! Riley's going to freak," I say, remembering that she's not here. "Where *is* Riley?"

"She went to get a coffee," Eva says.

Right on cue, Riley comes sauntering out the rotating doors, making her way to the front door of the Winnebago because she called shotgun. Once she's seated, she says, "What just happened to y'all?"

"Ask Skye," Eva chirps. "You're not going to believe it."

I see Mom in the rearview mirror, and she's staring forward, suspiciously *not* bragging to Riley. Clearly, she's still a little giddy.

Then Mom puts a lead foot on the gas as she tears out of the parking lot.

30

The Net

Monday morning, I'm back in my closet office with three layers of cover-up on my black eye, and somehow, this place is growing on me. The air conditioner buzz has become a comforting white noise.

Woody stays in his corner, I stay in mine.

And Riley comes to see me *all* the time. West pops in, too.

It's weird to think that Lucas isn't in the building anymore—or the same state for that matter—and that makes me feel like I'm missing something. Or everything.

I keep telling myself to forget him, but I don't think that's going to happen anytime soon. Or ever, on some level.

Love Buzz has me and my pink bra plastered on the homepage of their website. Headline, "Animal Rescuers Crash *Bridesmaid to Bride* Wedding… Half-Naked."

The subsequent article has all our pictures and a brief synopsis of our lives. So, I guess we are… famous?

It was the *Bridesmaid to Bride* film crew responsible for keeping the dogs in the hot van, not Fur Bebé—the dogs were extras for the reception. Urban Productions fired a bunch of folks, had to pay a fine, and have since made a very generous contribution to Georgia's animal shelters—surely on damage control to save the show and production company's reputation.

Speaking of reputations, Missy publicly apologized for hitting me and told me all was forgiven, surely so she looked like the kind-hearted soul that she is. You know, after hauling out and punching me in the face. I'm pretty sure the *Bridesmaid to Bride* producer told her she had to.

But I hardly doubt all is truly forgiven with Missy, and as soon as she returns from her honeymoon, each time I hear a knock at my door, I'll tense.

The silver lining of all this—since me and my pink bra hit it big—is that preorders are pouring in. Except there's no way I'm prepared to handle so many, so everything's backed up.

And I won't have Pet IQ's support until I can convince them to choose RezQ... which hasn't happened yet and won't for another week. But having too many orders is a good thing to mention in my pitch to them. A *very* good thing.

Riley comes busting through my door with West, who's carrying a metal box with cords hanging everywhere, like a robotic sea creature.

"I know how we can catch Missy," Riley says, skipping hello, as usual.

I want to scold her for not knocking with a visitor, but her offer is too good to pass up. "Really?"

"Westie, tell her the plan." Riley bounces on her toes.

"All right. You're not at Fur Bebé, so we can't put you on the network. But you are in the building." He lifts the box. "So, we're going to set you up with a fake server and network, making the WiFi open. Then, we'll give it a tempting name, like, 'RezQ-private.' After that, you're going to put a file on there with an even more tempting name, like 'Pitch-MadamePuucci.' Missy will see the open network, join, and steal your files."

My face pinches. "That's great, but is she really smart enough to figure all that out?"

"No," Riley cuts in. "But I'm going to help her along. At lunch, when she's microwaving her skinny popcorn, I'll pretend to be having a call with you where you're complaining about your network issues. I'll tell you that you'll just *have* to leave it password free for now."

"Nice." My smile is genuine. "Wow, thanks."

"No problem." Riley shrugs. "I'll also mention that what you're doing for your new wedding collection is off the hook. Then she'll steal it, but it's going to suck." Riley points at me. "You have to make it suck."

"Roger that. And I have just the sucky idea for her to steal."

31

The Dirtiest Dog

My wake-up alarm Thursday morning is Eva and Riley blowing through the Winnebago door, their faces twisted in shock.

"What's up?" I croak, blinking to focus.

Eva is in her pajamas. *Eva*.

This is bad. Very bad.

Riley doesn't say a word as she takes the remote and turns on the TV. She flips to the news, where a poofy-haired brunette reporter is speaking. "I'm here, live, outside the Yum Breath headquarters in Atlanta. As you can see behind me, animal rights activists are marching after our breaking report last night. The company continued to sell their product, even after learning that it caused thousands of animal deaths." The reporter addresses the camera, a look of controlled concern on her face. "Yum Breaths is a subsidiary of Pet IQ, which is run by the infamous Madame Puuccí, the premier petwear designer."

I gasp.

"Shhh," Riley scolds.

The reporter continues, "Ms. Puuccí has no comment at this time, but sources tell me she's resigned as CEO of Pet IQ."

"Oh, no!" Riley looks at me, her face frozen.

I have to practically scoop my jaw off the floor. "Did I hear that right? Madame Puuccí is responsible for the toxic Yum Breaths? And she's no longer Pet IQ's CEO?"

"Yes," Eva squeaks.

"So, when it's her name on things, she cares about animals." Riley's nose flares. "But when her name is shielded by a subsidiary, she cares so little that she sells a product that hurts them?"

"It seems like it." My cheeks burn. "I'm glad Mom and West took her down—and I'm proud of them for that. But I'm not glad I lost my pitch. *Very* not glad."

Eva begins to pace. "We need a plan to get your spot back. We need to talk to your mom."

"No way, Eva. Never wake my mom up this early with bad news. There'll just be a whole lot of yelling." I shake my head frantically. "Let her and her two sleeping dogs lie."

"All right." Eva wanders over and rests her head on the kitchenette island. "You should call Frank."

"Yes. Good idea—I will." I grab my phone and frantically dial his office. To my relief, his administrative assistant, Meredith, answers.

Putting the phone on speaker, I explain my situation to Meredith. Afterward, she says, "I'm very sorry, but I'm looking at Madame Puuccí's list right now. RezQ isn't on it."

"Oh, no." I shoot Riley and Eva a desperate look.

"I'd like to help you, Ms. Fox, but I'm absolutely sure nothing more that can be done." Meredith clears her throat. "Legally, all Pet IQ employees are not allowed to speak with Madame Puuccí because of the pending lawsuit."

Eva's eyes go round as she nods in agreement.

I thank Meredith before disconnecting.

Eva's tone is dire. "This is bad. *Really* bad."

I don't answer as nausea roils in my gut. This is worse than really bad.

"We'll think of something." Riley swats her hands in front of her face as if that will help her inhale. "But I don't have a clue of what that something is. Yet. Sophie?" She looks at me, desperate.

Right now, my brain is as dysfunctional as a laptop submerged in a pool. "I got nothing."

Riley slumps into an island chair. "This is why we need your mom."

"I'll tell her before I leave for work," I say, wondering what I'm going to actually *do* at work now. The answer is nothing, but I definitely can't stay here in the Winnebago.

# # #

When I get back from my once-a-year morning jog, I don't have to wake Mom because she's in the kitchenette cooking something. I walk to the counter and say, "Hey."

"Hi." She opens a cabinet and pulls out a box of macaroni and cheese. Mom's uncharacteristically quiet as she fills two small bowls with water, then dumps the pasta in.

"What are you doing?" I sit at the kitchenette's island chair. "Mac and cheese for breakfast?"

"Sure." Mom covers the bowls with paper towels. "And I'm microwaving the macaroni. I don't feel like cleaning up a pot and stove."

I pick up the box and read it. "It doesn't say that it's microwavable."

"Everything is microwavable."

I rest my face on my palm. "I see where I get my cooking skills from." I stare into space, still reeling over the fact that everything's in shambles. And Mom's clearly on edge.

Now that the mac and cheese is nuked and mixed, Mom heaps it in a bowl before pushing it front of me. "Here." She sets down a fork.

The idea of eating makes my stomach tighten. "No, thanks." I give a bite to Dolly and Llama before I scoot the food away. "I'm not hungry."

She lets out an exasperated sigh. "Eat. You're turning into a bag of bones."

I grab the bowl and glance at it. "I take it you heard what happened."

"Yes. Since I was the one who sent the information to the authorities, they called me before the story broke. So, sorry about that."

I twist my lips. "No good deed goes unpunished."

"Isn't that the truth."

I pick up the fork and scoop a bite, but then I poke it into the food. "So much for my pitch to Pet IQ."

Mom slams her bowl down on the counter. "I can see that you're not really eating. I'm not saying another word to you until you actually put food in your mouth. Are you trying to starve yourself?"

"Of course not!" I let go of the fork. "I don't feel like eating, jeez. I just lost my big shot at making RezQ a success. I'm out of money—I spent all my earnings from the shelter on material and supplies. I have preorders that I can't possibly fulfill because I have no infrastructure, I have absolutely no idea how I'm going to pay my own bills, and I blew my chance at getting my job back." I take a deep breath to hold the tears back. "What am I supposed to do now?"

"Keep eating. Keep fighting." She puts the bowl back in front of me. "You have to take care of yourself. I don't even wanna know how many pounds you've lost since all this started, and you barely sleep."

"I'm trying, Mother." My voice cracks. "And how am I supposed to sleep?"

"You eat and sleep because you know there are people around you that care about you. Whatever happens, we'll figure it out."

"I can't spend the rest of my life living here in a Winnebago. I'm sorry. I need to be back on my own."

"Right. In a place where you can shut everyone out."

"Here we go again." My throat tightens.

"It's true."

"No, it's not, Mom. I *let* Lucas in. I told him things," I cry out, my lip quivering. "Look at where it got me."

"Right. And now I'm terrified you'll shut every man out now for good." She shakes her head. "And I don't want to see you do that. I know you want a family of your own someday, and you won't have it if you keep letting your fears run your life."

The Winnebago suddenly seems claustrophobic. I stand and back away from her. "I wonder where I got those fears from? I don't know, let's see. Maybe from a mother who's been married five times?"

Mom comes within inches of my face, then wags her finger at me. "I admit I have bad taste in men. But I did a good job raising you, Sophie Jean."

I bark out a humorless laugh. "Really? You think good parenting includes a steady dose of humiliation? You have *zero* boundaries."

"It's nice to hear you finally admit how you *really* feel."

I ignore her and plunge on. "Remember that time I brought a date home in high school? When you barged in and pulled him into your pyramid energy party? In fact, you're so talented at scaring guys away, your face could be on a pro-abstinence billboard."

Mom bobs her head. "You seem to do a bang-up job with abstinence all on your own."

"Was that supposed to be an insult? That I don't sleep around?" I throw my hands in the air. "Who knows the psychological issues I have from you. *You're* the reason my life's gone to hell in a handbasket!"

Mom jabs my chest with her finger. "Your life's gone to hell in a handbasket because of *you*, Sophie. The universe is trying to teach you something, but you won't listen. You're gonna keep getting the same lesson until you learn it." She stares me down. "I know some of my beliefs rub you the wrong way, but if nothing else, I taught you to trust your instincts and fight for the ones you love. Somewhere along the way, you stopped listening to yourself and started keeping everyone at arm's length. When did a big career become the most important thing in your life? When did you start prioritizing that?"

Her words hurt, but not as much as a memory that haunts me. I push her hand away. "When I decided that being able to pay the mortgage was part of becoming a responsible adult. Maybe I wanted a roof over my head that doesn't require a parking permit. A career is the way to do all that." I take a breath to make sure I want to say the next words.

"What?" Mom looks like she's about to be sick. "Tell me what you were going to say." Her tone is desperate, and I have to answer.

I can barely get the words out as tears stream down my cheeks. "When I needed to prove to myself I was worthy after my own father rejected me. I met Dad, and you never told me. How could you keep that from me?" I meet her fiery gaze, my vision blurry with tears. "I found the picture. Dad and I had ice cream. You lied. My whole life you lied."

Mom's face goes as red as if I'd struck her, and she finally steps back. She stands silent for a few beats before she says, "Why didn't you tell me you found that?"

"Why didn't you tell me you *had* it?"

"I was trying to protect you." She shakes her head. "All it would do is hurt you more if you knew he'd met you. And what good was telling you about your dad after he was dead? You don't want anything to do with him now, anyway."

"Oh, here we go again with me talking to a dead person." My voice is so harsh I don't recognize it. "I was four years old, and you *knew* he'd rejected me at two. You took me to his house anyway, on my *birthday*. How did you think that was going to go? Were you trying to win him back or something?"

"Of course not, Sophie." Her watery eyes narrow. "Don't you *dare* say that to me. You've always been my first priority. Always." She looks away, and when she meets my eyes again, her lips tremble. "I wanted your father to be in your life so much that I took the chance to meet him when he was desperate to talk to me. He had to have changed his mind about being in your life, but unfortunately, we never got to find out for sure." Her tone goes lifeless. "You would've hated me if I hadn't let you two meet, so it was a no-win situation." Her voice softens when she says, "Will you just try to talk to him now? Write him a letter?"

"Ugh, Mother, stop it! He's dead."

"It will help you get your feelings out."

"What good will that do? Just stop it already."

"So, you think I'm off my rocker, then?"

Right now, yes. I don't answer; I just stare at the floor and watch my tears hit. I can't bring myself to look at Mom's devastated face for another second. Part of me wants to apologize, but I don't. The conversation cut too deep. I grit my teeth and say, "I have to go."

Mom storms into her bedroom, cracking the flimsy door when she slams it.

32

Free Falling

It's just before noon on Thursday, and I'm working feverishly in my closet-office. Mom and I haven't said a word to each other since our blowout fight yesterday.

Riley told me that Fur Bebé's abuzz with chatter since they and Whiffany are pitching at Pet IQ at their Buckhead headquarters at three p.m. today.

And I guess, so am I—or I'm going to try.

Just this morning, I decided to show up without an invite from Frank Franklin, Pet IQ's newly minted CEO. I know it's likely fruitless, but I have to do everything possible to fight for my dream. I need to prove to myself that I'll take this all the way, and maybe part of me needs to prove this to Lucas too. It's a hard lesson—that when our best just isn't good enough, we sometimes slog forward, anyway.

Maybe, you play the hand even when the dealer's got the win.

Maybe, you throw that twenty-yard touchdown pass with everything you have, even when it's the end of the fourth quarter and you're down by thirty points.

Because life isn't fair.

And just maybe, you practice hard at failing. Because you need to grow the calluses to push hard enough—and long enough—against failure until something finally cracks through the walls of injustice.

Maybe, you create your own fairness.

And that's why I dig back into my work, making headway. I still have a lot to do since I decided to crash the pitch session this afternoon. Excitement tingles through me for the first time since Madame Puuccí's resignation, and I'm not exactly sure why. It has to be because I'm fired up to barrel into the meeting and make a mess of things.

Maybe I've become my mother.

I'm punching away at my keyboard, making my pitch for my Vera Wag collection as amazing as possible in the hour I have left to polish it up. When there's a knock on the door, I say, "Can't talk now, West. I'll call you later." He's the only person it could be since Riley doesn't knock.

"Um, it's Missy, actually."

Oh, crap. Missy is back from her honeymoon. And she's *not* happy with me. "Oh," I fumble out, licking my lips. "Come in, Missy."

She steps in, and she's *not* scowling—a good start. I manage a tentative smile when I say, "Welcome back."

"Thanks." As she approaches, she shields her eyes, but her expression is unreadable.

That's terrifying.

I wince as I lean back in my chair. My eye smarts again, as though it knows it's about to take another licking.

Then... she bends down and comes in for a hug. "Thank you, Sophie!"

"What?" I choke out.

She pulls away, beaming. "That was the most watched episode of *Bridesmaid to Bride* in the show's history!" She claps her hands. "I've gained another *hundred-thousand* followers. It's a dream come true."

"Wow, fantastic." So, I've made another one of Missy's dreams come true? This is a pattern I definitely have to break.

Although, if this means the lawsuit is off—again?—then it's worth it.

She waves her bright blue nails around, like she's a fairy with a wand granting wishes. And, sadly, I'm sure she believes she wields that kind of power. She's never told no and always gets to skip the line. But maybe it's all a mirage—her power only a reflection of those with the *real* power who need her. Once their need vanishes, so does the mirage.

At the realization, I'm in disbelief at how quickly my envy turns to pity.

"Now—to land the Pet IQ opportunity for Fur Bebé," she says in passing, like it's already a done deal. "And I'm sorry for punching you and being so… icky before. I was going through a rough patch after Eben and I broke up."

"Thank you." I smile, glancing at my computer clock. It's almost twelve-thirty! Crap, crap, crap. I stand and escort Missy to the door, saying, "I'm really sorry too. I never would've interrupted your wedding on purpose."

"All's well that ends well," she says before breezing out the door.

It's far from the end, but sure.

Okay, deep breaths. I still have a solid hour and a half before I have to leave. Sweat beads on my brow as I compile the research data, which looks promising.

When Riley comes in, she sits on my table desk, making it let out an unnerving groan. Her big blue eyes fill with tears. "My parents kicked me out after finding out I was one of the wedding crashers. Which is fine because I can't live there anymore." Her lips quiver. "They cut me out of the will too. I think I'm done with them for good."

"Oh, Riles. I'm so sorry." I stand and shimmy around my desk before pulling her into a hug. "We can always move back in together. We make amazing roommates—and I've missed you." After I say the words, I'm not exactly sure how that's going to happen. I don't have any money for an apartment. Yet.

I'm sure Riley knows this, but her voice is upbeat when she says, "I've missed living with you too. So much." She pulls away. "What am I going to do?"

I have to fix this. I text Eva and ask her if Riley can stay the night tonight. Her response is instant. "Of course."

I'm so grateful that Eva's a part of our lives.

I smile. "For tonight, Eva said you could stay with her."

"Really?" Riley exhales so hard her shoulders relax. "Thanks, Soph. I'll write her."

When West comes flying in the door, Riley says, "Out! We can't talk right now. Emergency."

"Jeez, okay, Riles." He holds his palms up. "I'm leaving."

"Okay, we'll talk when I'm finished, promise." She swipes the tears from her eyes. "Bye."

"Bye." He starts to shut the door but then opens it again. "Just one question. Do you think I should ask Eva out?"

Riley exhales a slow breath. "I think she only dates Jewish guys, West. I'm sorry, but you're not that," she says softly.

"Fine." He shuts the door. Then I hear the bang and clash of him working on the computer equipment across the hall.

"Aw, poor guy. He's got it bad." I clasp my hands, trying to rush this along. "Let's meet and figure out a plan for you, okay?" I hate to cut things short with Riley when she's so upset, but I've got to get busy.

"Okay." She slides off my folding table desk.

The door flies open again, and Eva darts inside. "Okay, so I've been put on disciplinary leave at my firm because of the wedding crashing fiasco."

"Oh, man." The effects of the mess I made just keep rippling down. Some good, some bad. But why does it have to be bad for Eva and good for Missy?

And *what* is going on? I feel like we've all jumped from a plane, and we're fighting to get our parachutes open. Meanwhile, we're all in free fall.

Except I have really good news for Eva, which I was going to wait to share after my pitch to Pet IQ today. But after seeing her sad puppy dog eyes, I decide the news can't wait. "So, Eva, I have a surprise for you." I smile when I put my make-up compact mirror in front of her face. "Meet our new dog wedding caterer for Saturday! Raven hired you."

Raven's caterers fell through, and I used that chance to pitch Eva and her services.

"What?" Eva raises her perfectly manicured brow before the news seems to settle in. Then she throws her arms up, careful not to hit the shelves on either side. "No way!"

Riley's eyes bulge out of her head. "Are you serious?"

"Yup."

"Thank you!" Eva hugs me before doing a little dance. "You're inspiring, Soph. When life hands you lemons, add vodka."

"Did my mom teach you that phrase?" My head tilts.

"Possibly." Eva brushes some invisible lint off her dress. "Wow, this is so incredible. I was actually thinking about taking out a loan and starting a small catering company on the side."

"Now you have a great resume-starter," I say.

After Riley gives Eva a hug, she says, "So, you gonna go for it? Start it up?"

"I don't know! This is a risk, and I'm not a risk-taker. Plus, my dad would *kill* me." Eva shrugs, exhaling. "But you only live once, and this is my dream."

"So, that settles it. Tonight, we're having a celebration." Riley does jazz hands. "Eva, you being free from the law firm, at least for the moment, me being free from my parents, and Sophie, you for having steel balls that clink when you walk."

"Aw, Riles, that's so beautiful," I deadpan.

"I'll make us all dinner reservations at Fleur Sauvage," she says, not missing a beat.

There's a loud bang from across the hall. Then, West's voice echoes from outside the door. "What's this about Fleur Sauvage?"

"Yes, you can come too, leech." Riley rolls her eyes.

"Thank you!"

"Since you'll be at my place, Riley, we can play spades. There'll be four of us," Eva says, and I wonder if she's making an excuse to have West over to her place after dinner. That would be adorable.

"Sounds awesome." It's West from outside the door again.

"It does sound awesome." I stand, attempting to usher everyone away. My work time is evaporating.

Riley lowers her voice when she turns to me and asks, "How do you feel about facing Lucas at Pet IQ today, Soph?"

"Fine," I reply, an octave too high, rushing toward the door. "I mean, we'll both be in work mode, so that's good."

Eva rolls her eyes. "You are such a liar." Her voice has an edge. "It gets old. Anyway, I better head over to Novu Villa. I've got to start putting together the menu for Raven Monroe. Knock 'em dead, Soph."

"Back to work for me, too." Riley turns on her heel, her smile gone. "Bye, Sophie. Good luck today."

"Thanks," I croak, a sick feeling in my stomach. I wish they understood how hard it is for me to share relationship details. It's not them, it's me. And when it comes to that, I don't know how to let them in. It just feels too hard.

But, since I'm low on time, I push that aside as I frantically throw the data together. Now I just need to do the sales projections.

Come on, I'm almost there.

My cell phone buzzes, and it's a local Atlanta number. I ignore it, but when it rings two more times, I groan before picking it up. "Hello."

"Is this Sophie Fox?" the man on the other end of the line asks.

"Yes. Who's this?"

"This is Dr. Rosenberg from North Georgia Medical. I'm sorry, but your mother's here. There's been an accident."

"I don't understand," I say, my mind unable to process his words. Shaking my head, I continue, "What accident?"

"She fell off the roof of her Winnebago. She's unconscious. Please. Come right away."

The room blurs, and I drop the pen I'm holding. "I'll be right there."

33

The Dark Skye

Once I'm at the hospital, I rush through the corridors, looking for Mom's room number. Everything is hazy. It's all just... wrong.

Why was she on the roof? They don't know how serious her head injury is, and she hasn't woken up. But falling from the Winnebago—that's pretty high up.

And why wasn't I there to help her? Why didn't she ask me?

Then I remember, and the guilt hits like a tidal wave, knocking the wind clean out of me.

We got in a huge fight.

I said horrible things.

Of course she didn't ask me. I move even faster because I can barely stand to be in my own skin. When I burst into her room and see her, my knees almost give out. She's lying there, disturbingly still, bandages on her head, bruises on her arms, and a gash on one eye.

It's Mom, but it's not Mom. Her glow, her energy, her spark—the things that make her *her* aren't there. She's right in front of me, and I miss her more than I've ever missed anyone in my life.

Tears are threatening to burst, but I refuse to let them. I have to be strong for her. I drag a chair to her bedside and sit, taking her hand into mine.

A nurse buzzes in, her shoes squeaking on the polished floor. Clara, by her name tag, checks all Mom's vitals. I say, "Do they know any more?"

Clara shakes her head. "Sorry, darling. Right now, we're just waiting to see what happens, but it's important to talk to her."

"Okay."

Clara smiles empathetically. "Let me know if you need anything."

"Thanks." I've got to pull myself together because it sounds like talking is the only thing I can do to help Mom. And I have so much to tell her. I never apologized for the awful things I said in our fight. I never told her how proud I am of her. And when was the last time I told her I loved her?

How could I have been so harsh? So careless? And why did I take her so much for granted?

I can no longer fight the tears, and they stream down my face. "I'm so sorry. About everything." I squeeze her hand as a collage of memories blast through my head like a flip book. I decide to talk about them, one by one, to show her how they've become a part of me. The times she crawled into bed with me when I'd have nightmares, usually about my father dying. The time she drove me to the hospital when I broke my ankle. I was eight-years old and hysterical, but she was calm as she kept telling me that when it was in a cast, I could have as much ice cream as I wanted. By the time I left the ER, I was actually looking forward to the desserts and attention. The time she stayed up all night with me in college to help me study for a macroeconomics exam. I wasn't even close to being prepared because I'd been in bed with the flu for a week. She didn't know the first thing about economics, but she asked me the study questions and made the concepts stick in my brain by coming up with ridiculous mnemonic devices. In the end, I got an A-.

Only my mother would do all those things for me. And I cannot imagine a world where I don't have her.

I push the darkness away.

When I tire of the stroll down memory lane, I tell her she and I will move on to do great things together, no matter what happens. That we make a good team. No, we make an amazing team. My voice is hoarse when I run out of things to talk about, and she's still not moving.

I've been strong, but then—in a flash—I'm desperate for her to wake up. My skin goes damp, and there's a buzzing in my ears that seems to get louder and louder. I pace the room as the knot of anxiety that needs to escape has nowhere to go.

When the burst of panic wears off, that darkness crawls its way back in, and when the tears start up, they turn instantly into sobs. "I'm sorry, Mom. I'm so sorry. I love you." My voice breaks around the words. "So much. Just, please, wake up. I need you. We all need you."

Then, when my throat gets scratchy, I talk to her in my head, hoping with everything in me that her subconscious hears me like she believes it will.

I'm holding her hand in exhausted silence when I look to see Riley and Eva standing in the doorway. I wave them in, and they rush to Mom's bedside, their faces full of concern.

"Do they know anything?" Eva puts her hands on my shoulders.

I slowly shake my head. "No. We just have to sit and wait. Her vitals are stable."

The two take a seat, each taking turns talking to Mom with voices they're clearly forcing to stay even.

That's when it hits me—they're giving it all they have to stay strong. For Mom. But for me too.

And that means everything.

When there's a lull in the conversation, I automatically open my mouth to ask Riley about what happened with Pet IQ today, but I realize I don't care about that pitch, Fur Bebé, RezQ... any of it. In fact, it all seems so silly and ridiculous now, I wonder how I ever cared.

None of it matters without Mom.

At the thought, I swallow back a fresh wave of anguish. The darkness approaches.

Thankfully, Eva interrupts my thoughts. "Your mom would tell us to talk to her on the astral plane."

I force my brain to concentrate on the here and now. "She would say that."

We all close our eyes as we focus on reaching her there, and I regret not asking her to explain what the astral plane looks like so I could visualize it.

But I invent my own astral plane with lilacs, cool breezes, sunsets, and autumn-brushed hillsides.

When we finish, and no one has anything else to say, time seems to drag on to infinity with nothing happening.

I finally send the two of them away, telling them I'll let them know if something changes. They can't do anything more here except stare at Mom.

Riley heads back to Fur Bebé, and Eva promises to pick up Dolly and Llama and take them to her apartment.

I fall into another long drag of silence, so I decide to read Mom a book. I find a good Regency bodice ripper I have on my Kindle, putting some *umph* into the approaching intimate scene. Clearly, Mom would enjoy it if she could hear me. On the chance she can, I want to make sure she's entertained. I feign breathlessness as I read, "'Oh, you magnificent beast!' Lady Hemmingsworth cried out as the Viscount penetrated her engorged petals—"

"Sophie?" It's Eva.

I flip around. "What's wrong?"

"I'm sorry, but my key to the Winnebago isn't working."

"It's okay—it's tricky, and you have to jiggle it just right." I hesitate, torn on what to do. I can't leave the dogs without care. Finally, I say, "Actually, it'd probably be good for me to come with you. I could use a quick shower and a change of clothes."

"Okay, hon. Thank you."

I'm slow to walk out, hoping Mom wakes up, but also hoping she doesn't so she won't feel scared or alone.

But I'll race right back.

# # #

When I return, there's a gigantic bouquet of wildflowers sitting on Mom's bedside table. When I check the note to see who it's from, there's no name, but it reads, "I'm practicing the visualization techniques you taught me, which is how I know you're going to be just fine. Thank you for this gift of peace, and I'll see you when you wake up."

Lucas. My heart somehow simultaneously pinches and expands at the very same moment, and I'd do anything to be in his arms right now.

I wonder if he sent this arrangement, or if he stopped by? He's in town for the Pet IQ pitch.

Nurse Clara walks in to check vitals, and I sit down in the chair. "Any update?" I say, my breath catching. I ache to hear that there's been something, anything.

"Sorry, sweetie. Sometimes these things just take time." She pats my hand. "But boy, is your mama sure loved. There was a mighty handsome young fellow here while you were gone. He was chatting it up with her like they were just the best of friends."

I manage a weak smile through the pinpricks at the back of my eyes. "They are."

When the nurse leaves, Mom gets a visit from Vorian-5, Shannon, the manager at the shelter, and Roach and his pregnant wife too.

Indeed, Mom is very loved.

Then I continue reading the bodice ripper to her until delirium settles in. It's worrisome that she's still asleep, although I keep pushing that out of my mind because I have to.

If only I could get comfortable in this recliner chair.

Thinking about how Mom wanted me to eat, I nibble on my sandwich from the cafeteria, unsure of what to do next. I peer out the window, which is a view of a bricked wall. Dusk is setting in, and the sky, at least what I can see of it above the wall, is transforming into an orange-red blanket of shadowy clouds. The gods of distraction are luring me outside, but I can't go. Leaving before was torture—all I could think about was if Mom was waking up without me. Or taking a turn for the worse because I wasn't here. Nope. I'm not doing that again.

A text message pops up on my phone. It's from Lucas, and my pulse speeds up.

Lucas: *Just wanted you to know I'm keeping your mom and you in my thoughts. And I'm sending you this because I know you can't go outside right now.*

The next text is an image.

My heartbeat gushes in my ears. As I tap on it, a photo of a postcard-worthy sunset appears. The deep shades of the sinking sun dominate the sky. Trees of countless shapes and sizes cast their shadows against the vibrant backdrop.

Then a new image appears, almost identical to the first, but with the scene shifted downward.

My breath hitches before stopping entirely.

Lucas is taking pictures of each moment of the sunset and texting them to me. This is better than dinner at a five-star restaurant, or jewelry, or anything else any man has ever done for me.

Before I can even process what that means, another image pops up. The sun's vanished, and a deep, blood-red shade blankets the sky. But by now, thoughts of Lucas rival the photos for my attention.

How does he know just the perfect way to soothe me? How can he make an unbearable situation almost bearable?

What I assume to be the last picture appears on my screen. All that remains of the display is a rusty sky tinted with a pearly mist, a lingering sparkle brushing the edges of the clouds. This looks more like an abstract painting than the real-life picture it is.

Lucas—a walking contradiction with his sharp suits, cowboy snap shirts, and impossibly ugly sandals. The guy with zero sensitivity on the job, but a sixth sense otherwise.

He's the one—the only one—who bandages my ouchies right along with my bruised and battered heart.

I have no idea what to reply. I sit, trying to calm myself enough to find the right words to respond, realizing there are none that are sufficient. I settle on:

Me: *Wow. Thank you.*

Lucas: *No problem. Just didn't want u to miss it, that's all.*

Me: *Glad I didn't.*

Lucas: *I know this sounds hocus-pocusey, but I feel like your mom's going to be okay.*

Me: *I believe you.*

My fingers quake, and I struggle to type those words. Not because they're not true, but because they are. I *do* believe him, which is comforting, but at the same time, deeply unnerving.

I sit motionless, desperately hoping to see the reply from him I've been aching for since the day he helped me pitch Madame Puuccí in the bathroom of Chateau LeBlanc's lobby.

I'm falling for you, too.

It never comes.

# # #

I must've finally drifted off, because I'm jarred awake by Riley's voice. "Sophie?"

"What? Who?" My eyes dart to Mom, who's still asleep.

My heart plummets, but I turn and meet Riley's empathetic gaze. She says, "Has she woken up yet?"

"No." My shoulders sag. "What time is it?"

"Around four," she says.

"Four? Mom and I have slept all day?" I scramble to look at my phone.

"Four *a.m.*" Riley touches my shoulder.

"Oh, good." My head is still clearing. "Wait, why are you here at four a.m.?"

Riley wrings her hands. "Well, I managed to sneak past the front desk. I wanted to stop by to see Skye, of course. But I also wanted to give you an update. About Pet IQ."

"Okay." I'm sure she's going to tell me Pet IQ selected Fur Bebé, and honestly, I don't care. But why would she come at four a.m. to tell me that?

I realize that this is the first time I've even thought about the implications of the Pet IQ meeting. Clearly, everything that I thought I ever cared about means nothing right now.

Riley sighs. "The meeting was delayed until eight a.m. today."

"Come again?"

"It was put on hold. Lucas delayed it because of a 'family emergency.'"

Shocked, I blink. "Lucas had a family emergency too?"

"No. He was referring to your mom. He left the meeting to come see her."

"What?" I know it's been the longest fifteen hours of my life, but Riley's saying ludicrous things right now. Something warms my chest when I say, "Lucas thinks of Mom as family?"

"Yes."

When I'm past that realization, another one hits. "Lucas postponed the most important meeting of his life to come see Mom?"

"Yes."

"Why would he do that?" I blurt, my lips now numb.

"He said because someone taught him that doing the right thing is more important than the bottom line."

I put both hands over my mouth, my heart doing that cymbal thing in my chest again. "He really said that?"

"Yes."

"Would you and Lucas just get together already? I'm getting too damn old for this." Mom squeaks out, croaky.

My head whips toward her, amazed. "Mom, you're awake!"

"Skye." Riley's voice shakes. "You're back."

"Who could sleep with you two yammering on like old hens?"

I chuckle, inhaling my first real breath since all this happened. "So, what's the date today?"

"I don't know." She looks around, then back at me. "But I never know. No, wait." She glances back and forth between Riley and me.

"It's October twentieth. The day Pet IQ's picks RezQ to be in their stores. But I've been asleep for a while. Maybe that was yesterday."

"No." I smile.

She rubs her head. "So there really is something wrong with my noggin'? Great."

"No, you were right about the date. That *was* yesterday. But Pet IQ didn't select RezQ." My smile grows. "Yet."

"Or Fur Bebé," Riley adds. "The pitch meeting has been rescheduled for today."

"Well, then. Let's go." Mom fumbles as she tries to throw her covers off.

"No, you can't get out of bed!" I push her back down. "You have a nasty concussion. You fell off the Winnebago."

"Oh, yeah." She touches her bandaged head. "You were right, Soph. The Winnebago's roof has mold. When I stepped on it, it started to cave, so I jumped away. That's when I fell."

I cringe, icy shivers running through my veins. My chest is tight when I say, "Mom, promise me you'll never go up on the roof by yourself again."

"Promise," she mumbles.

Wow, that was way too easy.

Clara comes in to check on Mom, thrilled to see her awake. While she's checking Mom's vitals, Mom asks, "So, can I go now?"

"Not yet, darlin'," Clara says, taking the stethoscope out of her ears and letting it fall to her shoulders. "We need to keep you overnight for observation. You're just gonna have to take it easy, okay?"

Mom taking it easy. *Right.*

"Humph." Mom nods toward the door. "Sophie, can you go to the cafeteria to get me something to eat? I know these places serve crap food, so I just want cake or ice cream. Something they can't screw up."

"Got it." I pat her arm and stand.

"And then after that, go do that pitch. I have a good feeling."

I don't respond because I can't agree to that. I'm not leaving her.

Mom glares at me. "If you don't go, I'm gonna walk out of this hospital and drag you there. Do you want that?"

"No."

"Then go do the pitch."

I gulp in some much-needed air. "Okay."

"Good." Mom grabs her phone and starts punching at it. "I'm telling Lucas I'm okay."

I nod. "Great. He came by."

"I know," Mom says without looking up from her phone.

Before I can ask Mom how she knows that, Riley says, "Uh, Soph, there's a reason I got here early," her voice tentative. "We need to get your presentation down to two minutes. I realized that's probably all you've got since you're not supposed to be at the pitch meeting."

"Right. Good point, Riles."

Her eyes narrow. "Yeah, well, I want a job at RezQ when Fur Bebé goes under."

"You got it."

34

Snaked

I enter the vast ballroom wearing my lucky gray Fendi long-tailed blazer and carrying my briefcase of samples. With my chin held high, I march past the Bebé's executives on one side, Whiffany's executives on the other, and continue toward Pet IQ's team at the intimidating, marble table up front.

Making my way up the infinitely long aisle, I feel smaller and smaller as tension whirls in the air. The buzz of chatter stops, leaving the room dreadfully quiet.

Frank Franklin peers at me over the rim of his glasses. "Sophie Fox. You have a habit of showing up to places uninvited."

"That might be true, but I *was* invited here, sir." I sniff. "Madame Puuccí extended me an invitation at the *Bridesmaid to Bride* wedding. I have the same right to be here as everyone else. She loved my portfolio—and that's because what I have to offer is about to disrupt the industry."

His eyes bulge. "That's quite a claim."

Alice Jones, Pet IQ's new VP of Products, scoffs. "Ms. Fox, you're not on Madame Puuccí's list, and we don't have extra time in our schedule today."

"Now hold on," Frank cuts in. "I think we can spare a few minutes to hear about something that may disrupt the industry..." he trails off, side-eying me.

"Oh, It will. Definitely." I smile brightly.

Alice Jones frowns. "Take a seat, Ms. Fox. Our team needs to discuss this."

My pulse kicks into top gear, but I force it into neutral—I can't get my hopes up too high.

"I'm sorry to interrupt, but it's pertinent." Hugh stands. "I feel obligated to remind this distinguished committee that Sophie Fox broke into Missy Mulligan's computer and stole a presentation. I would question her integrity and originality."

"No way." Lucas flies up out of his chair, hurt and fury coiled on his face. "Uncle Hugh, you know that's not true."

My heart crashes around my ribcage as I lose the battle to tame it. My skin ignites, and I begin to see the scene around me in high definition. The words come easily. "If you really believe that, Hugh, why did you offer me my job back at Fur Bebé?"

Hugh's lips twitch as he clearly fights to come up with a response. Finally, he puffs his chest and says, "It's my obligation to this industry to ensure Ms. Fox doesn't do more harm."

Alice Jones cut in with, "I'm sorry, Ms. Fox, but after everything happening with Madame Puuccí, we can't risk any more threats to our reputation. We need to play it safe and side with Hugh Nevarez."

Lucas's eyes skim the room, desperate. "Ms. Fox never stole anything. As demonstrated time and again, she's a brilliant idea person with no need. In fact, it's Ms. Fox who had *her* presentation stolen. She was set up to take the fall."

"You'll have to excuse my nephew." Hugh's tone vibrates with suppressed rage. "He's quite fond of Ms. Fox and is struggling to see the situation clearly."

"I'm seeing clearly for the first time since I took this job." Lucas's jaw clenches, his whiskey eyes shadowed.

"I got this, Lucas," I say. Here he goes again, risking his job again for me. "I have grown a strong, solid reputation with RezQ, and have a devoted following. I'd bring Pet IQ all my socially conscious goodwill and fans, both things that *boost* reputations."

Hugh stands. "Ms. Fox has no infrastructure. It's all marketing hullabaloo."

Lucas groans. "Hugh, it's evident that you and a few others on the Fur Bebé board will lie, cheat, and stomp on heads to climb to the top." Lucas's nose flares as he hesitates, his face torqued in dismay. "I can't work for a company without scruples."

My pulse feels like it's in a high-speed car chase—and mixed with the amount of heat flowing through my body—I could almost be engulfed in a carbeque.

Hugh shoots Lucas a glare so fiery, it's almost as though flames lick his irises. "Sit down, Mr. Nevarez. Or you're finished."

"Not a chance." Without missing a beat, Lucas packs up his things. "No more, Uncle." He marches across the infinite room to stand beside me in my lone seat.

I break into shivers, as though my fever broke, and the heat evaporated. I turn to meet Lucas's eyes, sending him a thousand thank yous in an adoring gaze. I'm too numb to do anything else.

All I know, in this moment, is that he has my heart, all of it, for as long as it beats.

Our gaze locks, and I swear, by the intensity of his eyes shimmering gold, he feels the same. A moment passes between us where it's just him and me, an infinite connection. It's as if there's no one else in the room.

But then, adrenaline kick-starts my mouth into motion. "If this distinguished committee can spare just two minutes, I can tell you everything you need to know."

After conferring with his team, Frank Franklin says, "Once we hear from Fur Bebé and Whiffany, you've got two minutes, Ms. Fox."

"Thank you." If I could do a cartwheel right now, I would.

Whiffany & Co is up first, and I guess Smithy Baldwin must've gotten good feedback from his lingerie modeled at Le Chienne Couture, as he went all in on it. Unfortunately, Pet IQ is clearly unimpressed, bordering on insulted.

Frank Franklin rubs his eyes. "Okay, Fur Bebé, let's see what you've got."

Missy approaches the podium, and for the first time, she doesn't look so confident. "Hello, Mr. Franklin, distinguished Pet IQ executives. The Fur Bebé team and I prepared..." she trails off, glancing at Hugh. He gives her a nod, and she swallows hard. Her cheeks go rosy, and her voice lacks its usual luster when she says, "We prepared one pitch, but after seeing that dog weddings are trending like a tidal wave, I'm going to present a new pitch—a much more exciting one."

"*Dog* weddings? What makes you think dog weddings are trending?" Alice says, frowning.

"You may want to hold off on that question until you see the data." Missy flips up a chart I created, which is actually accurate and persuasive—because that helps me.

"Wow, if that chart is true, then you're right—it is." Alice nods, eyebrows perked.

"I told Missy that she couldn't present this," Lucas whispers. "But I guess now that I'm gone..." he trails off, shrugging.

"Good call," I whisper back. "Looks like Hugh's making her."

Missy's face contorts into a feigned smile. "So, without further ado, allow me to introduce Fur Bebé's exclusive wedding attire—snakeskin gowns with matching bow ties and cummerbunds."

I purse my lips to hold my face expressionless as I hear a collection of gasps.

Once again, she stole my presentation, verbatim. Except now, my words are ridiculous, which she seems to understand. It's Hugh that doesn't.

I glance at Fur Bebé to see Brock's and Mark McCoy's faces contort in shock. Unsurprisingly, Hugh's doesn't.

"Here are our snakeskin cowboy boots for those country dog weddings." Missy's voice cracks as she holds up a sample and spins its tiny spur.

"Okay." Frank Franklin puts a hand up. "Snakeskin wedding wear?"

"It's a bit out there, I realize." Missy laughs nervously. "But as the first to introduce designer pet wedding wear, we need to solidify ourselves as trailblazers."

Another line of mine.

"That's not trailblazing, that's just... tacky—I gotta be honest." Alice's irritated voice echoes through the room. "Not to mention you're killing animals in these designs. An animal company killing animals?"

Frank Franklin pinches the bridge of his nose. "That's the daftest thing I've ever heard."

"We can make them with faux snakeskin." Missy's voice trembles. "Here, look at this fang-toothed tiara made from crystals."

Frank Franklin squeezes his eyes shut. "All right. I've seen enough."

"If I may," Hugh cuts in. "We have another presentation on our formalwear that we think you'll love."

"Your time is up, Fur Bebé." Frank Franklin's voice is firm.

Hugh goes to argue, but when Frank points a finger at him with a stern expression, Hugh stops and slumps in his chair, red-faced.

I step up to the podium, nerves exploding in my gut as I look at the Pet IQ executives in crisp, designer suits, all eyeing at me with derision except Frank Franklin. I'll just focus on him.

I pull out the dress Raven had me make for her newly adopted shelter dog, Princess Dogana. "This is a dress that will be worn next Saturday, at Novu Villa country club, for a very exclusive dog wedding."

"Wow, another presentation about dog weddings. And what makes y'all think dog wedding wear will be good in Pet IQ stores?" Alice's frown is deep. "When we're not targeting the ultra-rich?"

"Great question, Ms. Jones." I flip up the poster board that Riley and I made. "Because we're not just dealing with the uber wealthy, we're dealing with famous people. Raven Monroe, fitness star, is hosting tomorrow's wedding with several high-profile guests. Eli Monet, host of Project Fashionista and major influencer, just purchased three items from the Vera Wag collection. He's *the* trend-setter. Everyone and their dog, pun intended, will want dog weddings after this."

"Good answer, Ms. Fox." Frank Franklin smiles.

Kristen Yale, Pet IQ's CFO, brushes a twisted lock of graying hair from her face. "But how are you, alone, in any position to fulfill orders, nationwide?"

"That's a weak spot, I admit. But that's just logistics. What you get when you get me is the creative mind that disrupts industries. Isn't it worth juggling a few logistics for that?"

She tilts her head in approval. "I've got to say—you make a compelling argument."

"Thank you." I walk back to my seat, hopeful for the first time since Madame Puuccí resigned.

After a short dismissal, the Pet IQ team returns to the table, and my nerves ratchet back up again.

Frank stands before he says, "We want to thank each of you all for your time and efforts today and allowing us to hear your ideas for what we should carry in our stores. And because this was an extremely difficult decision, we still need more information."

And my heart sinks again, like the downspin of the yo-yo.

Frank clears his throat. "Sophie, Lucas, can you join me up front?"

And the yo-yo that's my heart spins back up.

Frank Franklin wants to talk to us alone. That's good, right? Inside, I'm squealing. Outside, I'm glowing as I shoot Lucas a hopeful smile.

Once we're in front of Frank Franklin, he says, "Sophie, we love what you're doing with RezQ. We think the brand will fit in our stores, and we want to be a company that gives to animals in need. Our problem, as we mentioned, is logistics. We aren't prepared to take on all the needs of another line when we have our own. What we want to know is if you're interested in raising capital and getting the cash flow to get operations up to par?"

I open my mouth but close it because I don't want to promise something I can't deliver. I've never sought any capital, nor do I know the first thing about creating investor packages. But that doesn't mean I'm not willing to try.

Before I can respond, Lucas says, "I'm highly experienced at seeking angel investors and getting promising companies off the ground. It's what I do."

"Right." Frank Franklin interlaces his fingers. "Would you be willing to do that for RezQ?"

"Absolutely." Lucas doesn't hesitate.

My heart, back on the upswing, feels like it's almost in my throat. My pulse roars in my ears, and I'm not sure I heard right. Did Lucas just offer to lead my company?

Frank's eyebrows arch. "Sophie, how do you feel about partnering with Lucas?"

My mouth is numb, but I manage to say, "I think that's a great idea." I glance at Lucas. "We make an excellent team."

"Well, then." Franklin clasps his hands. "If you're both willing to do that, then Pet IQ is willing to partner with you."

My mouth says, "Howdy, partner." As soon as my brain catches up, I close my eyes. "Bad joke, sorry."

I open them to see Franklin grinning. "Eh, I have a soft spot for corny jokes. I do that myself." He extends his hand.

I shake it.

"Count me in." Lucas nods before pumping Frank Franklin's hand.

I turn toward Fur Bebé's team to see a table of stunned faces. Hugh looks like his head is about to explode, and Missy is about to cry. Nope, she *is* crying.

Lucas offers to walk me out, and as soon as we're out the rotating doors of the building, he pulls me into a hug, lifting me and twirling me around as I squeal. "I knew you could do it," he says. "And you amaze me."

I pull out of the hug to meet his eyes. "You're pretty amazing yourself."

"So, that was you? Behind the snakeskin thing."

My mouth curves into a conspiratorial smile. "Possibly."

"That trailblazing comment. That sounded like you," he says. I bust into a laugh, and Lucas joins me. He shakes his head when he says, "You got Missy good."

"It seemed like it was your uncle behind it, actually."

His tone turns heavy. "After what I saw today, I'm certain it was my uncle who was behind it. And he was probably who helped Missy from the beginning. It makes sense. He was an IT guy before starting up Fur Bebé, so he knew what to do."

"Wow. Hugh's really something." I decide to ask the question that's been eating me for a while. "Why did you come to Atlanta to help him?"

Lucas hesitates. "He's family, and he supported me a lot after my mom died and my dad was checked out, drowning in grief. Uncle Hugh took me under his wing and taught me about business. I wouldn't be where I am without him, that's for sure. He can be a heartless jerk, but I owed him. Or I thought I did. Until I had to draw the line."

"Right."

"I'm sorry." He touches my shoulder.

I put my hand over his. "I'm sorry too. I mean, that Hugh let you down so much."

"Yeah, that sucks. But I'm glad he and Missy both got what they had coming."

"As my mom would say, cosmic boomerangs are heartless shrews."

"Your mom knows." He grins. "And I'm so glad she's okay."

"Me too." I move my hand to give him a hefty pat on the back. "Well, welcome to the team, Lucas Nevarez. CEO of RezQ."

"I like the sound of that." He tilts his head. "I guess my personal and professional life just collided." His grin spread. "In the best possible way."

That they sure did.

35

The Puzzle

I park the bling machine, then rush over to wrap a supportive arm around Mom's back and help her from the car into the Winnebago. She doesn't want help, and she probably doesn't need it, but tough.

Getting Mom settled on the couch with some hot tea, I take a seat next to her, touching her bruised face. She looks at me with an expression I don't recognize when she says, "I can't believe you'd blow the most important meeting of your life for me."

I furrow my brows. "Of course I did. You're my mom."

Doesn't she know how much I love her? But can I blame her? I took her for granted for far too long. And I owe her a long overdue apology—I'll never wait on that again. "I'm so sorry about the things I said." I take her hand.

She runs a finger over my hair. "You have the right to be angry that I didn't tell you about that picture and the story behind it. I don't know if I'll ever forgive myself for that. I'm sorry, although I know sorry isn't enough."

"You were trying to protect me. Like always." I sip my tea. "You know, today and these last few weeks have helped me understand something about myself." I swallow hard. "I've been caught up in the idea that if I had career success, then I'd be better than the world I came from. But you can't outrun yourself or leave behind who you are. Everything that's happened, us launching RezQ, helping animals get adopted, getting the truth out about Yum Breaths. And helping Missy hang herself. We did that."

"We did do that, Soph. You should be proud."

"I am." I smile. "I *am* proud of who I am and where I came from. And I'm proud of both of us for what we had to overcome to get to where we are."

Mom reaches out and pats my knee. "I'm sorry that I didn't do better by you. Give you every opportunity..." She blinks back tears. "I failed you."

"No, you didn't." I scoot closer to her and cover her hand with mine. "Do you realize how special you are? You figured out that a company was poisoning animals. You make friends with everyone, and they all respect you for your abilities."

"So, you admit I have abilities?"

"Of course, Mom. You have a magnetic personality. You help people every day, saving puppies, stopping people from jumping off cliffs, finding love for the lonely, giving your clients something to believe in. The truth of the matter is you're a better person than I'll ever be."

"Oh, honey." Mom grabs my hand, a tear tumbling down her cheek. "You're a wonderful person. You've made some mistakes, but not nearly as many as I have."

"Like you told me, maybe all the things that happened to us were for a reason. We make a great team."

Mom gives me a weak smile. "You were a little lost, just like I've been my whole life. And I didn't want you to end up like me. Old and still drifting around. But you're finding yourself. My Sophie's a fighter and survivor." She brushes my hair away from my eyes. "But now, look. You're pulling off sting operations. And you're intuitive, you just haven't been open to it. But you're getting there." She nods in satisfaction. "More every day."

"You're very strong, Mom."

"So, are you, Soph."

"Well, I got it from you. How many daughters can say their mothers make the cover of *Hog Honeys*?"

"I'm pretty bad-ass, aren't I?" Mom snickers. "Sorry that I have terrible taste in men. But apparently, you don't. At least not any more."

I nod. "Maybe you're right. Ahhh, Lucas. Sometimes I love to hate him."

"The man you love to hate is your greatest love of all."

"True. How come you're so wise except for when it comes to yourself? Why can't you follow your own advice and find the love you help others find?"

"I've tried, Soph. At this point, I'm lucky to find a man who can drive at night and has a little unemployment left."

"Your lesson in life is to learn that you deserve the love you think everyone else deserves."

"Maybe you're right." She yawns, still looking terribly worn out. "But that's for another day."

Mom makes a toast with her teacup, and I study her as I see her in a new light. I'm not so sure what to think about her anymore. I still don't believe she's "psychic," but she has an amazing talent for reading people, feelings and situations. Her intuition is her gift, seeing nuances beyond what the rest of us can. Maybe she isn't kooky after all, but way ahead of her time. Maybe it's the rest of us who aren't enlightened enough to see her talent.

Mom touches her cup to forehead and says, "And a toast to you too, third eye."

Nah, she's still kooky.

# # #

The next morning, Mom tries to get up from my dining table bed herself, and I push her back down, saying, "What do you need?"

"Coffee—please."

"Sure." As I stand, she heaves out a breath and stares into the distance. Worried, I ask, "Are you feeling okay?"

"I'm fine. But Sophie, there's something I need to tell you."

As I head to the kitchenette, the front door flings open, and Eva and Riley come busting in.

Eva's carrying the crate with Dolly and Llama in it, and when she unzips it, Dolly and Llama run straight to Mom.

She cries out in joy, cuddling her two babies.

I get a text from Lucas telling me to check my email. I'm nervous as I get on my laptop and go to my account. It's chock full of unread emails, but I only click on his. The subject is, "You Aren't Gonna Believe This..."

The first line has a link that takes me to the sales of the Vera Wag collection. I gasp when I see what appears on the screen—sales have shot through the roof. I was expecting that to happen when Eli Monet posts his dog wedding photos, but that's not until next week. So, I go to Lucas's other link which takes me to Billy Road's FaceSnap account. The picture is of him, his trademark gray ponytail slung over one shoulder as he stands, grinning, between a lab and a shepherd. The dogs are decked out, head to paws in Vera Wag dresses, and RezQ is credited for everything. It says, "Getting ready for our first dog wedding today."

"Holy smokes," I mumble. "This can't be real."

After I show everyone my computer, Eva and Riley sit in shock. Mom has an unreadable expression on her face.

"Billy Road. The amazing singer." Eva shakes her head. "Just advertised our stuff. He has it bad for you, Skye."

Mom sits, quietly. When the silence from them gets to be too much, I say, "What's going on?"

"Did you ever register for OriginLinx.com?" Mom's voice goes creepily soft.

"Oh, yeah. I got the email, but I've been so busy doing RezQ stuff, I forgot to do that yet." That's not entirely true. Okay, that's an outright lie.

"You need to. Right now." Mom's tone is weird as she jumps up, fetches my laptop, then boots it up before she hands it back to me.

When I find the email, I click on the link. It takes me to my account that I have to finish setting up, but there's a message in my account's inbox. After clicking on it, I say, "I have a 'family' request from a Maddox Winter."

"Holy crap on a cracker." Riley's mouth is open so wide it looks like a Venus Fly Trap in full bloom.

I accept the request, then I say, "I don't understand. It has us linked up as half brother and sister."

Riley's voice is hoarse. "Maddox Winter is Billy Road's son."

My ears ring from the blood gushing through them so fast. My palms clam, and it almost feels like I'm floating out of my own body. "I don't understand."

Mom shoots Riley a look, and Riley puts her hand on Eva's back before saying, "We're gonna go for a jog, right, Eva?"

"Um, sure. Yeah—let's do that."

After the two are out of the Winnebago, Mom lets out a long exhale. "Billy Road is your father," she whispers, her eyes misting.

"But my father's dead. He overdosed on drugs." I'm furiously shaking my head.

Mom's voice is even, gentle. "Billy is short for William, and Road is his stage name. His real last name is Winter. He had a twin brother who overdosed twenty-four years ago—named Henry."

"Henry Winter." I hear myself say. My dad. Or who I thought was my dad.

Mom says, "When I saw Billy Road in the parking lot of Chateau LeBlanc, I recognized him. I mean, I never did on TV or on stage because he looks so different from how he did before he got famous. Apparently, they had him completely redo his look to be more mainstream. But up close, in person, I knew those eyes and that charisma anywhere. *He* was the guy I met at the LGTBQ rally. After all these feelings I've been having about something not being right about your dad, I asked him if he'd been at that rally, and if he remembered me from that night. He was, and he did—I couldn't believe it." She swallows hard. "Then I asked him about the day I came to talk to him two years later when he was playing drums in Midtown. He didn't remember me that time, and told me he's never played drums, but his twin brother did."

I can't feel my lips, but I manage to say, "So, the man who rejected me was Billy Road's brother."

"Yes. Henry said he didn't remember me from the rally, and I thought he was just trying to get out of being responsible for you. But he really didn't remember me because he wasn't there."

"Holy moly."

"Right. Then I asked Billy Road why he told me his name was Henry. He said it was a stupid thing he and his brother did at the time, telling girls the other's name to cause each other grief."

Her words are echoed, like I'm in a tunnel, and I can't grasp what's happening. "I still don't get it. Why did Henry ask you to his place when I was four?"

"I don't know, honey. Maybe he wanted to help figure this out for his brother."

My brain is spinning so fast, each thought flashes through my mind as the next one hits.

My father is alive. *Alive.*

As I stare at the beige walls of the Winnebago, I think about the biographies I watched about Billy Road, and how he stopped doing drugs after his brother overdosed. Then he fell off the map for a while after a couple of stints in rehab before one finally stuck. When he reemerged into the spotlight, he was a different person and a different artist. A much better one. "I just can't believe this," I mumble to myself. "I need air."

I walk out the door and sit under the awning, letting the morning air brush my face. Every neuron in my brain swirls as it fights to process all this.

Thoughts hit my mind like gunfire, one after the next. My father is Billy Road, one of my favorite artists. One of the most talented musicians on earth. And Mom was with him.

When I hear the Winnebago door open, I turn to see Mom on the front steps, holding two whiskeys on the rocks.

"Mom, you can't be drinking after your injury!"

"I'm just going to have a little bit. Get off my back. We both need this." She shuffles over and hands me one.

She's right about that. "Thank you." I stand and help her into the other collapsible chair. Then I say, "Were you one of his groupies?"

"No way! I was with him before he was famous." She sighs. "I don't do the star chasing thing."

"You don't. That's why I was surprised you seemed so starstruck when Billy was at your window."

"I was in shock."

"Do you think I'd be good at the guitar?" I have no idea why I asked that question. It just kind of came out.

"Now, how would I know that, Soph?"

"I dunno. You're psychic." I take a sip of the whiskey, letting it burn before I hack out a cough.

"I believe you can do anything you set your mind to."

I see Eva and Riley jogging together, and I wave them over. After I catch them up on the conversation. Riley says, "So, the Urban Productions—that's Maddox Winter's company."

"Ohhh." I go bug-eyed. "So, that lawyer. He wasn't trying to serve me papers because Missy was suing me. He was reaching out because of Maddox?"

"Seems like it." Riley nods.

"But how would Maddox know to come looking for me?"

Riley shakes her head. "We were trying to figure that out too."

"He must've gotten a clue from somewhere," Eva adds.

After we all tire of straining our brains, I give up and say, "So, what are you two doing now?"

Eva hitches a thumb over her shoulder. "We'll just be at my place. Call us."

"You'll both be there?" I ask.

Riley looks at Eva before she returns her gaze to me. "Eva's letting me stay with her longer term. Until I'm back on my feet."

"That's great news!" I smile, my eyes glossing over. "We really are a family, aren't we?"

"Yes, y'all are my only family now." Riley's eyes glisten. "I hope that's okay."

"More than okay." I stand and pull the two of them into a hug. Then, we don't want to leave Mom out, so we shuffle over to her and include her in the group hug.

After a few seconds, Mom says, "Okay, get off me. I can't breathe, maggots." Mom's voice is gruff, but the mist in her eyes tells the true story.

36

Princess Bride

We're back at Novu Villa to celebrate the nuptials of Princess Dogana and Ludwig Von Steak.

I'm thrilled to be here—especially when October is taking its final bow—because the place is stunning. And today is a perfect day for a wedding—dogs and humans alike. The crew is with me: Mom, Riley, Eva, and West. Since Lucas wasn't already wrapped into this as "staff" like the rest of us, he'd have to pay the hefty price tag to attend. Plus, he has to work today—it's critical he finish the investor funding packets so RezQ can seal the deal with Pet IQ.

The twinkling lights and floating lanterns take on a golden glow, a reflection of the autumn's blooms.

And the bride, Princess Dogana, a white Pomeranian, stuns in her ivory Vera Wag mermaid wedding gown of sequins, lace, and pearls.

The best man, Mr. D, couldn't be more handsome in his custom, freshly designed RezQ tuxedo.

That's right. Fur Bebé officially found another face of the company, allowing me to finally adopt Mr. D. They said they wanted a "fresher face." And now, I can bring Mr. D with me on my adventures.

Today's guest list is impressive, and we've even got a couple of bigger names that we're excited to meet. A B-list actor, a cooking show host, and a FaceSnap fitness sensation who's a close friend of Raven's.

I cannot believe that this event raised enough for animal shelters to make a real dent in the problem, at least locally. It feels amazing.

After my team and I prepare the dogs and walk them through their rehearsal, using treats, the guests filter in and fill the white satin-covered chairs.

The string quartet starts, and I shake off nerves.

The dogs have been properly trained, so it's out of my hands now. It'll go how it goes.

Canon in D plays while, one by one, different members of Raven's family walk the two groomsmen and two bridesmaids down the aisle, or in this case, over the moat. But I'm the one who has the honor of escorting Mr. D.

Raven, glowing in her mother-of-the-bride matching gown, is next to Princess Dogana, and they begin their march as the string quartet plays an original rendition of "Here Comes the Bride."

Raven's eyes mist as she escorts Princess Dogana over the moat, the bride's long train of sequins shimmering in the sunlight.

Our dog training pays off, and each member of the wedding party stays in place. All the groomsmen and bridesmaids sit neatly in a row, doing just as they should, the only mishap occurring when Lady Paw Paw veers off course to eat a giant fly.

After an exchange of barked vows, the officiant—an animal rescue veterinarian—leads the guests through a slideshow of the way their donations will be spent to help animals in need, with pictures of those still waiting to be rescued.

When the reception kicks off, I can finally relax. Eva's bustling around with food and drinks, West is on the dance floor, and Riley and Mom are at the bar doing a flight of top-shelf drinks.

Mr. D and I sit at our reserved table, which is adorned with gold silverware and crystal water and wine glasses. The centerpiece is a fire hydrant statue made of dog treats to keep our four-legged guests fed and happy. Eva's doing an amazing job catering. Together, Mr. D and I soak in the scene.

The dancing bodies, dressed in bright colors and textures, move around the floor like scarves in the wind. The tiny twinkling lights scattered about almost appear to be fireflies in the burnt orange sky. Dance music fills the air, harmonizing with the croaking frogs and chirping crickets.

After giving Mr. D a good head rub, I look up to see Lucas approaching.

My heart trips and falls over its next beat. He paid the two grand to attend this thing? *Late?*

Lucas is only a silhouette—the bright sun creating a warm halo around him—but I'd recognize that thick hair and those broad shoulders anywhere.

As he transforms into a three-dimensional person who's grinning at me, my lips stretch into a smile.

Mom wanders over and hands him a drink, saying, "Here's your martini with a lemon twist—and get this: Chopin vodka, your favorite."

"Oh, wow. You remembered. Thank you." Lucas raises his glass to her.

Really? Mom knows his favorite drink?

"So, Lucas, your aura is violet today, which is angelic." Mom clinks her glass on his before looking at me. "See, Soph, you should've trusted me. I was right about him."

I meet his gaze, feeling like I'm glowing myself. "Yeah, maybe you were." Mom's right about most things, and I didn't give her enough credit before. That stops now.

When she flutters away, I stand and approach him. "I can't believe you're here."

"I wouldn't have missed it. Well, after I got those investor packets sent."

He and I return to the table, and after he gives Mr. D a good scratch, he pulls out my chair for me. "May I offer you a seat?"

"Of course. And thank you, good sir."

After I sit, he takes a seat beside me before he raises his martini glass. "Cheers. To the remarkable woman who made all this happen."

"Thank you. But I couldn't have done it without you."

"I think you could have. It just might've taken you more time. And a few more bruises."

My smile's so big it almost reaches my eyes. "Thank you for saving me from further injury."

After a toast, Lucas leans back, his mouth curving when he says, "You know, I never did get a chance to tell you this. But hot-pink lace bras look good on you."

"Maybe I'll have to model it for you later."

He swallows hard. "Won't argue with that."

It's approaching dusk, and Lucas and I sit and enjoy the surrounding scene, debating whether we should join the dancing couples, or the playing dogs, for that matter. But we opt for a stroll through the botanical gardens.

Walking hand in hand with him feels perfectly right, like we've done this for years, even though it's our first time. It doesn't hurt that there's a rainbow of flowers scattered on the grounds around us, filling the air with citrus, honey, and freshly cut grass. I feel content... almost. There's something I have to ask Lucas. My stomach clenches when I say, "So, if you're staying here, what about Boston? And your dad?"

"Atlanta is growing on me. It's much warmer here. My dad can fly in anytime—he's got his own private jet." Lucas shrugs, a conspiratorial tug at the corner of his mouth. "And I've been offered a really important job. It's with a company that donates five percent of proceeds to charity."

"Now, that's a great idea. Props to the person who came up with it."

"She *is* pretty brilliant, I must say." An adoring glint flashes in his eye. He stops walking, his brows pinching as he seems to consider his words. Sure enough, his lips twitch before he says, "I need you to know this, though. I'm staying for the job. But I'm also staying for you." His Adam's apple bobs as he swallows hard, then he meets my gaze with eyes like melted caramel. "I'm in love with you, Sophie Fox."

My heart gallops like a pack of wild horses. Lucas is in love with me. *In love with me.* Others have said those words before, but it hadn't felt like this. Nothing has ever felt like this. Breathless, I rest my forehead against his when I say, "That's good to know. Because I'm in love with you, too, Lucas Nevarez."

He doesn't respond, at least not with words. He pulls me close before he brings his lips to mine.

Lucas is kissing me, and it's everything. Fiery and warm, natural and electric, urgent and easy. It's incredible. In a blissful haze, my lips yield to his tongue. He wraps his arms around me and pulls me closer. I would analyze it to death if I could form thoughts, but the only thing I can manage to do is breathe.

All the built-up tension rushes out, and this beautiful contrast of everything makes me wonder how any kiss has ever satisfied me before. As the warm Georgia breeze blows around us, I fall deeper into his arms, wanting to feel more of him. He grips me tighter too, opening himself up to me. Not able to stop, I take it all in.

Between breaths, I say, "We could go back to your place?"

"Oh," he says raggedly. "Good idea. Great idea. But just so you know, the sun's about to set."

"I see that. Do you wanna wait?"

He blinks. "Do you?"

"It looks like it's going to be auroral—the best kind." My brow perks.

"I'm good."

"Me too."

We miss the auroral sunset tonight.

And neither of us is one bit sorry.

37

Rolling Stone

"Are you ready for the best picnic ever?" Lucas loads a collapsible cooler into his car alongside some blankets.

"Absolutely." My smile must be glowing. This is the last step in celebrating our official partnership with Pet IQ. Last weekend, I took Lucas on a motorcycle trip that was *exactly* what we both needed—riding all day, the cool wind on our faces, then sleeping under the stars at night.

"So, now that you got a big partnership bonus, are you getting your own place?" Lucas says.

I shrug. "I'm actually gonna live with Mom a while longer. I had to use that check for something else. And believe me, it's something impossible to miss."

He smiles conspiratorially. "I can't wait."

Once we're both in the car, Lucas drives for a while, surprising me when he turns onto the freeway entrance. "We're going on quite a trek for a picnic." My curiosity piques.

"It's the perfect spot."

Soon we're in the middle of a traffic jam, so I sit up tall to peer as far down the highway as I can. "What's all this for? It's Saturday evening, and I don't see an accident."

"I'm not sure." Lucas keeps his eyes on the road.

Off in the distance, the Lakewood Amphitheater comes into view. "Oh, that's why. There's probably a concert tonight."

"Probably."

"Wait." The light flips on in my head. "This weekend Billy Road is playing. His November show."

Lucas glances at me, his face nervous. "Skye told me you wanted this. But if you don't, we can turn around. No problem at all."

After a few weeks thinking about it, I've decided watching my father play would be a great first step. I lean over and kiss Lucas's cheek. "Nope. I do want this. And you really are the best."

When we arrive, I should be surprised at what I see parked in the most remote corner of the amphitheater parking lot, but I'm not.

Mom's Winnebago. Except it's her new, WindWorm 2000 triple slideout that she'd been dreaming about. I point at it when I say, "I see you invited my mother."

"I did. And I see where your bonus went." He chuckles, shaking his head.

Lucas pulls up beside the new Winnebago before Mom steps out with Mr. D, who comes running into my arms.

"Well, hello, Mother." I readjust Mr. D, who's so excited he's about to fling out of my grip. "I see you were allowed to take up four parking spaces."

"I got a whole bunch of food and drinks too." Mom winks. "For free."

"Well, you did bang the lead singer, so—" I stop speaking as Riley, Eva, and West all step out of the Winnebago.

Riley approaches and grabs my hand. "We're all here for you."

I pull her into a hug. "Of course y'all are. You're always here for me. I love you, Riles." I don't miss the chance to tell my friends to tell them that anymore.

"Love you too."

Eva and West join in the hug, and West seems a bit too happy to be close to Eva.

Pulling away, Eva looks at me. "Your mom got us backstage passes. But only if you want."

I bite my lip. "I'm not sure."

"Then they're gone." Eva holds them over the trash and starts tearing them.

I dart over and snatch them away.

"Good." Eva smiles. "Then they must be what you really want."

"I guess I do."

I turn around to see Ted approaching me. I go wide-eyed. *Ted?* He's all cleaned up wearing an usher's jacket. "Hey, Sophie," he says with a glowing smile.

"Ted!" I beam. "So, you working the concert?"

"Billy gave me this job so I could finally have something to put on a resume. Plus, it's some cash for the week and free food."

My eyes go round. "I didn't know you knew Billy Road."

"I met his son when he came looking for you."

"So, his son was the young handsome fella asking for me." That makes sense. I talked to Maddox on the phone, and he said he came himself when his lawyer couldn't locate me. Maddox explained that he'd found a note from his late uncle that compelled him to reach out. So, it seems that Henry Winter *was* trying to get to the truth before he passed.

"I'm glad you came to see your dad, kid." Ted winks, turning and shuffling away, as only Ted can do.

We make our way to the hillside and take our seats on the grass. Mom on one side of me, Lucas on the other. He pulls out the blankets, flings one over us, then hands Mom the extra.

Mom puts on her biker jacket, and when she does, something falls out of the pocket. I look down to see the stone I collected when Lucas and I rode the Harley to the lookout point. Neither of us have worn the jacket since that day.

I pick it up, and hand it to her. "I found it and decided to keep it. It spoke to me."

Mom takes it. "Turquoise." She hits it up against another rock on the ground. A corner breaks off, revealing a brilliant aqua blue color underneath. "This stone symbolizes friendship. It means you've got a solid wingman in your life."

A warmth rushes through me as I take the rock from her and study it. When I picked it up, I didn't see its beauty or meaning. It was just another dull rock on the outside, but a gem on the inside.

In the past, I would've felt it was all a coincidence. I don't feel that way anymore. "Friendship," I say, taking Mom's hand. "And I do have a solid wingman. My wingmom."

Mom's eyes brighten the dusky sky. "Wingmom. I like it."

When Billy Road kicks off his show, he leans into the microphone and says, "This first song is going out to my daughter, who's here tonight."

The crowd roars, right along with my pulse racing in my ears.

Billy's voice goes raspy when he says, "We missed out on a lot, but here's to hoping we don't miss out on anything more."

I smile wistfully, hardly able to process that Billy Road is dedicating a song to *me*. His daughter. When he starts singing, I can't stop the tears from falling. Tears of joy, mostly, but a few tears of sadness too. I wish we hadn't lost out on so many years, but I'm beyond happy he wants to change all that, just as I do.

We all watch Billy Road in the typical incandescent Atlanta evening. Mom's "vision" had been right: I'm not sure about the soulmate part, but I *have* found someone who understands me and appreciates me for me. And I understand Lucas and appreciate him for him.

No more pushing each other away. No pretenses. Just a perfect fit.

Like his tattered, awful Birkenstocks.

Also by Terra Weiss

BLUE VINE STORIES

A Sweet, Small-Town RomCom Series

Finding Yesterday, Blue Vine Book One

Claire...My veil dangles from my fingers as I hightail it into a wine cellar instead of down the aisle. My caterer, famous bad boy chef, Jack Brady, provides a bottle opener and a listening ear. But the tragic past lingers between us like the smoke from a Southern barbeque. Buried secrets could send our dreams up in flames.

Cutting Chords, Blue Vine Book Two

Emma...Eight years ago, I had two loves: music and the awkward yet brilliant guitarist Will Evans. When he ghosted me, I lost both. Now, Will's back, admitting a secret had his heart locked away. The fire between Will and me reignites as we make music together again. But I have a secret of my own that could close Will's heart forever.

Restoring Hearts, Blue Vine Book Three

Charley...When my dead husband's best friend, Grant Bresser III, comes to town, the last thing I expect is to find him on the steps of

Town Hall trying to steal my grandfather's mountaintop estate. As Grant and I restore the place where my heart lives, I wonder if he's falling for more than the town of Blue Vine. But the bombshell lie my husband took to the grave threatens to leave our lives in ruins.

# # #

Join my readers group at for updates on the next Blue Vine Story and a brand new series. You'll also get two free novelettes, bonus content, short stories, and special giveaways!

About the Author

TERRA WEISS

Terra Weiss is a romcom author with a knack for witty banter and gift for capturing authentic family dynamics. Readers love how her stories steer away from typical romcom cookie-cutter formulas and show how real-life people find real-life love.

When Terra's not spilling the tea on what happens in the big and small towns that live in her heart, you'll find her with her spunky daughter, mad scientist husband, wacky and wonderful mother, and the two six-pound dogs that run her house. She enjoys jogging at a snail's pace, reading from her iPhone, and piling bright orange mountains of squeezy cheese on her crackers.

Acknowledgements

Wingmom is the book that inspired me to become an author. If there was one close to my heart, this one is it. And dare I say, my personal favorite.

My biggest thank yous go to my husband, Dave, and my daughter, Alexa. I love you both to the moon and beyond. You two really came through with plotting ideas and even some jokes on this book. Kudos! All my love and thanks to my writing and brainstorming partner, my biggest fan, and my example—Mom. Many thank yous to Dad, who's always there via text, cheering me on and letting me know that I'm so truly loved. To Terry Ann, my step-mother, who encourages and supports me. And a big thanks goes to my mother in law, Philippa Strum, whose encouragement and careful editing on all my books have helped bring them to the world. Thank you to my in-laws, Herbert and Sevana, who are always rooting for me, ready to step in to help when needed. To my sister, Christina, who always is happy to read each and every one of my books and support me. To my sister, Paris, who cheers me along.

To the Sassy Scribblers. Deena Short, Brenda Lowder, Jill Cobb, Shelby Van Pelt, and Jenny Ling. Deena, who helped plot this book to fine tune the characters, and everything between. And, as always,

I can't thank her enough for reading through countless pages, more times than anyone should. Deena, thank you for caring for my books as they're your own. To Brenda, who helped me make this funnier and more sparkly. Brenda, you have a gift for that! Thanks to Jill, who championed through this book from its humble beginnings so many years ago, to now, always helping me make sure the plot stays sound. Jill, so grateful for your awesome marketing advice for this as well. To Shelby, who helped me bring the characters alive through her many gifts and mastery of details. To Jenny, who always adds dimension to my ideas and beauty to my words.

To Tory Bunce, who cheers me on, encourages me, and always makes me want to keep going, even on days I *really* don't want to. She always makes this journey fun, hope-filled, and motivating. Thank you for always being there with your marketing genius to help me kick off each new book.

To Grace Wynter, thank you for being there from the earliest days and the very beginning of this book when it was in rough shape. You saw its potential, way back then, and never stopped encouraging me. I know I can count on you to pull me through, holding my hand, when sometimes I just can't do it on my own.

To Katina Ferguson, who's always just a phone call away, for *whatever* I need, using her jack-of-all-trade skill to talk me through just about anything. Katina, thanks for all of the personality and jokes you gave to this book as well.

To Deb Lacativa, my self-publishing partner in crime.

To Eliza Peake, for her continued advice and support.

To Chris Lowder, the IT expert who helped me devise a solution to catch Missy. Phew! What a lifesaver.

To Curt Shannon and the other members of Atlanta Writes who helped me on the earliest drafts of this book.

To Mel Todd, the amazing author who helps, supports, and inspires me. And quickly answers any and all text messages I send her randomly.

A gigantic thank you to my wonderful and amazing editors, Reina from Rickrack Books and Marcia Migacz from Final Edit.

A world of thanks to my cover designer, Michelle Fairbanks from Fresh Design.

Copyright © 2022 Terra Weiss. All Rights Reserved.

No part of this book may be reproduced in any form or by any electronic or mechanical means including digital storage and retrieval systems, without written permission from the author.

This book is a work of fiction. Names, characters, specific locations, and any incidents are either imaginary or used fictitiously. Any resemblance to actual persons or events is coincidental.

Published by Autumn Sky Books.

Cover by Terra Weiss and Michelle Fairbanks at Fresh Design.

Editing Services by Reina from Rick Rack Books and Marcia Migacz from Final Edit.

TerraWeiss.com